Reservations Required

La Cocina
MEXICAN FOOD

HELP WANTED

Estela Bernal

PIÑATA BOOKS
ARTE PÚBLICO PRESS
HOUSTON, TEXAS

PIÑATA BOOKS

Reservations Required is funded in part by grants from the Alice Kleberg Reynolds Foundation and the National Endowment for the Arts. We are grateful for their support.

Piñata Books are full of surprises!

Piñata Books
An imprint of
Arte Público Press
University of Houston
4902 Gulf Fwy, Bldg 19, Rm 100
Houston, Texas 77204-2004

Cover design and illustration by Mora Des¡gn Group

Library of Congress Control Number: 2021934784

Printed in the United States of America
Versa Press, Inc., East Peoria, IL
August 2021–October 2021

4 3 2 1

Though no one can go back and make a brand new start, anyone can start from now and make a brand new ending.

—Carl (Bard) Sandburg

Para mis amorcitos: DF, GH, Gris (y todos los demás).

Dedicated to the Lucys, Luckys and Bertas out there,
who, given the chance, will add their warmth,
love, and light to our world.

Acknowledgements

As always, my sincere thanks to Dr. Nicolás Kanellos, Marina Tristán, Dr. Gabriela Baeza Ventura, Adelaida Mendoza and all the staff at Arte Público Press for their continued support and guidance.

❦   ❦   ❦

I'm grateful to Chef Eduardo for his review of *Reservations Required*. His own story serves as an inspiration to us all. Be sure to check out his website and recipes:

www.montanamex.com

CHAPTER ONE

Home, Sweet Home

There were only four survivors left in Nana's garden—the rosemary, mint, a fig tree and me—all barely hanging on. I crushed a brittle rosemary sprig between my fingers and held it to my nose. The aroma brought back memories of Nana's roasted vegetables, generously seasoned with the herb. Tears clouded my eyes when I saw that, in the two weeks since her funeral, weeds had begun to choke the plants. It was here that my dream of becoming a chef was born, and I couldn't let anything choke that dream.

At the sound of Mrs. Lara's voice next door calling her dog to dinner, I dropped the watering can I was holding and ran the four blocks home, getting there just as Mom was setting a bubbling pan on the table.

I held my breath, my hands clutching an empty plate as Dad stabbed his fork into the lasagna. "What's this?"

Mom flinched and kept her eyes on her clasped hands. She usually served the frozen kind—pretty hard to ruin, even for her—but this time it looked like she'd started from scratch and forgotten to boil the noodles. Dad grabbed the spatula and started jabbing the dish again and again until the half-cooked noodles broke, splattering hot sauce all over his hand and wrist.

A low rumble built to a loud roar as he grabbed the foil pan and flung it against the wall. The pan slid to the floor, leaving a trail of cheese, tomatoes and mushrooms behind.

"When are you going to learn to cook a decent meal?" He jumped up, knocking his chair to the floor, his face red and ugly.

Mom sat with her elbows on the table and her face in her hands, shoulders shaking. I tried to swallow the lump in my throat. My brother Mario and I had learned to keep our mouths shut during these blowups. A single word in Mom's defense or even a questioning look were enough to send Dad into a frothing rage.

We sat like statues until Dad turned on his heel and stomped out of the house. A minute later we heard the screech of tires as he sped off in his beat-up Explorer. Every time he raced away like that, I sent a telepathic warning to any kids who might be playing in the street: Out of the way! Run for your lives!

Mario rolled his eyes at me before he disappeared into the kitchen. I soon heard him scrounging around in the fridge.

I reached across the table and put my hand on Mom's arm. "It's okay, Mom. I'll help with dinner from now on."

She gave me a vacant look, her eyes red-rimmed. "You?"

"Sure. I learned a few things from Nana."

Until Nana got sick, I'd mainly served as her assistant, helping pick fresh produce from her garden, chopping vegetables, measuring ingredients and watching her work her magic. Now it was time to start creating my own.

"Clean up the mess before he gets back." Mom got up and stumbled out of the room.

I took the dustpan and a roll of paper towels from the kitchen and cleaned up as well as I could.

Home, sweet home. Living in our house was like living on a volcano. Whenever Dad was home, Mom, Mario and I did our best to stay out of his way. Even when he wasn't home, Mario and I had to be careful creeping around the shadows thrown by the candles Mom kept burning day and night on the hokey little altar she'd set up in the living room. Her voodoo dolls, different types of cards, incense and dried flower arrangements, along with a jumble of other odds and ends, made the room look like a dusty shrine to the Queen Witch. Witchcraft was her explanation for every-thing she didn't understand—and there was a lot she didn't understand.

❁ ❁ ❁

I found Mom sitting at the kitchen table drinking coffee the next morning as if nothing had happened the night before. I asked her if I could have twenty dollars to buy ingredients for enchiladas. She walked to the counter, took the money out of her purse and handed it to me—just like that. No questions. No lecture about spending Dad's hard-earned money. *Nada.*

"Thanks," I said. "See you after school."

I stuffed the money in my back pocket and walked the five blocks to Patti's house. I got there just in time to see her come prancing down the steps, swishing her curvy hips, holding her books against her chest with her left arm and swinging her right arm like a model.

"Hey, short stuff," she said.

She was only a couple of inches taller than me, but that morning, she looked like a giant. When she reached me, she balanced on one leg and stuck out the other so I could see her new shoes.

"From Daddy. He sent me the money after I wrote to tell him I had to have them since all the other girls at school are wearing them."

"I haven't seen anybody wearing anything that looks even close," I said.

Patti giggled. "He doesn't need to know that."

With Patti's new walk in the ridiculous shiny red shoes that made her stand four inches taller, it took us twice as long to get to the bus stop. As she boarded the bus, the guys started whistling while the girls oohed and aahed.

By mid-afternoon, I noticed she was wearing her gym shoes—good thing, since she'd offered to walk with me after I told her I needed to stop by the grocery store on the way home.

"Come in for a minute," she said when we got close to her house. "I want to show you something."

"I really need to get home and start dinner," I said.

"Oh, come on. You're not your parents' slave."

"One good thing about having them as guinea pigs is that cooking for them is good practice for when I have my own restaurant," I said as I followed her inside.

"Lucy's Gourmet Kitchen," Patti said. "I'll be your best customer."

Everything in Patti's room reflected her dream of studying fashion design and her obsession with clothes, shoes and make-up. She'd started making clothes for her dolls when she was about seven. The summer before our freshman year, she'd switched to making clothes for herself. Now, mirrors of all shapes and sizes were scattered throughout the room. A dress form on a stand stood next to her sewing machine and her closet took up a whole wall on one side of the room.

"Be right back." She threw her books on the bed and made her way to the kitchen.

While she was gone, my thoughts drifted back to the night, a month ago, when we'd celebrated our seventeenth birthdays. Mom hadn't put up much of a fight since it was Patti's mom who was taking us out to dinner. That night Patti had insisted on "coloring me up a bit."

"Don't waste your stuff on me," I said when she sat me in front of her dressing table and started painting my face. "You know I can't go home looking like this."

"It's not like you'll be going home drunk or stoned out of your mind."

"Whoa! There's an idea. Then I wouldn't care what Mom and Dad said, would I?"

"Now you're talking, girl." Patti snapped her fingers and, in her best Selena imitation, shimmied her shoulders and shook her hips. "Enough about them. Tonight we're going to PARTY."

Nana always told me I looked just like Mom. I'd never seen the resemblance . . . until then. As Patti transformed me with brushes, liners and cotton puffs, Mom's large dark eyes and full lips appeared on my face. I didn't mind looking like her, as long as I didn't start acting like her.

My daydream evaporated when I saw Patti waving her hand in front of my face. "Yoo-hoo! Want a Jarritos?"

"Thanks, but I really don't have much time. Dad'll be home soon and . . ."

"You've got to have the worst parents on the planet. How can you stand it? I'd die if Mom didn't let me date or talk on the phone."

I bit my lip. Her boyfriend Fernando was my brother's best friend. Did he know how Dad treated Mario? If Patti got a whiff of how he treated all of us, she'd be on her cell calling the police and spilling all the secrets she knew about our home life.

"I can handle it for one more year." I sounded more confident than I felt.

"With your brains and your looks, you'll be going places as soon as you get away from those creeps."

How could she be so sure? I didn't talk much about my after-graduation plans. I'd be happy to still be in one piece. While Patti created sexy dress patterns, I dreamed of creating recipes that would make Nana proud.

Patti handed me a drawing of the outfit she was working on. "What do you think?"

"It's gorgeous!" The low-cut blouse and hip-hugging skirt she'd designed were perfect for her.

"I wish you didn't have to leave so soon," she said when she saw me looking at the clock on her nightstand.

"Me too." I picked up my backpack and the bag of groceries and walked out before she could find something else to show me. "See you in the morning."

❧   ❧   ❧

Mom was nowhere in sight when I got home. She stayed in her room while I dipped tortillas in sauce from a can, stuffed them with store-bought roasted chicken and smothered them with shredded cheese. I cringed at the thought of Nana turning over in her grave if she could see that the only thing I'd made from scratch was the rice. Dad wouldn't even notice, though. With a layer of hot salsa and a dollop of sour cream, this meal would set his taste buds buzzing.

Mom appeared after I finished cooking and right before Dad pulled into the driveway. She set the enchiladas, rice and refried beans on the table while Dad was in the shower.

We ate in silence, as usual—at least Dad and Mario ate while Mom and I picked at our food. I breathed a sigh of relief when, after his second helping, Dad went to park himself in front of the TV.

Mom didn't thank me, although I could see she was glad when I offered to start planning a weekly menu. I started by making a list of everything I needed for her to get at the supermarket. From then on, dinner became my responsibility. Mom never offered to help and hardly ate anything. At least things were quieter. For a while.

CHAPTER TWO

No Time for Goodbyes

Dinner was always a tense event at our house. We were expected to sit down to eat at six. If we were late, we didn't eat. There was no chit-chat allowed unless Dad had something to say. After Nana died, though, Dad started acting like he'd lost his very last marble. He had a beer as soon as he walked in the door, another with dinner and who knows how many more before he went to bed. Some nights he didn't even make it to bed.

We had just finished eating, about two weeks after I'd taken over the cooking, when Mario walked in from soccer practice.

"Sorry I'm late." He dropped his bag by the door and started walking to his chair.

"Sorry doesn't cut it. You know the rules."

"I said I was sorry. Coach asked us to . . ."

"You think I'm going to keep supporting you while you're wasting time playing games?"

"I'll lose my scholarship if I don't play"

"You lazy bastard!" Dad yelled. "Get out of my sight."

"I'll just make a sandwich."

"I said get out!"

Dad jumped up and grabbed Mario by the throat. He must've weighed twice as much as my brother, but he was mostly flab. Mario was thin but quicker than Dad could ever hope to be. Before Dad could figure out what was happening, Mario kneed him in the crotch. Dad let go of him and, as he started to double over, Mario kicked him in the head as if he were kicking a soccer ball. Dad's head bounced back. He stumbled and tried to right himself before crashing to the floor.

I saw everything in slow motion—every frame of the action frozen still for a few seconds before the next frame came into focus.

Mom screamed and dropped to her knees beside Dad.

I grabbed my throat, trying to keep my heart from jumping out.

Mario knocked down a chair as he ran for the door. He was almost there when Dad sprung up and went straight for his neck again.

My trembling fingers curled around my fork handle. I didn't know what to do but felt like I had to do something.

Dad's fist hit the wall when Mario ducked out of the way at the last second and ran out the front door, slamming it shut behind him.

Dad's eyes were bloodshot and bulging, and his head looked like it was about to explode.

Mom reached out to help him. He shoved her against the table, making the dishes rattle and pinning me against my chair.

I watched him stumble to his car, not caring what happened to him. But worry about Mario made me tremble. I started sobbing so much I could barely see as I collected the dishes and carried them into the kitchen. Mom was standing at the sink, washing her hands and staring out the window.

You can stand there and wash until your skin peels off, I felt like screaming. Nothing is going to change until you leave that monster. Then, I reminded myself that I could stand there and scream until I turned blue, and she would never leave him. Realizing how little I knew about my own mother, I immediately regretted directing my anger at her. She had to be more terrified of the unknown than of the nightmare we were all living every day. Somehow, I had to find my own escape. I had to follow my dream.

※   ※   ※

I tiptoed down the hall to my bedroom, opened the window and sat there watching and listening for any sign of Mario. Despite the heat, I shivered, trying to imagine where he might be. We couldn't run to Nana for shelter as we had when we were young—when Mom had seemed like the bigger threat.

I lost track of time but figured it was pretty late when I started nodding off. Other than the corner streetlight and the headlights of passing cars, it was already dark.

Wherever you are, Mario, I hope you're safe. Please come back for me.

On that hopeful note, I lay down and fell asleep.

※   ※   ※

The next morning, I stopped by Patti's on the way to the bus stop. Noticing that she was unusually quiet, I tried to make small talk. Had she finished writing her essay on the red-eyed tree frog? No. What did she think of Ms. Salinger's new hairstyle? She hated it.

"Are you okay?" she asked as we stepped off the bus at school.

"Sure," I said. "I just miss Nana . . . a lot."

"What about Mario?"

"I'm sure he misses her too. . . ."

"Come on, Lucy! I thought we were friends."

"What are you talking about?" I asked, even though I knew the answer.

"I've been waiting for you to tell me what happened, but I guess I never would've heard about it if Fernando hadn't driven Mario to the bus station."

The hope I'd been holding onto until then turned to panic. I grabbed her arm. "Did he say where he was headed?"

"He didn't know. Fernando borrowed two hundred bucks from his dad and gave it to him. I guess he'll go as far as that'll take him."

I closed my eyes, trying to hold in my tears.

Patti put her arm around me and pulled me along. "Don't worry. He'll be all right. He'll lose his scholarship, but at least he won't have to put up with any more shit from your parents. He wanted you to know he's sorry he didn't get a chance to say goodbye."

"Thanks."

I tried to smile, but it's hard to force a smile when your heart's been shattered. It was true there had been no time for goodbyes, but I didn't want to say goodbye. I wanted to go with him.

"I always thought your mom was the witch in the family and your dad was just a bully."

"They're both nuts." Thoughts of Mario and where he might be going filled my head.

"Mario wouldn't tell Fernando what happened. He just said he was fed up with your dad and couldn't take it anymore." She stopped, wrinkled her brow and said, "Does he ever hit you or . . ." a look of disgust twisted her face, "try to . . . touch you?"

"Yuck! No! But he's a real jerk to Mom and likes to terrorize all of us every chance he gets."

"You have to get away from there, be around normal people. Why don't you come stay with us, at least until we graduate? With your grades, you won't have any trouble getting into a good college. You can get financial aid or a part-time job." She laughed and waggled her eyebrows. "You might even meet Mr. Right."

"Thanks, Patti, but I can't just move in. Besides, how long do you think it would take them to find me only a few blocks away from their house?"

"So what if they find you? Mom's not afraid of them."

"It won't be long before I can put it all behind me."

Patti made it all sound so easy, and I tried to sound confident, although I had no idea how to get out of my nightmare.

"Five minutes can be a long time when you're living in a loony bin."

Every minute is hell now that Mario's gone. How could he leave me alone in that nut house?

☙ ☙ ☙

With Mario gone, I expected Dad to zero in on Mom and me with a vengeance, but things were eerily quiet for several weeks. Dinner time began to feel like sitting at a wake. Other than the clink of dishes and silverware and the disgusting noises escaping from Dad's mouth as he scarfed down his dinner, it was deathly quiet. The only sounds from

Mom and me were made with our forks as we pushed our food around our plates.

"Pastor Negrón called," Mom said as we ate dinner one evening. "One of his parishioners is interested in renting your mother's house."

"K'ungh!" Dad choked on the mouthful he tried to swallow before he'd finished chewing it. Between coughs and sputters, he said, "Tell them all to go to hell. If I ever see anybody sniffing around her house, I'll . . ."

"Mom's just the mess—" I started to say before I could stop myself.

I turned my head when I saw his beefy hand fly off the table, headed in my direction. He slammed it against my ear, making my brain rattle. For a minute, I just sat there, stunned. He was practically foaming at the mouth, lips flapping a mile a minute, shouting obscenities I could barely hear.

I leapt out of my chair but, before I reached my room, he grabbed me by the hair and sent me sprawling onto the floor. I scrambled to my knees and tried to stand up. Before I could, he knocked me down again and pinned my arms with his knees. His fingers gripped my face so tightly, I was sure he'd break my jaw.

He brought his face close to my ear and whispered, "Don't ever disrespect me again, you little shit."

I tried to turn away from his filthy, hot breath. I only succeeded in stretching my neck further than I ever thought possible, hoping I would pass out, maybe even choke myself or break my own neck.

"From now on, you'll keep your mouth shut if you know what's good for you. And don't even think about running away because I'll find you and you'll regret it for the rest of your life."

By then I was whimpering, shaking and praying that he would just kill me. But when he loosened his grip, I opened my mouth and sank my teeth into the side of his hand. I shook my head from side to side like a rabid dog, until he smacked me upside the head with his left hand. Since he was right handed, the blow wasn't as hard. Although it stunned me for a couple of seconds, my teeth had stunned him even more. He cursed and pried my mouth open, pulled his hand away and ran out moaning like a wounded beast.

Instead of comforting me or even checking on me, Mom disappeared into her bedroom.

I waited until I heard his car drive away before I got up and limped to my own room and slammed the door behind me. I sobbed and raged into my pillow, calming down only when I thought about my brother. *Mario, I'm glad you got away from these freaks.*

At ten that night, when things were dark and quiet, I unlocked the window screen and jumped out. The dry grass was prickly on my bare feet, but I didn't dare go back in for my shoes. I ran out into the street and kept running without knowing or caring where I was going. I wanted to keep going until I fell off the face of the earth.

On the outskirts of town, I saw a sugarcane field and headed into it, holding up my arms to protect my eyes. The blades and stalks scraped and tore at my skin. I went just far enough to hide from the road traffic before I collapsed into a heap and, between gulps of air, started sobbing until I cried myself dry. While lying on the ground, I thought about what I would do if Dad ever attacked me again. I scrapped each idea that occurred to me once I saw how ridiculous it was. Whatever I did would be like trying to stop a train with a feather. Buying the sharpest knife I could find would only provide him with more weapons to use against me. He'd probably snatch it away from me before I had a chance to use it on him. Besides, if I succeeded in . . . I didn't even want to go wherever that thought was leading.

I had no idea how long I'd been there but knew I had to get out before daylight. I couldn't let anyone see me in this condition. The very thought of what I must look like scared me.

I forced myself to get up, made my way out of the field and back to the road. This time I headed toward Nana's. Even if Dad had run to hide there last night, he would be gone by now. It was a chance I had to take.

I crouched behind a patch of weeds when I saw a car heading my way. After it passed, I jumped up and ran the rest of the way.

Although Dad's car wasn't in Nana's driveway, I snuck in the side gate just in case. Mrs. Lara's kitchen light was on, but it was dark enough that she wouldn't be able to see me. I opened the gate just wide enough to let myself in. Nana had always left the small bathroom window halfway open. She figured it wasn't big enough for a prowler to crawl through. It was big enough for me, though.

I needed something to boost me up to reach the window. The only thing I could find was a plastic bucket Nana used for washing potatoes and carrots after she dug them out of the ground. I carried it to the window and flipped it over, then felt around for a stone with which to pry the screen off. I removed the screen, pulled myself up and wriggled my way in.

I didn't dare turn on the light. If Mrs. Lara saw it, she might call the police. Or worse, my house. Instead, I went to Nana's bedroom and took the small flashlight she kept by her bed. In the bathroom, I peeled off my filthy clothes and stood under the shower with the water turned to the hottest temperature I could stand. Afterward, I looked through the medicine cabinet until I found some peroxide and cotton swabs. The tears started flowing again when I remembered the many times Nana had tended to my childhood wounds the same way.

I checked my face in the mirror and saw that, although my face had been red and swollen when Dad beat me, there were only a few bruises, and the scratches I'd caused myself. After I cleaned up, I wrapped myself in a towel and threw my clothes in the washer, glad Dad hadn't bothered to shut off the utilities

I went back to Nana's bedroom and lay down on her bed. The minute my head hit the pillow, I fell asleep and was quickly swept up in a current of swirling brown water. Stuff flew through the air and electric wires dangled dangerously close to the water. I screamed and grabbed a passing log, but the current carried us both downstream. When I saw I was headed straight toward a boulder, I started kicking and trying to roll away from it. I hit the floor with a big thump. That woke me up. Sweat covered my whole body, and the sheets were sopping wet.

Still shaking, I grabbed the pillow and curled up on the floor.

At six, I got up and put on a long-sleeved shirt Nana used to wear when she worked in her garden. Then I stripped the bed and headed to the laundry room to wash the sheets and put my clothes in the dryer. On the way there, I stopped to feel around under the kitchen sink for the spare key Nana kept there. When I saw the three beer cans sitting on the counter and two more on the kitchen table, I ran to the laundry room, threw the sheets in the hamper, grabbed my clothes out of the washer and put them on without bothering to dry them.

I was about to let myself out the front door when I remembered the screen. I went to the back door and, staying as close to the wall as possible, where I knew Mrs. Lara couldn't see me. I crept back to the bathroom window, replaced the screen and put the bucket back near the door. Realizing I hadn't made the bed, I went back in, took a fresh set of sheets from the linen closet and put everything in order in the bedroom before running home and crawling into my bed. Crazy thoughts and images kept crowding my brain.

I was sure mom had burned Dad in effigy many times, oblivious to the fact that her potions, rituals and amulets were about as effective as her rubbing an egg all over our bodies to draw out the bad energy when we were children. If she wanted to stay out of fear or whatever else kept her from leaving, it was her choice.

But me, I was barely seventeen. What could I do? I'd be jumping from a known evil into a jungle full of strangers, like walking around with a sandwich board announcing open season to any pervert or predator looking for a victim. Still, there had to be a way out, and I needed to find it. Fast.

I lay awake planning my escape. *Where would I go?* The only possibility was El Paso. Dad's older sister lived there. But I barely knew her. Nana, who in my eyes was the perfect grandmother, rarely spoke of her. The last time I'd seen Aunt Delia was a couple of months earlier, at Nana's funeral. She'd come to pick up the key to Nana's house and stayed one night. She and Dad kept their distance from each other the whole time.

At five that afternoon, Mom came to my door. "What's going on? Your father will be home in an hour and you haven't started dinner."

When I didn't answer, she came in, walked to the bed and yanked the covers off me.

"I think I have a fever," I said, moaning a little, trying to sound as weak and pathetic as I could. "Two kids at school have come down with mono. I may have caught it from them."

Mom's eyes widened. She looked at my crumpled clothes, which made me look like I was sweating, before she turned and practically ran out of the room. A short time later, the smell of incense wafted into the room. I heard her banging pots and pans in the kitchen, and soon the sickening aroma of burning grease started mingling with the incense.

The phone rang.

"She's sick and can't get out of bed," Mom said before slamming the phone down.

It had to be Patti. She must really be worried. What was I going to tell her when she started interrogating me the next time I saw her?

Dad's car pulled into the driveway just then.

"How many times have I told you not to burn that crap in the house?" he yelled as soon as he walked in the front door. "Open the windows and let in some fresh air."

"Lucy has some kind of virus," Mom said. "How's your hand?"

"Never mind my hand. Where's dinner?"

"I'm heating up the leftover spaghetti. It'll be ready when you come out of the shower."

"Forget the leftovers. Go get me a burger and fries."

"But Pedro . . ."

"And while you're out there, get me a six pack of Bud."

My fake mono infection kept me safe the rest of that week. Mom avoided me like the plague. I'd wait for her to leave the house each day before I got up, showered, brushed my teeth, ate a bowl of cereal or a piece of fruit and went back to my room.

The following Monday, thinking I'd heard Dad drive off earlier than usual, I went to the kitchen to make myself some toast. I jumped when I heard a tiny clink and turned to see Mom standing by the fridge, watching me.

"What?" I said.

"Why do you aggravate your father so much?"

"I . . . WHAT?"

"You heard me. He couldn't even get up to go to work today."

"And how is that my fault?"

"We've done everything for you and Mario. All you've done is given us grief."

"Mom, why do you put up with him? You deserve better."

She started to cry and, for a second, I almost felt sorry for her. I put my hand on her shoulder. She shrugged it off.

Without bothering to take a shower, I went to my room and changed. It was way too early for the bus and, although it would take me twice as long to get to school, I decided to walk.

The campus was empty when I got there, except for a couple of maintenance trucks and their drivers. As I hurried across the parking lot before they could see me and ask what I was up to that early in the morning, I heard someone behind me call my name. I turned to see Art Treviño getting out of a car I hadn't noticed until then.

"Hey, Lucy. Haven't seen you around lately. How are you?"

Art was a senior at Las Nubes High. He'd been voted the student most likely to succeed, and I had no doubt he would—big time. He not only had the brains, but he was also the most handsome guy I'd ever seen. Although he wasn't an athlete, the school's cheerleaders, along with most of the other girls in town, acted like a bunch of groupies when they were around him. I was surprised he even knew my name.

"Hi, Art. I'm okay. What are you doing here so early?"

"I could ask you the same question, but since you asked first, I'm tutoring a student who has some catching up to do. This is the only time we can meet because he has to work after school."

"Oh. That's nice. Happy tutoring." I waved and started to walk away.

"I haven't seen Mario for a while," he shouted. "Tell him I said hello."

"Thanks, I will." He must think I'm an idiot, I thought after he waved and headed off in the opposite direction. *Happy tutoring?*

I saw Patti running toward me just as I was about to sneak into my first period class. At the beginning of the school year, she'd tried to talk me into taking drama and theater arts with her. But I couldn't imagine memorizing lines and standing in front of people spouting words that would never naturally come out of my mouth.

"Okay, then. Let's take dance," she'd said when she heard my reasoning.

"How about choir?"

"I can't sing."

"Neither can I, but at least in choir, my lack of talent won't be as noticeable."

She ended up choosing dance. I stuck with choir. It was the only class we didn't have together.

"Where have you been?" she asked when she caught up. "I called your house and the *bruja* wouldn't let me talk to you."

"I had some kind of bug," I said, coughing a couple of times to prove it.

She put her right hand on her hip, looked at me with a big smile on her face and batted her eyes, making her bangs bounce every time she opened and closed them.

"So, what other secrets have you been keeping from me?"

"What do you mean?"

"I'll give you a big hint. Art!"

"What about him?"

"Just that he stopped me in the hallway yesterday and, before I had a chance to wink or blink or turn on the charm, he said, 'Where's your buddy, Lucy? I never see one of you without the other.' Anyway, for once I didn't know what to say. I couldn't tell him that you live with Looney and Tooney, who won't even let you talk on the phone, so I just said you were out sick."

"Sorry Mom hung up on you."

"You. Need. To. Get. Away. From. Them!" It's not like you don't have a place to go."

I took a deep breath. She had no idea how right she was, at least about the craziness at home. The last thing I wanted to do, though, was to move in with her and her family. Her parents divorced when her mom discovered Patti's dad was having an affair. Now, she worked two jobs to take care of Patti and her younger brother Pete. Pete didn't even have his own bedroom, so it wasn't like they needed me to move in and crowd them even more. Besides, I knew what Dad was capable of and couldn't put them in that kind of danger.

"Thanks, Patti. You're the best. I'll be okay." I gave her a quick hug.

She pecked me on the cheek. "Well, this will brighten your day. Mario called Fernando from Galveston."

"How is he? What's he doing there?"

"He's okay. Thinking of joining the Navy. Until then, he's working at some grocery store. He asked about you. What should we tell him if he calls again before he sails away?"

She made it sound like Mario was going to be whisked away on some ship as soon as he enlisted.

"Is there some way to contact him?"

"He called from a public phone. Since he can't call your house, he'll call Fernando whenever he can."

"Tell him I'm okay. Tell him I miss him. Tell him . . ." Before the idea had fully formed in my head, I blurted out, "Could I use your phone for a minute?"

Patti handed over her phone, curiosity written all over her face.

I pulled the page I'd torn out of Nana's address book from my pocket and called Delia. Her phone rang about ten times before she picked up.

"Hi, this is Lucy. I need to get out of the house and was wondering if I could come visit you for a while." I blurted out.

Delia didn't say anything for a long minute.

While waiting on pins and needles for her to answer, I closed my eyes and tried not to cry as fear crept up my spine.

Finally, she said, "How are you planning to get here?"

"I can probably borrow the money for a bus ticket," I said, turning to look at Patti.

Patti wrinkled her brow and mouthed the words, "Who's that?"

"If you can wait until tomorrow, I can drive down and pick you up," Delia said.

Stunned and relieved, I said, "Thanks, Tía Delia. That would be great!"

"I can try to be there around noon. Where will I be picking you up and how can I get a hold of you when I get there?"

I gave her Patti's number. "I'll be waiting for you in front of my school."

Patti gave me a wide-eyed look when I handed her the phone. "Can you trust her not to call the loco-loonies and turn you in?"

Hmmm? I hadn't thought about that. "I have no choice."

Patti let out a sob. "Oh, Lucy. I don't blame you for leaving, but it sucks that you have to go." She blew her nose. "This may be our last day together. You need to stay with us tonight."

"I need to go home after school and get my stuff. I'll come by your house to drop it off after they go to bed."

❧   ❧   ❧

I don't know when Mom had last shopped for groceries, but there were slim pickings as far as ingredients for dinner. I found three potatoes, a couple of eggs, half a tomato and an onion. As I peeled the potatoes, I thought of Mario. I was glad he was okay and that he was thinking of me. Since he'd lost his scholarship, maybe the Navy would offer him another way to get through college.

After I'd fried the potatoes, I mixed in the rest of the ingredients, topping it all with a thick layer of cheese.

"What is this?" Dad asked when we sat down to eat. "We're having breakfast for dinner now?" He scarfed down the first fat burrito in five or six bites and kept going until he'd eaten everything but what was on my plate and mom's.

After dinner, I quickly cleared the table, washed the dishes and locked myself up in my room. I went to my closet and folded my clothes in a small pile. Then I sat on the floor and tried to read for a while but kept thinking about Delia. What had driven her away? How did she really feel about me suddenly barging in on her?

At ten-thirty I opened my bedroom door a crack. The only sounds, other than the blaring TV, were Dad's gasping, rasping snores. Figuring Mom was already asleep, I tiptoed across the hall into Mario's room. The smell of mothballs walloped my nose. Whew! Mom must've planted them throughout the room when she realized Mario wasn't coming back.

"It's my turn to get away, Mario," I whispered into the darkness.

I felt around for the light switch. The room looked exactly as he'd left it. I opened the top drawer of the small chest next to his bed, where he still kept his old baseball cards and the few other treasures he was allowed to have before Mom told him he was too old for such stuff. Mario had never been much of a reader, but he did like stuff like *The Avengers* and *Cirque Du Freak* when he was younger. I pulled out *Pantalones, TX*, the one comic book still left there and stuffed it under my shirt like a shoplifter before rummaging through his closet looking for a suitcase. All I found was an old duffel bag I'd never seen before. I dumped its contents on the floor and took the bag to my room.

I packed some books, my toothbrush and my own little treasures in my backpack, then put the comic book, a couple of cooking magazines and my clothes inside the bag. My belongings only filled half of it.

Other than the doll Nana had given me for my fourth birthday, I had one memento she gave me when I turned fifteen.

"I don't know if I'll be around on your wedding day," she'd told me. "If I'm not there physically, you know I'll be thinking of you, wherever I happen to be. This has no special value to anyone but me, and I don't know anyone but you who will appreciate it."

I'd taken the small stone out of its pouch and run my thumb over its cool, smooth surface. It was translucent red with crimson veins running through it.

"It's beautiful, Nana," I'd said.

"My brother-in-law gave it to my twin sister on their wedding day. Since they had no children, she gave it to me just before she died."

"That's a strange gift to get from a bridegroom."

"It's an agate stone. Ágata's husband wanted to have it made into a pendant, but she insisted on keeping it intact."

Nana had taken an old photograph from her dresser and held it out to me. "If you look closely, you'll see the small pouch hanging from her neck. Ágata was my best friend. That's why, when you were born, I asked your parents to name you after her. It's an old-fashioned name, but I hope you don't mind it."

That made me feel a little better about my first name, but I still preferred to go by my middle name. Although marriage was not even on my radar when I got the agate, I'd sewn my own pouch for it and fastened it to a red cord.

I held the stone for a moment. It reminded me of Nana's last days. She'd had a stream of visitors from her church when she was in the hospital, and everyone who knew her had been at her funeral to say goodbye. The songs we sang, the tears we cried, the words that were spoken were all real. I couldn't imagine anyone attending Dad's funeral when he died—maybe Pastor Negrón and Mrs. Lara, out of respect for Nana. But there wasn't a single neighbor Dad hadn't gotten into a fight with. None of them had anything good to say about him. I was sure he was probably as big a shit at work as he was at home, so his co-workers would probably celebrate rather than mourn. But why waste my time thinking about him, especially now?

I put the pouch back in my backpack and threw the duffel bag out the window, jumped out behind it, picked it up and ran all the way to Patti's house. She must've been watching and listening for me because she opened the door before I had a chance to knock.

"Your aunt called. She said she'd call us tomorrow when she gets here."

I dropped the bag by the door and threw my arms around her. She squeezed me to her and we held on, each of us sobbing into the other's shoulder.

I reluctantly loosened my grip after a while.

Patti sniffled. "I hate to see you go." She pulled some crumpled bills out of her pocket and offered them to me. "Here's twenty-three bucks. Sorry I don't have more to give you."

"I can't take your money. You've already . . ."

"Don't be silly." She smiled. "And don't piss me off."

"Thanks." I squeezed her hand. "See you in the morning."

I could've used one of Mom's Excedrin PMs to knock me out that night, but I wasn't taking any chances of oversleeping.

CHAPTER THREE

Escape

As soon as I heard Dad drive off the next morning, I got up and checked my closet one more time to make sure I hadn't forgotten anything. After a quick shower, I rummaged around the kitchen looking for something edible to take on the trip. I found cheese and tortillas and made a couple of quesadillas. I packed them, an orange, a bunch of grapes and two bottles of water in my backpack.

Patti and Fernando were sitting in his car in front of her house waiting for me. Patti jumped out to let me slide into the back seat.

"Your bag is in the trunk." Fernando reached back and grabbed my hand. "We're going to miss you, but I know Mario will be glad to hear you got away."

"I'm going to miss you too." I gave him a lopsided smile and quickly looked away, hoping he wouldn't notice my puffy, bloodshot eyes.

I went through the morning feeling tense and jumpy, my brain still too stunned for my body to notice how exhausted I was.

Patti and I ate our lunch in Fernando's car while waiting for Delia's call.

"Call me when you get there," Patti said. "Call me every day."

I reminded her I didn't have a phone.

"If your aunt's willing to drive all the way here to pick you up, she won't mind letting you use her phone every once in a while."

"I'll try, but I'll definitely write until I get my own phone."

"Wow! Does anybody even write anymore? Besides texts and e-mails, I mean?"

"Maybe just people like me who're still stuck in the dark ages."

Patti wiped away a tear and reached for my hand.

※　※　※

We watched students heading back to class when the bell rang, every minute seeming like forever.

Finally, the phone rang. I answered on the first ring.

"I'm parked right in front of the school," Delia said.

I climbed out of the car and scanned the No Parking area until I saw her green Subaru and gestured to Patti, who was pulling my bag out of the trunk.

Delia had gotten out of her car and was stretching her back. I gave her a quick hug and turned to introduce Patti.

"I'm going to miss her, but I'm so glad Lucy's got a safe place to go," Patti told her.

Delia nodded and turned to me. "We've got a long drive ahead. You ready?"

"Yeah. Thanks for driving all the way here to pick me up."

"I happen to be off today," she said as if she'd had nothing better to do than drive however long it took her to pick me up. She opened the trunk. Patti dropped my bag in and gave me one last hug before I climbed into the passenger seat.

"Call me!" Patti yelled as we pulled away.

I waved and kept on waving until she disappeared from view.

"So, you've finally had enough of Pedro," Delia said once we were on the road.

"He started getting worse after Nana died. Now, he's turned into a real monster."

"The monster's always been there. Mamá tried to trick people into seeing him through her rose-colored glasses. What you see now is the real Pedro. I don't blame you for wanting to get away from him. Under the circumstances, I guess you could use a change of scenery. I can't promise it'll be any better, but it'll give us a chance to get to know each other. Mamá would be pleased."

❦ ❦ ❦

We drove in silence for a while. Traffic was so light at that time that it seemed like the only others on the road besides us were the long-distance semi drivers and a few delivery trucks. Delia turned on the radio and switched from one station to another and another before turning it off again.

"Don't you have any decent radio stations around here?"

I shrugged. "I don't listen to the radio much."

"There's a high school not far from where I live. You should be able to transfer there."

"Maybe." Transferring to another school hadn't even crossed my mind. I wondered how much she knew about us—Mom, Mario and me—but I wasn't about to volunteer any information. Instead, I tried to keep the spotlight on her.

"What do you do in El Paso?"

"I work in a nursing home . . . been there for years. Mamá had big dreams for Pedro and me, but I was never a very good student. Pedro was even worse. Mamá always bragged about how smart you are, though. You must've gotten your brains from Sara. She was always a good student. If I'd known she was going to marry Pedro, I would've told her she'd be better off joining the Army. What do you plan to do with your life?"

"I love to cook. Someday I'd like to be a chef."

"We're going to get along just fine then." She patted her big belly and laughed. "Bet you'd never guess it, but I love to eat."

She went on and on for a while, giving me every detail about her job and everyone she worked with. Before long, I started nodding off. Around six, I woke up to the sound of doors slamming shut and engines starting up. We were at a truck stop.

"Hungry?"

"A little," I said. "I packed some food for us, quesadillas and fruit."

"Cold quesadillas aren't going to do it for me," she said. "We still have a ways to go. Let's see what we can find at that little dump up ahead."

After she filled the tank, she drove to a place nearby that advertised fish and chips as their specialty.

"Where in the heck do they get fish?" she said. "Must be frozen, but it's probably best not to ask any questions. You think you can stomach that kind of stuff?"

"Sure."

It felt good to stretch my legs when we walked across the restaurant parking lot.

The waitress led us to a booth and pointed behind her with her thumb. "Our menu's listed on the board by the cash register. While you decide, what can I get you to drink?"

Without bothering to ask me what I wanted, Delia asked for two orders of fish and chips and two iced teas. "Oh, and extra tartar sauce, please."

As soon as the waitress walked away, Delia turned back to me. "I don't know about you, but I'm about to pee my pants. Back in a minute."

While Delia was gone, I tried to picture the scene back home in Las Nubes. By now, they'd noticed my absence. Had they called Patti yet? I looked around the restaurant. Most of the other diners were men, probably truck drivers. They sat at the counter, talking and laughing like old friends.

The waitress dropped off our drinks and started to walk away, almost running into Delia, who was right behind her.

"You some kind of pee camel or something?" Delia said as she slid back into the seat across from me.

I smiled. "I can wait until after we eat."

While we waited for our food, Delia checked out the pictures on the wall. Most were of people toasting the camera with a beer mug in one hand and a plate of fish and chips in the other. Others were kids, their faces smeared with ketchup, their cheeks bulging, as if they were storing food in them for a long, cold winter.

Our waitress soon reappeared, carrying two plates piled high with fried fish and potatoes. It all looked pretty greasy but smelled good. I cut my fish into bite-size pieces and, as I waited for it to cool, I watched Delia pour half the contents of the ketchup bottle on her fries and gobs of sauce on her fish. If she kept eating this way, it wouldn't be long before she turned into a lard tub like her brother.

I ate a few bites of fish and half of the fries, minus the sauce or ketchup.

"I must've been hungrier than I realized," Delia said after she'd eaten every last crumb on her plate. "You didn't eat much, though."

"I've had enough."

"You need to put on a few pounds, or else you'll get blown away by the wind."

"Would you like the rest?" I asked when I saw her eyeing my plate.

"I shouldn't, but I hate to waste money and perfectly good food."

She pushed her empty plate aside and dug into my leftovers. The food actually wasn't bad, nothing like the fish sticks Mom fed Mario and me when we were kids.

"If . . ." I started to say Mom or Dad but decided they didn't deserve to be called that. Neither of them was really a parent as far as I was concerned. "If Sara or Pedro calls you asking about me . . ."

"No chance of that," Delia said. "Don't worry. I wouldn't have made this drive just to turn you in."

A soft, warm blanket of relief wrapped itself around me. "Thanks. What will happen to Nana's house now that she's gone?"

"I'm sure Mamá left it to Pedro, and there's no telling what he'll do with it. Or when."

She didn't sound upset. It was like she'd expected it all along.

❦   ❦   ❦

While Delia paid for our meal, I went to the restroom. She was by the front door waiting for me when I came out.

"I tend to get sleepy if I drive right after a meal," she said on the way to the car. "Mamá always said you're a big reader. Got anything to read? It might help me stay awake if you read to me."

"I have some books and magazines in my bag."

"Good."

Mothball fumes escaped from the trunk when Delia popped it open. The stink must've saturated my old bedroom too but, with all the other strange smells in that house, I hadn't noticed it until now. I held my breath while reaching in to grab my backpack. Then, I slid into my seat, took out a book and threw my pack behind Delia's seat.

"Have you ever read this?" I asked, holding up *The House on Mango Street*.

Delia glanced at the cover before she started the engine. "Nah, I don't have much time for books these days. Truth is, even in school I only read what I had to read to get by. Now, all I read is the paper every once in a while, if somebody leaves one lying around at work."

I opened the book to "What Sally Said" and started to read. "He never hits me hard. She said her mama rubs lard on all the places where it hurts. . . ."

Out of the corner of my eye, I saw Delia turn to look at me. I kept reading.

❦   ❦   ❦

"That's enough," she said after a while. "You're starting to sound like a frog."

I took a sip of water and looked out at the mountains in the distance.

My heart did a double flip when I saw a checkpoint ahead.

"I don't have my birth certificate with me," I said. "All I've got is my student ID."

"Don't worry, they only stop traffic on that side of the highway."

Whew! I pulled the sack lunch out from under the seat and offered Delia some grapes.

"You eat them," she said. "I'm still stuffed. Besides, you need them more than I do."

An hour later, we drove into a barrio a lot like the one where I'd grown up. Delia parked in front of a small corner house and turned to me.

"It's not much," she said, "but it's home. Come on in."

The front yard was bare, except for a few sorry-looking bushes on each side of the front steps. As soon as we walked in, I saw that the inside wasn't much either. I could see the kitchen from the living room. There were no pictures on the walls and very little furniture in either room. Still, the house looked even smaller than it had from the outside. I guess since she'd never married or had children, she didn't really need much.

"You'll be sleeping in here," Delia said, pointing to a door next to the kitchen.

I followed her into what looked like a storage room. Although there was a twin bed in it, there were also bags, boxes and old appliances stacked up and crammed into the small space. Next to the bed was a low nightstand with a shade-less lamp on top and two drawers underneath. Delia pulled open a long curtain in one corner of the room. Hanging from a wooden rod were a few wire hangers holding a robe and some shapeless dresses.

"I'd forgotten I still had these old things." She yanked the clothes off the hangers. "You can put your stuff in here."

She walked into the hallway and came back a minute later. "I have to be at work by seven tomorrow morning and I'm exhausted. I'm going to take a shower and go to bed. If you get hungry later, see what you can find in the kitchen."

"Thanks. Um . . . may I use your phone to call Patti? I'm afraid Sara and Pedro are going to cause trouble for her."

"¡Ay, Dios mío! Poor girl. I only have the cell, so plug it back in when you're done."

Patti answered after the first ring. "Lucy?"

"Hi. I can't talk for long. Just wanted to make sure you're okay."

⁂ ⁂ ⁂

"You know those freaks don't scare me. Sara called at six. I could hear Bigfoot spouting shit in the background. I yelled, 'Wherever she is, I hope she's gotten away from you maniacs for good!'" She laughed. "She hung up without bothering to say *adiós*."

"I guess it's a good thing Pedro and Delia don't talk to each other."

"Good for her and definitely good for you. So how was the trip?"

"Okay." A sob escaped from me without warning. "Sorry. I'm still kind of numb. I miss you already. But I don't know when I can call again."

"Oh, Lucy!" Patti sniffled. "You know I'm here anytime you need me."

"I love you," I blurted out and quickly hung up. It was the first time I'd said those words to anyone other than Nana.

❀ ❀ ❀

Delia came out of the shower wearing a bathrobe, a towel wrapped around her head. She pulled a ten-dollar- bill out of her pocket and plunked it on the coffee table, along with a piece of paper and a key.

"You'll probably still be sleeping when I leave in the morning. Eat whatever you can find while I'm gone. I'd advise you to not go anywhere, but if you have to go out, don't wander too far off. And, for pity's sake, don't be chatting up the nosey neighbors. Here's my spare key. I wrote my work number down for you, but only call me in case of emergency. I'll be home around four-thirty." She seemed to have forgotten I didn't have a phone.

"Thanks, Tía. I need to do some laundry in the morning. Where can I . . ."

"The washer's out on the back porch. You'll find the detergent under the kitchen sink. I don't have a dryer. You'll have to use the clothesline in the backyard."

After Delia went to bed, I stacked some bags and boxes on top of others and pushed them against the wall to give myself a little more space. I started to put my stuff away and, realizing it had picked up the mothball smell from the bag, took it back to the living room. I went to the window when I heard loud music coming from the house next door. A woman yelled at someone in Spanish, and a dog barked in the distance. There didn't seem to be much else going on outside.

I turned on the TV with the volume so low I could barely hear it and switched from one channel to another. All I could get were staticky reruns of old sitcoms, a few *telenovelas* and one commercial after another. *Yak, yak, yak. Click.*

In the kitchen everything looked old and worn: the dull beige linoleum, the yellow Formica counter and tabletop, the chairs with little and not-so-little rips in the upholstery. The fridge looked like it had come from the time when they'd been called iceboxes. I figured Delia must've dug it up at some junkyard. A cockroach skittered along the wall and disappeared behind an old clock, which was stuck at 11:07.

Since I was still wide awake, I turned on the porch light, walked out the back door and sat down on the step. The backyard looked just as dusty as the front, except it was full of dry weeds. In one corner stood a rusty metal shed. Big pots with dead plants were scattered here and there.

What would Nana have thought of all this? Nana, with her doilies, throw rugs and frilly curtains had always kept her house spotless. Her garden had been full of color—spring, summer and fall. Still, I was glad to be here.

I went back inside and tried the TV again, this time with the sound turned completely off. When I heard music coming from a different direction, I opened a front window to listen. It was coming from the building kitty-corner from Delia's house. I tried to tune out the noise from the neighbor's house and focus on this other source of music. I recognized a hymn we'd sung at Nana's funeral: *In the Garden.* She used to hum it all the time when she gardened.

I stood there until the church music stopped and the worshippers started leaving.

Despite the noisy neighbors and the lumpy bed, I fell into a deep sleep.

I woke up to the sound of Delia rushing around, getting ready for work. I got up as soon as I heard her drive off. Though I hate to admit it, one thing I'd inherited from Sara, besides her looks, was a touch of her OCD.

I found a sponge and some kind of spray cleaner under the sink and set to work, cleaning the bathroom. In the kitchen, I tried to pull the fridge away from the wall. When it wouldn't budge, I stuck a damp paper towel on the end of a broom handle and slid it into the spaces between the fridge and the cabinets, pulling out balls of black gunk from both sides. I scrubbed and mopped until I'd gotten rid of all the dirt I could reach. As I worked, a plan began to take shape in my head.

I checked the cupboard and found a can of chili beans, a jar of spaghetti sauce, a box of bran cereal and some stale bread. On the counter were a couple of overripe bananas and an onion. In the fridge, I found spoiled milk, peanut butter, mayo, wilted lettuce and a sliver of dried-out cheese. Even Betty Crocker would have trouble fixing a decent meal with those ingredients.

After I finished cleaning and scrounging around in the kitchen, I showered, changed and decided to go out and explore. I crossed the street to get a better look at the now-vacant church, Iglesia Libre del Buen Pastor. Next door, a small dog came to the fence and barked. Since there were no sidewalks, I walked along the gutter. The houses all looked like Delia's, except they were painted different piñata-bright colors. A few were a dull gray like they'd never been painted at all.

Three blocks away, I stumbled upon a little neighborhood market. The selection of groceries was pretty limited, but I bought a few things with Delia's ten dollars. Back at her house, I went through the cabinets looking for a skillet. The only one I could find was just big enough to fry an egg. I kept looking until I found one small pot and one medium-sized one. After scrubbing them a few times, I searched through drawer after drawer, looking for a knife and spoon. Under a bunch of outdated phone directories and catalogs, I found a paring knife and a wooden spoon along with two mismatched forks, two teaspoons and a butter knife.

I almost sliced off the tip of my thumb while trying to cut up the vegetables but managed to slice and dice everything and fit it all in the medium pot, using the smaller one to cook rice. Delia didn't seem to own a can opener, so I punched holes around the can of beans and pried it open. I'd seen her blood pressure medicine in the bathroom cabinet that morning and went easy on the salt.

Delia walked in the door that afternoon and went straight to the stove. She lifted the lid off the bigger pot and gave me a suspicious look.

"You made this?"

Duh! Either that or the galloping gourmet must've whipped it up when I wasn't looking. "Yeah, I went shopping at a nearby market."

"Smells great."

"Stew. Made with beans, vegetables and a spice mix. It's a recipe from one of my cooking magazines. The market didn't have Cajun spices, so I used some stuff you had in your cupboard. We're having it over rice. I hope you like it."

She ran her hand over the counter. "You've been busy, haven't you?"

"Hope you don't mind, but I did a little cleaning."

"Sorry, the place is such a mess. I never seem to find the time to clean."

❈ ❈ ❈

I ladled the stew into a couple of bowls.

"Very tasty," Delia said after she'd polished off her second helping. "Got any more recipes up your sleeve?"

"I can probably get some. Is there a library in this part of town?"

"There's one a couple of miles away. I've never been there. Only know it's there because I drive past it on my way to and from work."

Before going to bed, Delia gave me another twenty dollars and the library's address, along with a vague idea on how to get there.

The next morning, I slept in a little longer. After my shower, I went to heat up the leftovers for breakfast. They were gone. Delia had either eaten them or taken them for her lunch. I ate a couple of slices of toast instead.

❧ ❧ ❧

I stopped to ask for directions to the library a couple of times and finally found it an hour later. It was small but had a nice selection of magazines, including some of my favorites—*Sunset* and *National Geographic*—and several cooking magazines. It also had a decent cookbook section, which made me feel like a whole new world had opened up and was just waiting to be explored.

I read one of the most current copies of *National Geographic* while keeping one eye on the clock to make sure I left enough time to shop and cook. On my way out, I got a library card.

"You'll like Aarón Sánchez's cookbooks." The librarian said when she saw the two cookbooks I was checking out. "He's one of El Paso's most famous native sons."

"Thanks. I'm looking forward to reading them and trying the recipes."

I took my books home and started reading the Sánchez books that very night. Until then, I'd never really missed not having a TV. Now, I wished Delia had cable and a decent set so I could watch The Food Network.

❧ ❧ ❧

Saturday morning, Delia slept in. She looked rested and was in a good mood when she got up. She seemed to like our unspoken arrangement. I was her new live-in maid and cook. She bought the groceries and left it up to me to plan the menu. Aarón's garlic-chipotle love recipe became my main magic ingredient from then on.

"You're starting to spoil me with all these good eats. After being on my feet all day changing beds and wheeling people around, the last thing I feel like doing is coming home to cook. Why don't we go to a bigger grocery store and pick up whatever you're going to need for the week?"

"I'll make a list but I'll still need to buy a few things during the week, so they'll be fresh when I need them."

"Fair enough." She handed me twenty-five dollars. "Let me know if you need more."

Although we went up and down every single aisle at the Big 8 Foods she took me to, I spent most of the time in the produce section. I half expected her to question how I could possibly need to buy anything else during the week, but she just paid the bill and let me load the groceries in the trunk of her car.

I didn't buy any more groceries during the week. Instead, I put the money in my duffel bag with Patti's twenty-three dollars and distracted my aunt by bombarding her taste buds with exotic flavors and textures each night.

On Friday, we had just finished eating our stuffed artichokes and were about to start on the minestrone when

Delia said, "I hate to upset you, but Sara called to tell me Pedro had a stroke a few days ago."

The food I'd just eaten suddenly threatened to come right back up. I gulped down half the water in my glass.

"Don't worry," Delia said. "I didn't breathe a word about you being here."

"Does she expect you to go see him?"

Delia shook her head. "She knows better than to ask, but now that he can't work, she's thinking of selling Mamá's house. Apparently, someone made an offer, even though it's not on the market yet."

The word about Pedro's stroke must've reached Pastor Negrón, probably through Mrs. Lara. *Could it be the same potential renter who now saw a possible bargain?*

"You're trusting Sara to sell Nana's house?"

"It's Pedro's house now. Besides, a real estate agent will actually be selling it. Sara just has to sign all the paperwork."

"So why are they selling now when Pedro didn't even want to rent it out before?"

Delia took a deep breath. "I guess they expect the medical bills to start piling up and Pedro won't be going back to work anytime soon. They've transferred him to a rehab facility because he's still having trouble talking and getting around." She gave me a quick glance. "He somehow managed to ask about you, though. Probably wondering why you haven't stopped by to see him."

My fork clattered to the floor and the room started spinning.

Delia rubbed her eyes as if the whole thing was giving her a headache. "I can't imagine it's been any fun living with those two," she said. "I don't blame you or your brother for wanting out of there."

I picked up my fork and busied myself collecting the dishes and putting away the leftovers.

※　　※　　※

That night, I lay awake thinking of Nana and Mario. I suspected that, except for them, I was descended from a long line of losers, that the world would've been a better place if my family tree had been pulled out like a weed. Of course, that wouldn't have been fair to Nana. Without her, I might've not inherited any good traits at all. And where would I be without Delia now? She had been a lifesaver when I most needed her, but I couldn't see staying here now that the ghosts of my life in Las Nubes were rearing their ugly heads. It was time to grow a backbone, start planning my second escape and get serious about realizing my dream. If I was ever going to learn to be a chef, I sure wasn't going to do it by serving as a maid for my parents or my aunt. With Mario and Nana gone there was nothing to stop me from wiping the slate clean and starting over.

Chapter Four

Maguey

I continued to cook, clean, and visit the library every day. The topic of my transferring to a local school never came up again, but the news from Las Nubes had really rattled me. Since I was too distracted to read, I spent most days looking out a window. Guilt had been gnawing at me lately because I hadn't yet written to Patti. So one night, I asked Delia for directions to the nearest post office. After she went to bed, I wrote a short note.

Dear Patti,

Sorry I've taken so long to write, but things haven't been all that great here. Delia's okay, but I'm still too close to the fire. You've probably heard about Pedro's stroke. Sara called Delia and told her he'd asked about me. Not sure what's going to happen next. I'll let you know.

Love,
Lucy

I stuck her twenty-three dollars inside the note and sent it without a return address, thinking I wouldn't be hanging around El Paso much longer.

❈   ❈   ❈

"You deserve a break from all the cooking you've been doing," Delia said one day, while I did the dishes and she soaked her feet. "Let's go out tomorrow night. We can have an early dinner and do our grocery shopping afterward. I'll leave it up to you to pick a place."

"Italian okay?" I said remembering that a week earlier she'd raved about "Fideo a la Italiana," a pasta recipe I'd revised to give it a Mexican twist. She'd liked it so much, she'd even shared the leftovers with her co-workers.

"Perfect."

❈   ❈   ❈

Friday night, we were sitting at Pierleoni's, both wearing our Sunday best, which for me was a denim pencil skirt and a royal blue pocket tee Nana had given me a month before she died.

"You seem a little preoccupied lately," Delia said after we placed our orders.

"I've been thinking it's time for me to move on," I said.

Delia frowned. "Just where are you thinking of going?

"I've been considering Los Angeles."

"And here I thought you were the only one in the family with a brain in your head." Delia unfolded her napkin and placed it on her lap. "You planning on cooking for the stars?"

I tried to smile but didn't quite succeed. "I figure I can wait tables to pay for cooking classes."

"You can probably find a cooking school right here."

"I can't stay here much longer. I need to . . . I just have plans that I can't keep putting off."

I never thought I'd see my aunt pass up a chance to eat whatever was set before her, but when the waitress brought our food, we both just picked at it.

"At least hang around until you've thought things through," she said. "After all, it's not like you're going to get to LA and walk right into a job. I can start giving you a weekly allowance."

"I don't want to take your money."

I didn't tell her I was already taking it. Instead of spending what she gave me each week on groceries, I'd been saving for a bus ticket, food and a place to stay for a few days once I got to LA.

Delia's reaction planted a seed of doubt in my mind, though. Not very convincingly, I said, "I can probably get a part-time job somewhere here and save enough to get by for a while once I get to LA."

"Whatever job you're able to get won't be worth the trouble you'll have to go through," Delia said. "You're saving me a lot of time by cooking and cleaning."

"It's the least I can do since I don't pay for room and board."

"I never like to plan too far ahead. When you came to stay with me, I decided to take one day at a time." She looked down at her plate while she searched for just the right words. "The last thing I want is to stand between you and your dream. It sounds like you've made up your mind anyway." She tossed her napkin on the table. "Look, I'm getting a monster headache. Just promise you'll stick around for a while and think about this a little more before you run off like your brother did."

He has a name, I wanted to yell at her, but she was the only ally I had and I couldn't afford to piss her off.

"If I hired someone to cook and clean for me, it would cost me a lot more than I can afford, but I'll start paying you whatever I can spare each week. I'll even get rid of the stuff in your room to give you a little more space. I don't remember what's in those bags and boxes anyway, so it can't be that important."

"Thanks, Tía." I immediately warmed up to her suggestion, thinking it would give me more time to plan and save.

"I should be thanking you. I've got so much more energy since I stopped eating the junk I used to eat. I'd given up hope of ever losing weight, but just last week I had to exchange my size 16 uniform for a 14."

I didn't tell her that, while she lost weight, I managed to gain five pounds, now that I was actually eating and wasn't so stressed out. I was now tipping the scales at a whopping one hundred and ten pounds. Since I'd moved in with her, I'd done a complete reversal of the diet I'd fed Pedro, switching to baking, broiling and steaming—never frying. Of course, almost anything would've been an improvement to her diet of fast food and just plain junk. I never served dessert unless we were celebrating something. When I did, it was mostly fresh fruit, low-fat puddings or sorbets, which I made using the blender I'd convinced her to buy.

I must've fallen asleep with my eyes wide open that night. One minute I was staring at the ceiling and the next I was standing on a street corner with people bumping into me as they hurried past. Horns honked and radios blared while the bumper-to-bumper traffic crept by and pedestrians darted across the street. Not sure which way to go, I let myself be carried along by a wave of humanity. The army of people marching to the noisy beat threatened to trample anyone who slowed them down. Before long, my breathing became ragged and my legs started cramping. I sat up in bed, gulping mouthfuls of air until my heart rate returned to normal.

I was still tossing and turning when the phone rang. I ran out to shut it off before it woke Delia up. Instead, I pressed the answer button when I recognized Patti's number.

"Hi, Patti." I walked out to the back porch with the phone.

"I've been worried sick about you. Your letter didn't exactly ease my mind. Can you talk?" She sounded more like her mother than herself.

"Yeah. Delia's asleep."

"So, how are you *really*?"

"I'm okay. Delia's place is a dump, but at least it's a quiet and safe dump."

I let Patti ramble on and on about school and what she and Fernando had been doing lately. When she stopped to catch her breath, I asked about Mario.

"He called right before he left for boot camp. He asked about you, and Fernando gave him your aunt's number. You should be hearing from him soon."

Knowing that she'd have a million questions I wouldn't be able to answer, I didn't mention my plan.

❧   ❧   ❧

Other than getting rid of the junk in my bedroom, Delia and I kept going just as we'd been doing since I'd moved in, except that I started getting a hundred-dollar weekly allowance. That meant I earned less than fifteen dollars a day for cooking every night of the week and doing some light cleaning most days. On the plus side, I didn't have to put up with any grief. Or pay rent.

Delia pulled double duty Thanksgiving Day to cover for a co-worker who was going out of town. I worked all that day cleaning, baking and cooking a special dinner: stuffed acorn squash, a spinach soufflé, Brussels sprouts with caramelized onions, poppy-seed cornbread and, as a special treat, red velvet cake with coconut icing.

"This house has never smelled so good," Delia said as she walked in the door late that evening. "And look at that table."

I'd decorated her raggedy table with the tablecloth and placemats I'd picked up at a local thrift store. I'd even bought seat cushions to cover the tears in her old chairs. In the center of the table, I'd placed a harvest basket with small pumpkins and gourds of various colors, shapes and sizes.

"Mamá was a great cook," Delia said while we ate, "but even she would have to admit this would be hard to beat. Why do you need to go to cooking school? You could probably teach your own classes."

Delia's compliment was better than a twenty percent tip to me.

"If it weren't for Nana, I might never have learned to cook, but there's so much more I need to learn." I looked across the table at Delia, but she was busy crumbling her cornbread and sprinkling it over her Brussel sprouts.

"Will you be working overtime again on Christmas day?" I asked.

She nodded. "I've been doing it for years. It keeps me busy, and the few extra bucks I make come in handy."

"That explains why we never saw you at Nana's during the holidays."

Delia got a faraway look in her eyes. "As long as Pedro was there, I don't think it made much difference to Mamá whether I showed up or not."

"I'm glad you came back for her funeral."

"Of course, I had to be there. She was a good mother, just had a blind spot when it came to Pedro." She stopped eating and looked at me. "I can't imagine what it must've been like for you and . . ."

"Mario," I said. "It was a nightmare."

"I don't blame either of you for escaping the first chance you got. Do you ever hear from him?"

"Only through Patti and her boyfriend Fernando. According to them, Mario enlisted in the Navy."

Delia patted my hand. "Well, he's welcome to come visit you here anytime."

I wondered if this was another attempt to keep me from leaving. But I just said, "Thanks. I hope you don't mind that Fernando gave Mario your phone number the last time he spoke with him."

"Good. Maybe he'll call you soon."

❀   ❀   ❀

That weekend, I hung Christmas lights around Delia's front porch and tried to make our Christmas a little more festive by decorating a miniature tree. My nonexistent budget, plus the fact that I knew so little about my aunt, made it hard for me to find a gift for her. Then it dawned on me. Since she was always complaining about her feet, what better gift than a foot massager? I went out and got her one, wrapped the box in bright red paper and tied a green bow around it. The gift was almost as big as the tree.

On Christmas Day, Delia walked in with a beautifully wrapped package and placed it next to the little tree. After dinner, we opened our gifts. Mine was a set of fancy kitchen knives—perfect for an aspiring chef.

❧   ❧   ❧

By New Year's Day, I'd saved twelve hundred dollars, more money than I'd ever seen at one time. It probably wouldn't go very far in LA, but hopefully, it wouldn't take long to find a job and a place to stay when I got there.

"I think this is a good time for a new beginning," I said as we ate the pumpkin-spice pancakes I'd made for breakfast.

"I wish there was something I could say or do to change your mind," Delia said.

At that moment, I thought I caught a glimpse of Nana in my aunt's eyes. The resemblance disappeared as suddenly as it had come.

"Tía, I don't know what I would've done if you hadn't let me stay with you when I had no place else to go. I . . ."

"Having you here has been the best thing that's happened to me in a long time. You're welcome to stay as long as you want. You don't have to cook and clean as much as you do now if you decide to go back to school."

"I don't want to cause any problems between you and Pedro."

"Things have never been good between us. Nothing you do can make them worse."

"What would it have taken to change your mind when you left home?"

"Nothing could have kept me from leaving."

❧   ❧   ❧

At the bus station that night, Delia pulled a small box out of her bag and held it out to me. "Let me know how things work out in LA."

Inside, I found a cell phone. Under it was a one hundred dollar bill.

"My coworkers' recommendations," she said, "so you can blame them if you don't like it. I added a new line to my plan and got a good deal because I also bought a new phone for myself. Your number and mine are in the address book inside the box. You're all set. Now there's no excuse for not staying in touch."

I didn't know what to say, and not caring whether she was a hugger or not, I threw my arms around her. I couldn't stop my eyes from tearing up.

She clung to me longer than I expected, then gave me a gentle push. "You better go before the bus leaves without you."

She was still standing there as the bus pulled away from the station. I waved one last time, then stared out the window at the shadowy figures hurrying past in the dim light. Once we were out of the city, I turned away from the window when the darkness outside threatened to suffocate me. Across the aisle, a woman had turned on the overhead light. Her little boy, who looked about four years old, leaned against her. Her arm rested protectively around him. I wondered about their journey, picturing the boy's father, or maybe his grandmother, waiting for them, eager to greet them when they reached their destination.

Using my jacket as a pillow, I leaned my head against the window and closed my eyes, trying to drive away the thought that no one was waiting for me in LA. But every muscle in my body remained awake, every nerve fully alert.

With all the stops at every little bump in the road, it was hard to tell how far we'd gone. The little towns we passed seemed like clones of one another. In Tucson, I got off the bus to use the restroom and buy a Pepsi. Although I was thirsty, I only took a couple of sips and saved the rest when I remembered it might be a while before the next pit stop.

Back on the bus, I kept one eye on the door as the other passengers started boarding. While the last passenger, a drunk, made his unsteady way down the aisle, I kept repeating under my breath, *Please don't come near me. Please stay away.* I took a quick look around to see what other seats were available. There were only two, both in the back, but the characters I'd have to sit next to didn't look any better than the drunk.

"Ain't you a little young to be travelin' alone?" he said as he planted himself in the seat next to me.

I ignored him, closed my eyes and turned toward the window.

"Where you headed, anyhow? Maybe we could team up and travel together. Ain't nobody gonna mess with you, long as you're with me."

I slid further down in my seat and pretended to doze off.

He yammered on and on. I did my best to ignore him until he laid his head on my shoulder and started snoring, as if each breath he took might be his last—wishful thinking. I covered my right ear and tried to push him away, but he kept rolling right back. I finally put my jacket on my shoulder and that helped a bit.

I don't know how long we traveled that way. It was hot, and I was tired and growing more anxious by the minute. Here I was from a little hick town in Texas, headed for a city that made up a tenth of the whole state of California with only a vague plan—a dream, really. Delia was right. What had I been thinking? I'd be surrounded by total strangers in a city I only knew through television and magazines.

I'm going to be a chef. I'm going to be a chef. I repeated my mantra over and over in my head, when my hands started getting cold and I was close to hyperventilating.

Early in the afternoon, as we approached the next town, I sat up and looked around. *Welcome to Maguey, population 3,600,* the city limit sign said.

My eyes zeroed in on a restaurant with a Help Wanted sign in the front window. The sign on its awning identified it as La Cocina, magic words to me. The kitchen, like the library, had become my cocoon, my safe place.

Pushing the drunk up with my arm and shoulder, I pulled my small bag toward me with my feet and leaned forward just far enough to pick it up. Not caring about the drunk's reaction, I shoved his dead weight off me with every ounce of my weight. Keeping the bag between us, I squeezed past him and into the aisle. I hurried to the door and jumped onto the sidewalk. The only passenger who'd been waiting at this stop boarded quickly.

After watching the bus disappear in a cloud of dust and shimmering heat, I set my bag down, shielded my eyes from the sun and looked around at the squat old buildings that lined what looked like the town's main street. The bus had stopped in front of a small post office. Next to it was a bigger building, Maguey State Bank and Trust Company. *Invest in Your Community,* a big sign in front of it said.

Other than the restaurant sign, what had compelled me to stop here? I couldn't really explain it. Sara would've called it *brujería.* I quickly put her and her witchcraft out of my mind, picked up my bag and made my way to the restaurant.

The door creaked as I pulled it open. The place was warm and dim, and the scents inside reminded me that, other than the sandwich and snacks I'd packed for the trip,

I hadn't eaten for quite a while. I ran my fingers through my hair, hoping I didn't look too wilted after serving as a pillow for the drunk on the bus.

"I saw your sign," I said to the lady behind the cash register.

Her round face lit up. She smiled and came around the counter to get a better look at me.

"It's a dishwashing job," she said. "Still interested?"

"Yes, ma'am," I answered, hoping my disappointment didn't show. *What an idiot! I hadn't even stopped to think about what the job might be.*

"What kind of experience do you have?"

"I've been washing dishes since . . . half my life," I said.

"Well, this is a little different from doing the dinner dishes at home. Don't you even want to know how much the job pays?"

"I'm willing to work for minimum wage."

The woman smiled again. "Good. Because that's what it pays." She looked at my bag and asked, "Where are you staying?"

"I'm new in town. I, uh, need to find a place to stay. But I could start tomorrow."

"This is a small town, in case you hadn't noticed," she whispered as if she were sharing a big secret. "You won't find any apartments or hotels here, but let's see what my husband says. He's the one who does the hiring."

She called out a man's name, and a tall, skinny cowboy walked in from another room.

"We have an applicant for the dishwasher job," she told him.

"*¡Carambola, Lola!*" he said. He adjusted his glasses and took a good look at me. "How old are you, anyway?"

I pulled my shoulders back, trying to look taller than my puny five feet. "I'll be eighteen in a couple of months."

He looked unconvinced. "Sorry, kid, but this is a full-time job. We need somebody who can just walk in and take over, the sooner the better."

"I can do it. I know I can."

"What about school? Come back when you're eighteen. If we still have an opening, we'll think about hiring you then."

Maybe Sara had been more skillful at her witchcraft hobby than I'd given her credit for. Had she cast some kind of spell on me that caused me to get off the bus in the middle of nowhere? How was I going to get to LA now?

By then I'd lost my appetite, but who knew when I'd get another chance to eat.

"Could I at least buy some lunch?" I said.

"We're closed until . . ." the man started to say.

"Have a seat," his wife said. "I'm sure there's something left in the kitchen."

I sat at the counter, trying not to cry.

The cowboy disappeared through a door behind the counter, and his wife soon showed up with a steaming bowl of *pozole* and a basket of corn tortillas.

"What would you like to drink?' she asked.

"Water, please."

She made her way back to the kitchen, her slippers swooshing softly against the floor.

I usually liked *pozole* but seeing the hominy kernels floating in the bowl like swollen teeth killed what was left of my appetite. I rolled up a tortilla, dipped it in the bowl and bit off the wet end.

The cowboy's wife stood across from me, watching me eat.

"I remember being seventeen . . ."

I tried to picture the seventeen-year-old version of her behind the lines that crisscrossed her face, and the gray hair pulled back into a braid with wisps of it falling across her forehead. The sparkle in her eyes was probably still the same. Her full lips and easy smile also made her seem younger than she looked. But too many years had passed, and too many layers of life had been piled onto that face to get a clear picture of what it had been like when she was young. Still, she seemed nice. And hoping I wasn't being too nosy.

"Do you have any children?" I asked, hoping I wasn't too nosy.

"No, dear." She sighed and looked at her hands as she massaged the red, swollen knuckles.

"Have you been washing the dishes yourself?"

"I tried to help out," she said, "but my arthritis got even worse. The assistant cook has been pulling double duty, and the waiting staff helps clean up the place. We've been managing, but just barely."

"Ma'am, if you give me a chance, I'll be the best dishwasher you've ever seen. I promise you won't regret it."

She looked toward the door through which her husband had disappeared, then turned back to me.

"Give me a few minutes. I'll be right back."

She walked back to talk to her husband. Pretty soon I started hearing his side of the argument.

". . . hire a kid who walks in out of nowhere telling you whatever she thinks you want to hear. For all we know, she could be a runaway."

Pause.

"And just how long do you think you can hide her in the kitchen? She doesn't look anywhere near eighteen to me. We have enough problems as it is. . . ."

Pause.

"What makes you think she can afford to pay rent? If you're finally ready to rent it out, there are plenty of people who'd be interested . . ."

I took another bite of my tortilla and pretended to be enjoying my lunch when I heard the shuffling steps headed back in my direction.

During the pauses, while I eavesdropped, I'd been trying to figure out what I was going to do if the old guy refused to budge. Where would I go? How far was I from LA? Where would I buy another ticket, and how often did the buses come through?

"I'm sorry, dear. I tried my best, but he's a stubborn one."

Remembering what I'd overheard about paying rent, I said, "What if I work for room and board until I turn eighteen? I won't actually be an employee until then."

She looked at me as if she were considering my offer.

"The room and board agreement sound fine. You'll be saving us money, and it'll be a big help to have you take over the dishwashing. When my husband and I first opened the restaurant, we used to live upstairs. The place is very small and, because it's right above the restaurant, I've resisted letting just anyone move in, although we could certainly use the rent money." She raised a finger and said, "Give me one more minute."

She shuffled back to the office. This time all I heard was, "Fine, then. If she turns out to be nothing but trouble, I'm sure you'll find a way to get us out of that mess."

She returned with a smile on her face. "You can stay upstairs."

Yes! I could've kissed her.

Before I could say anything, she added, "We haven't been there for a while. Why don't we go up there now and see what condition the place is in."

She led the way out into a weed-infested backyard and up a side stairway, her breathing getting heavier with each step. The sight of her thick legs, knotted with cords of varicose veins, made me wince.

"This is why we had to move," she managed to puff when she paused on the third step to catch her breath. "I just couldn't climb these stairs anymore."

I nodded, not sure what I was supposed to say. She took a few more steps and stopped again. The whole stairway was only about twelve steps high, but she could only climb three between breathing stops. After what seemed like forever, we finally reached the door. She pulled out a key ring from her apron pocket and tried one of the keys. When that didn't work, she tried another. On the third try, the door opened into a small living room.

My new employer plunked herself down on the first chair she reached. It creaked and groaned under all that weight.

"It's kind of musty in here," she said. "Let's open a few windows and air the place out a little. You can blow the dust off later."

I dropped my bag on the floor, opened the two living room windows and noticed two more in the next room. I opened those too and kept going from room to room, opening windows, wondering if shedding my old life and starting over would be as easy as airing out this place.

The whole apartment consisted of a living room, bedroom, kitchenette and bathroom, plus a balcony that could be reached from both the kitchenette and living room. The furniture looked like stuff I'd seen outside discount stores.

"There should be enough sheets and towels in there to meet your needs," The woman said, pointing in the direction of the bathroom. "You'll find a blanket or two in the bedroom closet. If you need anything else, I can probably bring it from home."

Suddenly, she got a worried look on her face. "Oh dear, here I've hired you and moved you in and I haven't even asked your name." She offered her hand. "I'm Mrs. Flores."

I took her hand and shook it once. "Pleased to meet you. I'm Lucy Sánchez."

"Lucy. What a lovely name." I had the feeling she would've complimented me even if I'd said my name was Kalamazoo.

She handed me the key to the apartment. "We're open from eleven-thirty to one-thirty for lunch and five to nine for dinner. You should probably come down around ten tomorrow morning, so my husband can explain how things work in the kitchen. He'll also want to know more about you then."

"Thank you for everything," I said. "I can start work today."

"Tomorrow's soon enough. You must be tired. Go ahead and rest. You'll have plenty of time to unpack later."

We both looked at my bag, something between an antique store reject and a bargain basement special I'd picked up in El Paso. It contained all of my worldly possessions.

I stood at the door and watched her as she went down the stairs. Going down seemed much easier and a little faster than the climb had been, although she still teetered at each step. When she reached the last step, I closed the door and started settling in. Mrs. Flores and her husband seemed to have just walked out and left everything as if they'd be returning any day.

The place was so small, it didn't take long for me to "blow off the dust" as she'd suggested. After I finished cleaning, I squeezed some rose-scented bubble bath I'd found under the bathroom sink into the big claw-foot tub and filled it with warm water until the bubbles started spilling out. The tub seemed out of place in the apartment. I couldn't imagine Mrs. Flores climbing in and out of it. Maybe that was another reason they'd moved. I sat in the tub, breathing in the scent of roses, trying not to worry about what Mr. Flores might ask me when I reported for work in the morning. I'd find out soon enough.

Chapter Five
On Probation

The sun shining through the window woke me up, making me feel like a salamander when the rock it's been hiding under is suddenly lifted. It took me a couple of seconds to figure out where I was. The bed, like the tub, was a big surprise. Since I hadn't slept the night before and the stress of the past twenty-some hours had worn me out, I'd fallen into a dreamless sleep right after my bath. I couldn't remember the last time I'd slept so well.

I put on a dark blue T-shirt and jeans and realized I would soon need to wash the few clothes I owned. The sheets and towels could also use a quick wash to remove their musty smell.

By ten, I was standing at the back door to the restaurant. I panicked when I tried it and found it locked. *Had Mr. Flores fired me before I even started? Maybe this was all a dream.* The apartment key in my hand was real enough, though. I knocked, stood on my toes to look through the glass pane and saw Mr. Flores walking toward me. He opened the door.

"Good morning," I said, as cheerfully as I dared.

He ignored me and headed back where he'd come from, the heel guards on his cowboy boots clicking loudly with each step.

"Good morning." His wife was sitting at a table by the cash register. I hadn't noticed it the day before because it was hidden behind a partition. "I hope you slept well."

"I did. Thank you."

Before I could decide what to do next, Mr. Flores walked back in carrying a pot of coffee. He pulled out a chair, and I took that as an order for me to sit. He sat across from his wife.

"If nothing else, I have to give you credit for persistence," he said.

"I promise you won't regret hiring me," I said.

"Unless I'm losing my memory, I think it was Lola who hired you. You even managed to convince her to let you move in upstairs."

I looked at Mrs. Flores. The smile on her face helped boost my shrinking confidence.

"Right. It's . . . perfect. I'll start paying rent as soon as I pass probation. Until then, you can just say this is my after-school job if anybody asks

"Now you want me to lie for you?"

I looked down at my hands. "I didn't mean it that way."

"We've managed without you for almost twenty years," Mr. Flores said.

His wife patted his hand and gave him a "be nice" kind of look.

He narrowed his eyes and looked at me sideways. "We'll show you around, and then you can make yourself scarce until two."

"Make that one-thirty so you can eat before you start work," Mrs. Flores said.

Just then, a man who looked a little younger than Mr. Flores walked in carrying a tray.

"Guerrero, this is the dishwasher Lola hired. She's starting this afternoon."

Guerrero put the tray on the table. "Lucy, right?"

I smiled and nodded as I shook his hand.

"Me and Guerrero, we do all the cooking," Mr. Flores said. "He's been helping out with the dishes since the dishwasher quit and moved away. He'll be glad to turn them over to you."

"I'm a fast learner," I said.

Mr. Flores leaned his elbow on the table and rested his chin in his hand. He looked at me as if to say, *We'll see about that.*

Mrs. Flores took the cups from the tray Guerrero had carried in, put one in front of each of us and started pouring coffee.

I gestured to her that I only wanted a tiny bit.

She pushed a plate full of pastries toward me. "You've still got some growing to do. We really should be serving you a more nutritious breakfast."

"Oh, don't worry about me," I said. "I plan to go grocery shopping later so I can have breakfast before I report to work."

"Nonsense, child! This is a restaurant for goodness sake. We've just gotten in the habit of having *pan dulce* every morning because it's convenient."

Guerrero laughed. "And because it's caffeine, we need more than food this time of day."

"Maybe she's the type who likes to sleep until noon," Mr. Flores said. "If I didn't have to start work until two, why would I come in at ten just to drink coffee?"

"I'm always up early," I said.

I helped myself to a pumpkin *empanada* and, although I didn't really like coffee, I drank half a cup after filling the rest of it with milk. The chocolate *concha* on the plate also seemed to be calling my name, but I didn't want to appear too greedy. After I finished my milky coffee, I was tempted to jump up and wash my dishes but, since I didn't know my way around, I waited and watched for the right cues. No one seemed in any hurry to start work.

"I hear you're new in town," Guerrero said. "What brought you to Maguey?"

"I, uh, was raised by my grandmother. She lived here when she was a child and used to talk about it." I surprised myself at how easily the lie spilled out of me. It had to be my survival instincts taking over my mind and mouth.

"And what is her name?" Mr. Flores said.

"Liliana Molina. She moved away when she was pretty young." *If you can't tell the truth, you better start coming up with more convincing lies,* I reminded myself.

"So, where is she now?"

"She died recently."

"I see." Mr. Flores gave his wife a see-what-you've-done look before he stood up. "Well, ready for the big tour?"

"Yes, sir."

As he led the way to the kitchen with me at his heels, a man even younger than Guerrero walked in the front door. Mr. Flores stopped and waved his hand in my direction.

"Meme, this is Lucy, the new dishwasher."

"Hey, Lucy, I'm Manuel Hinojosa. You can call me Meme. I'm Berta's assistant. Have you met her yet?"

Before I could answer, I heard a woman's voice coming from behind him.

"You all talking about me behind my back again?"

"Berta, we have a new dishwasher," Mrs. Flores said.

"Good. Now Guerrero can get back to his real job," Berta said without looking my way, or saying hello.

She went straight to a mirror at the end of the counter and started fluffing her honey-colored hair and dabbing at the corners of her lips with her left pinkie. In her short red dress with off-the-shoulder sleeves and French-maid apron, she looked like she'd stepped out of one of the telenovelas Nana used to like. I watched her and her long legs and swaying hips disappear behind the cash register and was glad that as the dishwasher, I wouldn't be expected to dress like her. With my flat chest and narrow hips, I couldn't see myself in Berta's uniform.

In the kitchen, Mr. Flores showed me the six-burner stove with the oversized oven, the industrial-size stainless-steel refrigerator and the pantry.

"And here," he said, pointing to a large double sink, "is your main workstation."

Next to the sink was a counter that sloped just enough to let the water run down from the drain board. A supply of dishtowels was stacked on a shelf above the sink and plastic containers filled with knives, forks and spoons were neatly lined up against the wall. Under the counter was the dishwasher. The hooks on the ceiling above my workstation held the biggest pots and pans I'd ever seen. On the stove side of the workstation were shelves where I was supposed to stack the clean, dried dishes. I couldn't have designed it better myself. But what did I know? This was the first restaurant kitchen I'd ever seen.

Guerrero explained the whole routine of washing, drying and stacking the dishes where he and Mr. Flores could easily reach them.

"Let me know if you have questions or need help," he said before he went to the stainless-steel island in the middle of the kitchen and started chopping onions.

I was about to offer to help, but Mr. Flores dismissed me before I could open my mouth. "See you at one-thirty."

He took an apron from a hook on the wall and walked to the stove.

"It's perfect," I said to Mrs. Flores on my way out. "I can't wait to start."

"Let us know if you need anything," she said as I went out the front door, figuring I'd go for a quick walk and see what I might've missed from the bus window.

I hadn't walked very far before realizing there wasn't much I hadn't already seen on the main drag. The rest didn't look that interesting. On the way back to the apartment, I saw a grocery store and stopped to buy bananas, peanut butter, snacks and a loaf of bread.

"Is there a laundromat in town?" I asked the cashier.

"Behind the post office," she said.

"What about a library?"

"Nope. If you want books, you have to go to Saguaro."

"Thanks. How far is Saguaro?"

"Ten miles up the road."

It was only noon when I got back to the apartment. I figured Delia must be starting to worry about me. Since there was no emergency, I sent her a quick text saying I was okay and would call her later.

I sat by the open bedroom window and tried to read. At one-thirty I went down to the restaurant. Mrs. Flores offered me a menu.

"Thanks, but I had a sandwich a little while ago," I said.

"I guess one-thirty is a little late for lunch when you only had sweets for breakfast."

"It's fine. I just wanted to see what it's like when the customers are here."

"You missed the rush. The only stragglers left are in no hurry to get back to work."

As soon as the last customer left, Berta threw her apron on the counter and disappeared without a word.

Guerrero was right behind her. "See you at four."

"I usually run home between lunch and dinner to check on my wife," Meme said as he got ready to leave. "We're expecting our first baby."

"How exciting! Congratulations."

"I take a little siesta in the office at this time while Beto does the paperwork," Mrs. Flores said. "Otherwise, I wouldn't make it through the rest of the day. But don't hesitate to knock on the office door if you have any questions."

"Thanks. I'll be fine. Have a good nap."

I went to my workstation and began loading the dishwasher before starting on the pots and pans. I was determined to keep my promise of being the best dishwasher they'd ever had.

After I finished with the dishes, I wrapped silverware in paper napkins, piled them in a big plastic tray and placed them on a cart, next to a stack of tumblers, beer glasses and pitchers. Then, I wheeled the cart out and parked it behind the bar.

Since it was still early and no one was around, I brought in a bucket and mop I'd found in the supply closet and mopped the floor. Mrs. Flores walked in just as I was about to put everything away.

"You don't have to do that," she said. "Every Saturday morning we all come in an hour early to give the place a good cleaning. The rest of the week, we just wipe up spills and sweep."

"Oh, I don't mind. It didn't take me long. I'll be happy to clean up after we close."

"Just do a good job with the dishes and we'll be happy."

❧   ❧   ❧

I called Delia right around the time she usually got home. When she didn't answer, I left a message saying I had a job, was okay and would call her back that weekend.

Once the restaurant opened for dinner and orders started coming in, the cooks forgot about me as they rushed around filling them. An hour later, I pushed a cart of clean utensils and glasses to the order window and retrieved another full of dirty dishes. I emptied the leftovers into a big bucket by the sink before starting the wash cycle again.

At around six-thirty, Meme popped his head in the door.

"Lucy, can you come out and help clear the tables?" He grabbed an empty bussing cart from the kitchen and pushed it toward a table with a stack of dirty dishes. "You need to make sure there's always an empty cart near the order window for the dirty dishes. Once we get busy, we don't always have time to bus tables."

"Sorry . . ."

"Don't worry about it," Meme said. "There's always a lot to learn your first day on the job. After you're done here, please clear table seven."

I walked over to where he'd pointed, cleared the table and was wiping it clean when Berta walked up behind me.

"Who are *you*?" she asked.

"I'm Lucy," I said. "The new dishwasher," I added when I saw the blank look on her face.

She looked me up and down. "Boy, Lola and Beto must've been more desperate than I realized."

Oh, stick it in that hornet's nest you wear on your head. The color probably comes from a bottle anyway.

She walked away and I went back to cleaning the table. On my way back to the kitchen, I saw her flirting with a bunch of rowdy guys at a table near the bar.

❧   ❧   ❧

Around eight-thirty, as I was pushing a cartload of dirty dishes past the bar on my way to the kitchen, I saw a man with a mustache that made him look like a bat had landed across his upper lip.

"Mmm, mmm, mmm. Where you been hiding all my life, *morenita?*"

I ignored him and kept going, hoping he wasn't a regular.

❧   ❧   ❧

Within a couple of days, I'd set up my own routine and even had time to help with other chores when I wasn't washing dishes. Mainly, I chopped vegetables and refilled salt and pepper shakers. Since Berta usually didn't report for work until the last possible minute, it was easy to avoid her at first.

❧   ❧   ❧

I walked in after lunch one day that first week while Mrs. Flores was handing out envelopes.

"Friday is payday," she said. "Something to look forward to."

Meme took his envelope and started to walk out. At the door, he stopped and turned to me. "Lucy, my wife, and I go to Saguaro practically every Sunday. Let me know if you ever want to come along."

"Thanks, Meme. Sounds great."

"Maybe next week?" he said.

"Maybe."

❧ ❧ ❧

On Sunday morning, I decided to call Delia again. She picked up on the first ring. "Lucy?"

"Hi, Tía."

"You met any movie stars yet?"

"No, not where I'm working."

"What was all that talk about cooking for the stars, then?"

I laughed. "I think that was *your* idea. Anyway, I never made it to LA. Instead, I had a chance to get some on-the-job training." I didn't tell her I was washing dishes. "I'm not sure where I landed exactly, but the less I tell you, the better. That way, if Pedro ever asks where I went, you won't have to lie to him."

"I'm glad you're okay and I don't care what Pedro says, but I hope you stay in touch every once in a while."

"Thanks, Tía. I just wanted to check in with you."

"Your buddy Patti called. She sounded very disappointed when I told her you'd left and I hadn't heard from you."

"Did you give her my number?"

"No. I figured you'd call her if you wanted to talk to her."

"I do and I will. Talk to you again soon."

Patti would want to know where I was and what I was doing. I'd have to call her later when I had time to answer all her questions.

❧ ❧ ❧

I hit the snooze button when the alarm went off at six-thirty the next morning. A half hour later, I stumbled out of bed and stuffed my clothes in one pillowcase and the linen in another. After a quick shower, I grabbed them both and headed to the laundromat.

Late that afternoon, I took a long walk in the outskirts of town and got a closer look at the different kinds of cactus plants, scraggly shrubs and stubby trees that grew in the area. Maguey was exactly the kind of town I'd been looking for, although I hadn't realized it until then. It wasn't exactly what I'd dreamed of, but I could learn a few things about working in a restaurant and save money for when I finally made it to LA.

I waited until ten-thirty that night to call Patti, hoping that she wouldn't talk too long since she had to be up early for school the next day. I got a busy signal the first two times and assumed she was talking to Fernando. On the third try, I got through.

"Your ears must've been buzzing," she said. "Me and Fernando were just talking about you. You didn't send me an address, so I called your aunt. She wouldn't tell me anything, except that you weren't there anymore."

"Actually, she didn't know where I was."

"What happened? Did you run away again?"

I laughed. "No. I just didn't see a future there." I tried giving her the same spiel I'd given Delia about my job and my whereabouts. But Patti wanted details.

"Wait! So where are you now?"

"In a tiny town somewhere in Arizona, working at a Mom and Pop restaurant."

"Have you met any cute guys?"

"You kidding? I haven't met anybody other than the people I work with. I'm kind of working under the radar for a couple of months."

"Don't let them take advantage of you just because you're . . ."

"Don't worry. They're great people . . . well, most of them, anyway. Has Fernando heard from Mario?"

"He got an e-mail from him a couple of weeks ago. He was someplace in Virginia. He'd called your aunt's number, but didn't get an answer and didn't leave a message because he was shipping out the next day."

After she gave me Mario's e-mail address, I only half-listened while Patti told me all about the dress she'd worn to Fernando's sister's wedding and how they'd danced until one in the morning.

She suddenly paused mid-sentence and switched gears. "Oops! I guess Mom's right. I'm so full of myself I don't know when to stop talking and just listen. Now, tell me everything you've been up to."

"I already have. Work takes up most of my time right now. I figure I'll get a little experience while I save enough money to get into a culinary program. I just wanted to let you know I'm okay. Since you have to go to school tomorrow and I have to go to work, I'll call you again next weekend."

"Does that mean I can't call you?"

"Sure you can. Sunday's the best day to call, though, because I really can't talk while I'm at work."

As soon as I got off the phone, I started thinking of setting up an e-mail account so I could send Mario a message. I wrote it out long-hand and stuck it in my backpack.

Dear Big Brother,

By now you've heard I was able to escape the looney bin soon after you left. Delia proved to be a lifesaver. I owe her big time.

Although I haven't yet made it to culinary school, I'm working at a restaurant in a little desert town called Maguey.

I think of you every day and can't wait to see you again. In the meantime, take good care and write whenever you can.

Lots of love and hugs,
Lulu

I added my phone number at the bottom.

❀   ❀   ❀

I'd just started loading the dishwasher the following day after dinner, when Berta burst into the kitchen. I was surprised to see her because she and Meme usually took off as soon as the last customer left.

"Beto, I hate to tell you this, but you made a big mistake when you hired that kid." She looked at me as if I were a cockroach she'd just found in her guacamole.

"What're you talking about?" Mr. Flores said.

Mrs. Flores shuffled in and stood at the door, trying to catch her breath.

"What is it, Berta?"

"Your new dishwasher's started swiping tips off tables when she's supposed to be clearing away the dishes."

I opened my mouth, but nothing came out. *Was she serious?*

"Go ahead and search her. She must have at least fifty dollars. She took it from the tables where the soccer team always sits."

Mr. Flores turned to me.

I pulled my pant pockets inside out to show they were empty, then slapped my back pockets to show that, except for my apartment key, they were also empty.

"Bet you stuck it in your training bra. God knows there's nothing else for it to hold in."

I patted my chest. "Go ahead and see for yourself if you don't believe me."

"*Pshhhhh*," Guerrero said, "it's been a long day. I'm sure the money will turn up in the morning."

Mr. Flores gave his wife one of his I-told-you-so looks. She probably didn't see it because she was looking at me, sadness clouding her eyes, disappointment making her lumpy body sag.

Berta spun around on her heel and walked out of the kitchen, her footsteps pounding the floor like a judge's gavel: guilty, guilty, guilty.

"I swear I didn't take her money. If it isn't found, you can take it out of my pay." Then, remembering I wasn't getting paid, I said, "Or I'll pay for it out of my own pocket."

"It has been a long day," Mrs. Flores said. "Let's go home. Things will be much clearer in the morning."

After everyone else left, Guerrero helped me dry the pots and pans.

"I don't know what really happened to that tip money, but I can't believe you'd risk everything for a few bucks. I'm sure Lola and Beto know that, too." He threw the towel over his shoulder and turned to me. "Berta's always been kind of moody and a little vain, but I was hoping she'd be nicer to you."

"Until now, she'd mostly ignored me. I'd rather she kept ignoring me than start accusing me of things I would never do."

"Don't let her get to you. You're doing a great job. I'll finish here and lock things up. You go home and rest."

I went home. But how could I rest while Berta came after me with such vicious lies?

CHAPTER SIX

Saguaro

I lay on the couch playing and replaying the scene in my head. Did Berta really believe I'd taken the money or was she just trying to get me fired?

I tossed and turned all night. At six, I got up and went to the bathroom. When I saw my bloodshot eyes and puffy eyelids, I filled the basin with cold water and stuck my face in it, like I was bobbing for apples. I resurfaced for a breath before dunking my head again and again, looking more rumpled and raw each time. I took my time showering and dressing, dreading going downstairs. Then it hit me. I couldn't hide out like a thief. My employers needed to hear my side. They needed to see that I'd been sideswiped by Berta and her lies.

Meme was there earlier than usual. He pulled out the chair next to him and gestured for me to sit.

"Thanks, Meme." I looked around the table at all of them. "I don't know why Berta accused me of taking that money. I may be young, but I'm no thief. I like working here and really need the job, so why would I do such a stupid thing?"

"So far, you haven't done anything to make me doubt your word," Guerrero said. "Berta, on the other hand . . . well, let's just say she tends to jump to conclusions."

"There's no way we can be sure what happened," Mrs. Flores said. "The money hasn't turned up, but you've proven to be a hard worker and you're doing a very good job." She pushed the pastry plate toward me, but even sweets didn't wake up my appetite that morning.

"Thank you. I just wanted you to know."

I shot a quick glance at Mr. Flores before I got up to leave. For once, he was keeping his thoughts to himself. Still, it was good to know Mrs. Flores, Guerrero and Meme were on my side.

❦   ❦   ❦

Meme was walking toward the exit when I reported for work that afternoon. I walked out behind him and saw Berta getting into a truck driven by the creep with the mustache.

I followed Meme to his car.

He saw me as he was unlocking the door. "Hey! You need a ride somewhere?"

"No, thanks. I just need to ask you something. Do you know why Berta hates me so much?"

Meme laughed and made a sucking sound with his teeth. He shifted his weight from one foot to the other, like the sidewalk was burning his feet.

"Whatever's going on with her, it's got nothing to do with you. Just ignore her."

"I try to stay out of her way, but . . ."

"How old do you think she is?"

"Huh? What's that got to do with anything?"

"Look, Lucy, don't worry about it. Just . . . don't worry about it."

He got in his car and started the engine. Before he backed up, he turned to look at me. "The bosses are happy with your work, and that's what matters." He waved and drove off.

I stood there watching his car until it was out of sight.

❧ ❧ ❧

The following week, I decided to take Meme up on his offer of a ride to Saguaro. I really needed to buy a few more work clothes and find a bookstore. I'd already read and re-read the books I'd brought with me.

"We usually do our shopping, catch a movie or both, but we don't really need an excuse to go to Saguaro," Meme said when I asked if they were planning a trip there soon. "Besides, Elena's looking forward to meeting you."

"And I'm looking forward to meeting her. I, uh, also need to set up an e-mail account. Maybe I can do that . . ."

"You can do that while we're at the mall, but you're always welcome to come over to use our computer."

❧ ❧ ❧

On Sunday, I was waiting in the parking lot when they drove up.

"You're so tiny!" Elena said when Meme introduced us. "Shopping for you must be a breeze. I love to shop. Meme's dreading the day I deliver this baby. Not that we're not excited. Don't get me wrong. It's just that after the baby shows up, once I get back to my normal size, I'll be making up for lost shopping time. Of course, I'll be lucky to get back into a size ten. What size do you wear?"

"Size six jeans and medium tees. I need to buy a few of each for work."

Elena talked non-stop all the way to Saguaro while Meme drove and I sat in the back, watching the desert landscape whiz by. Saguaros stood, like disembodied hands, among spiny shrubs and clumps of weeds. One of them looked like it was flipping us the bird. Every once in a while, I saw a few small trees with skinny branches and dry, straggly needles that made them look like they were having a bad-hair day.

As we neared the town, I noticed a cluster of buildings and trees set a short distance from the highway.

Elena had finally stopped talking while she looked through her purse for a tissue. "Darn allergies."

"Is that a school?" I asked while I had the chance.

"Saguaro Community College," Meme said. "It's a nice campus. You should check it out sometime."

I can't wait to do just that.

A few minutes later, he dropped us off in front of a mall and said he had some errands to run but would be back to pick us up in a couple of hours. When we got out of the car, my eyes zeroed in on Elena's enormous belly. She looked like she was ready to explode.

"Are you going to be okay?" I asked when I saw her swollen ankles.

She let out a big laugh. "Don't worry. I'm not due for another couple of months." She took my arm and started walking toward the mall entrance. "Did you have a particular place in mind?"

"I noticed there's a Target in the mall. I should be able to find the clothes I need there. Do you know if there's also a bookstore nearby?"

"I'm sure there is. Do you mind if we stop by The Fashion Spot along the way? It's a little pricey, but they always have such cute stuff."

Elena couldn't have been more than ten years older than me, but she acted like she was my mother. At the Fashion Spot, she took a dress from a rack and held it up in front of me.

"Check this out." She turned me around so I could see myself in the mirror. Good thing I didn't need a dress because I could see her taste in clothes, like Patti's, which was very different from mine.

We managed to finally walk out of the shop without buying anything. A few shops away, I spotted The Book Nook.

"I'll just pop into Babies and Tots while you shop for your books. Take your time," Elena said as she disappeared into a children's clothing store.

The Book Nook wasn't much bigger than the library I used to go to in El Paso. I walked around until I found the children's section. I grabbed a copy of Goodnight Moon thinking I'd keep it handy for when Elena's baby arrived. For myself, I got The Catcher in the Rye, which I'd never gotten around to reading since my English teacher had assigned it right before I left Las Nubes. I also picked up a copy of The Living. I'd tried to check it out from the library in El Paso, but there was a long waiting list for it.

From a display of desert postcards near the checkout counter, I picked out one of a roadrunner standing on a rock next to a bush of yellow flowers and another of a Saguaro in a big sombrero wiping sweat off its brow. I remembered Patti's birthday was coming up, so I got a silly birthday card for her with a naked mannequin looking through her closet, unable to decide what to wear.

After I'd paid for my books and cards, I connected to the store's wi-fi, set up my e-mail account, and sent Mario's message.

Back at the baby store, I found Elena sitting in a rocking chair with her eyes closed.

"May I help you?" the saleslady asked.

"No, thanks. I'm just meeting a friend here."

Elena opened her eyes. "Back so soon?"

"I can go finish my shopping while you rest." I turned to look at the saleslady to see if she had a problem with that.

"You stay as long as you want, dear," she told Elena. "You're doing us a favor by showing shoppers how comfy our little store is."

"Thanks," Elena said. "My feet are starting to complain, but I need to go sit near the entrance, where my husband agreed to pick us up."

"I'll only be a minute," I said.

Twenty minutes later, I'd picked out two T-shirts, two pairs of jeans, underwear, socks and even a hat.

When I returned, Meme was already there.

"How did you do that so fast?" Elena asked.

"I knew exactly what I needed—just a few more work clothes," I said. "Is anybody hungry? Lunch is on me."

"You're not even getting paid yet," Meme said.

Mrs. Flores must've told him about our little arrangement. Did Berta also know? Was that why she'd accused me of taking the tips?

"I will be in another month. Besides, I haven't spent any money until today and I have enough left to pay for lunch."

"In that case . . ." Meme started to say.

"How about that new Chinese place we've been wanting to try?" Elena said.

"Do you think your ankles can handle the MSG?" he asked.

"*Poco veneno no mata*, honey," she said.

I winced. A little poison might not kill her, but how much more swelling could those ankles take?

The menu was pretty thick. Good thing it said *No MSG* right under the restaurant name because Elena ordered wonton soup, potstickers, Chinese greens, chow mein, sweet-and-sour pork and walnut prawns.

"I think you just ordered for all of us," Meme said.

After we'd placed our order, Elena turned to me and put her hand on mine.

"I don't want to spoil your day, but let me just say one thing. Don't take any crap from Berta. She'll keep trying to trip you up, but just steer as far away from her as possible and you'll be fine."

I looked at Meme.

He shrugged. "Sorry. I had to tell her. She could see I was pretty pissed the day Berta made that big scene."

"I'm just glad Mrs. Flores and Guerrero don't seem to believe her," I said.

"Beto's being a little cagey, but he knows Berta and he's not swallowing her story either."

Although Elena had second helpings of everything she'd ordered, it was no surprise that we needed carry-out containers for the leftovers.

"Good thing you're eating for two, babe!" Meme kidded her.

"You mean good thing Lucy's picking up the check."

"Well, that too." Turning to me, he said, "You had no idea what you were getting into when you made your offer. Sure you still want to pay?"

"It's the least I can do in exchange for the ride."

"Chinese food, like pizza, is even better cold, so don't worry about any of this going to waste," Elena said.

Wasted leftovers were the least of my worries.

❧   ❧   ❧

The following night, Meme and the Floreses left as soon as things quieted down after the dinner rush. I was picking up the last of the dirty dishes when the guy with the bat mustache reached over and grabbed my butt. In my panic, I tried to run and, instead, stumbled into the wall like a drunk. Somehow, I managed to not drop the tray, but silverware went flying in all directions. The noise reverberated throughout the restaurant. Guerrero was in the kitchen and Berta was nowhere in sight.

"Hey, Tootsie, why're you playing so hard to get?"

"Asshole!" I hissed.

I put the tray on the cart and was backing my way toward the kitchen when Berta came hurrying out of the restroom. She stopped in her tracks when she saw me.

"Looking for more tips?" she said with a sneer.

I glared at her as she flounced out the door. The jerk slid off his stool, winked at me and blew me a kiss before he followed her out.

I locked the door and hurried back to the kitchen. My hands were shaking, and I could barely see through the tears burning my eyes as I crammed the dishes into the dishwasher. I was about to shut its door when I noticed a cup on the counter, reached for it and sent it crashing to the floor.

"I'll get that," Guerrero said. "You go on home. I'll finish cleaning up."

Before I could stop myself, I started to sob.

"¡Niña! What's wrong?"

"Why is that moron always hanging around?" I said.

"Rigo?"

"Berta's husband. I don't know his name."

Guerrero shook his head. "He's not her husband, but he *is* bad news. Beto's just looking for an excuse to ban him from the restaurant. If he said or did something to you, you need to let Beto know."

I was tempted to tell Guerrero everything the slime had said and done, but Berta seemed determined to get me in trouble and . . . the truth was, I was afraid. They were both so unpredictable.

"He gives me the creeps. They both do."

"Come on. I'll walk you home."

Guerrero led me out the back door and toward my apartment.

"Thanks," I said when we reached the stairs. "You don't have to come up."

"You sure you're okay?"

"Yes. Thanks."

I ran up the stairs. Guerrero stood there watching me until I reached the door. My hands were still trembling so much, I dropped the key. I knelt and felt around for it since my eyes were again filling with tears.

"¿Niña?" Guerrero started to climb the stairs.

My fingers finally found the key and, holding the knob with my other hand, I was able to open the door.

"Got it! Thanks. See you in the morning."

I went inside and collapsed against the door. By then, huge sobs were making my whole body shake. I don't know how long I stood there crying. When I finally stopped sobbing, I climbed into the bathtub, turned on the hot water and scrubbed my skin until I was covered with red streaks. Still dripping wet, I wrapped myself in my bathrobe, sat at the kitchen table and stared at the wall, wondering why Berta and her bully were after me.

I stood and paced the floor, sat down and held my head in my hands, then jumped up and paced some more. At some point I must've worn myself out because I finally lay down on the couch and closed my eyes. When I opened them again, it was eleven in the morning.

I took a shower and waited until the last possible minute to go down, hoping Berta would be gone by then. Meme and Guerrero were just getting ready to leave.

"Hey, what's up with you?" Meme said when he saw me. "You look like you were out partying all night."

I looked at Guerrero. He nodded but didn't say anything.

"I didn't sleep very well," I said.

"If you don't feel well . . ." Mrs. Flores started to say.

"I'm fine. I'll take a nap during the afternoon break."

Chapter Seven

Back to School?

That evening, I could feel Berta watching me each time I walked into the dining area. I was clearing one of her tables when she walked up behind me.

"If you know what's good for you, you'll stop flaunting your skinny ass around any man who bothers to look your way."

I turned around and immediately leaned back, away from her, when I saw how close she was standing.

"I wouldn't touch your sleazy boyfriend if he were the last man on earth. Why don't you tell him to keep his hands to himself?"

Berta clenched her right hand into a fist. She slapped it against her thigh, both of us knowing she would've preferred to slam it into my face.

"You expect us to believe you're just little orphan Annie all alone in the world? What are you really running from? What are you trying to hide?"

Just then, Meme called out to me, "Lucy, could you bring the cart over here?"

I shot one last look at Berta before I wiped the table and made my way toward Meme.

Somehow, I made it through the shift, but Berta's words kept running through my head all night. Had they been digging into my past? If so, what did they know?

❧   ❧   ❧

Soon after the shopping spree, I'd started walking every morning before work. I was growing used to Maguey's open spaces but still dreamed of Nana's garden—full of color, fragrance and life springing out of the ground. As usual, just thinking about her lifted my spirits. Memories of Mario and me straddling the brick fence next to her neighbor's mulberry tree, where we used to sit and gorge on sweet dark berries, made me smile.

One morning, I set out for my walk earlier than usual. The sun hadn't yet turned up its thermostat and, before long, I began to run. I hadn't run since I left school. After a couple of miles, sweat was trickling down my back. I walked the rest of the way and tried to come up with a plan. If I added half a mile to my run each week, I'd be back to running four miles in no time, like I had in school.

On my way back, Mr. and Mrs. Flores saw me crossing the street and waved.

"I have to plead and bargain with my body just to drag myself in every morning," Mrs. Flores said. "After work, all I want to do is go home to soak my feet. And here you are, pounding the pavement before you even start your workday."

"You come to work only because you want to," her husband said. "You know you could stay home and soak your feet all day instead."

With an exaggerated sigh, she said, "I know, *cariño*, but I'd be bored to tears if I did that." She turned to me. "The energy is what I miss most about being your age."

"I've been thinking of using some of that energy toward getting my GED so I can sign up for a class or two at Saguaro College—ones that wouldn't interfere with my work schedule."

"Excellent idea," Mrs. Flores said. "What kind of classes are you thinking of taking?"

"Not sure. I'll have to see what they offer. I'm mainly interested in using their library."

"SCC is not that close," Mr. Flores said. "Maybe a fifteen-minute drive. You'll need to take the bus."

"Great. I'll go pick up a class schedule and find out about their requirements." I waved and raced off toward my apartment. "See you in a few minutes."

❧   ❧   ❧

"Lucy's going back to school," Mrs. Flores said to Meme and Guerrero when I showed up for work later that day.

"Leaving us so soon?" Meme asked. "Was it something we said?"

"Oh, I'm not going anywhere, just thinking of taking a class at SCC if I can find something interesting."

Guerrero beamed at me. "There's always something new to learn. If I wasn't so old, I'd be signing up for classes myself."

Mr. Flores slapped his friend's shoulder. "Too late now. You know what they say about old dogs." They both laughed.

After the lunch shift, Mr. Flores locked the door behind Meme and Guerrero and disappeared into the office. His wife called me over to the employees' break area and asked me to sit down.

"I just wanted to tell you that you're doing a fine job, Lucy. Although Beto's too proud and stubborn to say so, I can tell he's glad I hired you."

"Thanks. I don't know what I would've done if you hadn't."

"I'm sorry that Berta's not very nice to you."

"I try to stay out of her way."

"She's got a big chip on her shoulder, and it seems to get bigger the older she gets."

Remembering Meme's reaction when I'd asked him about Berta, I realized this was my chance to learn more from Mrs. Flores.

"What about that creepy guy she hangs out with?"

Mrs. Flores closed her eyes and shook her head. "We make lots of allowances for Berta because she's a good worker and has had a tough life, but we'd just as soon Rigo didn't come to the restaurant. Beto's just waiting for a reason to order him to stay away. If Berta doesn't like it, she'll have to decide between him and her job."

I almost blurted out what Rigo had said and done, but stopped myself when it occurred to me, they might think I was just making up lies to get back at her.

Meme drove me to the Saguaro campus the following day. Although he made small talk about Elena, the baby they were expecting and a movie they'd watched over the weekend, he was careful to avoid the topic of Berta, which seemed to loom over us like a Goodyear blimp.

"Hey, listen, we get together with friends once a month, just some of the guys I jam with and their families. Elena asked me to invite you to join us next time, Sunday after next. We gave up inviting Lola and Beto a long time ago after they kept turning us down. They like hanging out at home on Sundays. I don't blame them. Guerrero will be there, though. He'll probably spend most of the time inside watching Univisión, especially if there's a soccer game on that night."

At the mention of soccer, I thought of Mario.

"Will Berta be there?"

"If I knew she wouldn't bring that loser along, and if she wasn't so nasty to you, I might invite her. Maybe."

"What should I bring?"

"Just your skinny little self. It's our turn to treat you. And Elena's made it her mission to fatten you up." He laughed. "I'll ask Guerrero to give you a ride. He has to drive past the restaurant to get to our house anyway."

"Good. We stay so busy at the restaurant that we never really have a chance to talk."

"He's a great guy. After my dad skipped out on me and my mom, Guerrero stepped in and stopped me from running wild."

I turned to look at him. "Sounds like Elena's done a lot of taming, then."

"Yeah, well, I was already semi-tame by the time I met her. Guerrero spent a lot of time with me right after I got out of juvie . . . you know, talking to me, taking me fishing, stuff like that. He's the one who got me my job."

"Where's his family?"

"His wife died a long time ago, and his daughter goes to Columbia. She plans to study medicine someday. Can you imagine going from Maguey to New York? For a hick like me, it would be like going to the moon. She got a full scholarship, too—that's how smart she is. I kind of wished he was my real dad, or at least that he and my mom would've got together before she started hanging out with Sam. Sam's all right, but I would've preferred Guerrero as a stepdad."

"You'd probably be at Columbia yourself if Guerrero had gotten a hold of you before you turned wild."

"Not me. I'm the kind of guy who likes to work with my hands."

※ ※ ※

We pulled into the SCC parking lot right then.

"Thanks for the ride."

"Sure you don't want me to wait for you?"

"I'm taking the bus back. Mr. and Mrs. Flores know I may be a little late."

"See you later, then."

I went straight to the Admissions Office and asked to see a counselor.

"You can put your name on the sign-in sheet and wait across the hall," said the cute guy who helped me.

"Are you a student here?" I asked him.

"Yeah—full-time. This is just my work-study job. What about you?"

"I'm thinking of signing up for a class," I said.

He handed me a schedule from the stack on the counter. "Let me know if you have any questions."

"Thanks." I was about to introduce myself, when an arm reached around me to grab a class schedule. I turned to see two students waiting behind me and quickly scribbled my name on the sign-in sheet before walking across the hall to wait.

I studied the schedule while I waited. About fifteen minutes later, I heard my name and looked up to see a lady wearing a long, loose red dress, a scarf around her head and bracelets that jingled and jangled every time she moved. As I followed her back to her office, I noticed her red high tops.

"Here," she said, "I'll just move these out of the way so you can sit down."

She took a pile of folders from a chair and stacked them on top of an already leaning tower of files. Mounds of papers and stacks of books looked ready to fall off her desk. The nameplate on top said *Ms. Svalinski.* Her office walls were lined with pictures. My eye was drawn to the biggest one, where she stood in front of a pyramid.

Ms. Svalinski pulled her chair to one side of her desk and sat facing me. Her lenses magnified her huge green eyes and made her look like she was peering out of a fishbowl.

"Now, then, how may I be of help?" she asked.

"I'm interested in signing up for a class, but I dropped out of school just before my senior year."

"Well, then, we'll need to schedule you for a GED exam. You'll also need to take assessment and placement tests. Once you've passed the required exams, you may enroll in any of the programs we offer. Have any idea what classes you might be interested in?"

"I was hoping you had a culinary arts program, but I didn't see any cooking classes on the schedule."

"We offer a few non-credit classes under our Personal Enrichment Program, also known as PEP."

"I think I'll focus on my GED first and then decide."

"Good idea. Here's my card in case you have any other questions."

"Thanks." I got up and went to get a closer look at the pictures. "Do you travel a lot?"

"It's my favorite thing to do. Although I love my job, I mainly do it so I can pay for my trips."

"Someday I'd love to see all these places," I said. "For now, I have to settle for reading about them."

"I used to do the same, saving my pennies until I had enough to travel to Mexico one year, Canada another and, over the years, the miles on my odometer started adding up."

I smiled. "Thanks for the information."

"You know where to reach me. Let me know when you're ready to take your tests."

On my way out, I walked by the counter, trying to catch another glimpse of the cutie who'd helped me, but he was already gone.

I sat in the waiting room to check for a response from Mario. Nothing.

❈ ❈ ❈

I felt like just another student walking around without a care in the world as I made my way to the bus stop. Seeing the kids sitting on the grass talking, horsing around, laughing or just reading or napping reminded me of Patti. It had been three days since I'd mailed her card, and her birthday was coming up in a couple of days.

That night, I kept thinking about my SCC visit. I'd been too busy trying to survive and hadn't given much thought to where or when I might meet someone. Until now. I couldn't stop thinking about the guy I'd seen there. I'd have to make up some excuse to stop by there again.

"Could he be my Prince Charming?" I asked the empty room. This reminded me of a song Patti's mom used to sing right after her divorce. "*¿Quién será el que me quiera a mí? ¿Quién será? ¿Quién será?*" Who will fall in love with me? The words kept running through my head until I fell asleep.

I called Patti at seven the morning she turned eighteen, knowing that she'd be trying to wake up right about then.

"I hope Fernando didn't show up at the crack of dawn to serenade you because I want to be the first to wish you the best birthday ever."

"Are you kidding? He's even lazier than I am." She sounded like she was covering up a yawn. "I wish you were here to celebrate with us. Mom won't take us back to Arturo's since he wouldn't let her pay for dinner last time we were there. She's taking us to Mickey Mac's instead. What are *you* doing for *your* birthday?"

"Not much, but you'll be happy to know that I'm thinking of getting my GED so I can sign up for classes at the local community college."

"When are you taking the test?" Patti asked.

"I need to study for it first."

"Study? I'll bet you'd ace it if you took it right now."

"You think? It's been a while since I've thought about any of that stuff, especially the math."

We talked for a half hour before Patti had to get ready for school.

"I better get up. I'll call you next week to serenade you."

"I've heard you sing. I'll settle for a plain old Happy Birthday!"

"It's not every day you turn eighteen. I'll send you a virgin margarita." She laughed and hung up.

❧ ❧ ❧

The following Sunday, I was waiting for Guerrero in front of the restaurant.

"I'm glad you agreed to come to the party," he said, when I got in his truck. "We've all been worried about you getting bored in such a little town, especially when you don't know many people."

"I haven't really had time to be bored. I spent one Sunday shopping in Saguaro with Meme and Elena, and I spend most of my free time reading."

"You and my Maricela would get along great."

"Meme told me she's going to be a doctor. You must be very proud."

Guerrero's face lit up. "She's all I've got. I'd be proud of her no matter what she decided to do with her life."

I could see why Meme would've liked to have a father like Guerrero.

"How long have you worked at the restaurant?" I asked.

"I've been there since it opened about nineteen years ago. Beto knew I couldn't afford to go in as a partner, but he wanted to hire me anyway."

"Meme says you're a soccer fan. You'd like my brother. He played soccer in high school."

"Where is he now?"

His question didn't make me feel like he was prying. Besides, I'd been bombarding him with questions, so I didn't hesitate to answer.

"In the Navy."

"You'd never guess by looking at me now, but I was once a Navy man. Back in the dark ages, when we sailed in wooden ships."

He laughed, and I had to laugh too, at the image of him bobbing around in the ocean with giant waves crashing all around his little ship.

"Hey, I could've walked here," I said when Guerrero pulled up in front of Meme and Elena's house.

"You don't have to drive far to get from one end of town to the other," Guerrero said. "Makes it convenient to get to and from work."

He rang the doorbell and we heard what sounded like people scrambling around inside.

"Maybe they didn't hear us," I said.

He rang again. This time the door opened and everyone inside shouted: "Surprise!"

"You tricked me," I said when I saw Mr. and Mrs. Flores standing there with Meme, Elena and a bunch of strangers.

"We didn't think you'd mind," Mrs. Flores said. "I hope our timing isn't too far off. When we hired you, you said you were turning eighteen in two months and it's been right around two months."

"Close enough. I'll be eighteen on Tuesday."

"This was a great idea, then," Elena said.

She hugged me and I had to blink back tears. I thought I'd never celebrate my birthday again since Nana, Mario and Patti had been the only ones who'd ever remembered it.

After we ate and listened to a little music, Mr. and Mrs. Flores and I joined Guerrero in the living room to watch the soccer game. While Mr. Flores and Guerrero hooted and hollered, Mrs. Flores knitted a baby blanket.

"I finally have a reason to knit again," she said. "Of course, it's taking me forever to finish this little blanket because my old fingers can only take it for fifteen or twenty minutes at a time."

"Was your last project a sweater for Mr. Flores?"

Mrs. Flores smiled and set her work down between us.

"Beto's never worn sweaters. I used to make them for Maricela, though. She was only four when her mother died, so we got to spend a lot of time with her until she started school. Beto and I are just as proud of her as if she were our own. It's been a long time since we've heard a child's laughter around our house."

"Maybe Elena and Meme will let us babysit their baby," I said.

"We'll have to get in line behind Elena's mother. This will be her first grandchild, and I'm sure she can't wait to start spoiling him or her every chance she gets."

"Hmmm! This is one lucky baby with all these people waiting for his arrival."

"True. What about you? Ever tried knitting?"

"No. But my grandmother used to knit, mostly doilies and stuff like that."

"I would've liked to have met her."

"I'm sure you would've liked her."

❦ ❦ ❦

Mrs. Flores stopped knitting again and turned to look at me. "I just had an idea. Why don't you come visit us next weekend?"

Oops! I hadn't seen that coming.

"Thanks, but I need to study for the GED exam, so I'll be ready as soon as the counselor schedules it."

The truth was that, although Mr. Flores had become a lot friendlier since he'd seen how eager I was to do a good job, I wasn't sure how he'd feel about me visiting them.

Mrs. Flores didn't give up. "The following weekend then. We promise not to keep you very long."

I looked at Mr. Flores, but he was too busy yelling instructions to the players on his team.

"Okay," I said. "If you're sure Mr. Flores won't mind."

To my surprise, when his wife managed to catch his attention, Mr. Flores took out the small notepad he carried around in his shirt pocket, scribbled something on, tore off the page and handed it to me.

"Here's the address and phone number in case you have trouble finding us," he said, before turning back to the game.

❦   ❦   ❦

I tried to leave when Guerrero left the Flores' home right after the game, but Elena wouldn't hear of it.

"You can't leave" she said. "You're the guest of honor."

I couldn't think of an excuse fast enough, so I stayed. We sat outside for a while, telling ghost stories. Or at least Meme's friends took turns telling stories while the rest of the group picked them apart.

"No ghost in his right mind's going to hang around the desert frying his ass when he could be in Acapulco or Ipanema sipping margaritas and riding the waves," said one guy who looked like he'd had more than his share of margaritas already.

The woman sitting next to him laughed. "Besides, if he runs into a saguaro or steps on a rattlesnake, he can kiss his fried ass goodbye."

"Snakes, cactus spines and sizzling heat can't hurt a ghost," one of the musicians said. "And anyway, they're mostly harmless, unless they scare the crap out of you." He laughed and started singing, "If there's something strange in your neighborhood, who you gonna call?"

"Ghostbusters!" everybody yelled before they burst out laughing.

"You guys are starting to get too silly for us," Elena said. "Lucy and I are going inside."

Even though we'd used paper plates and cups, we'd managed to make a mess. I started gathering the disposable dishes and dumping them in a large bag while Elena went to sit in the living room and propped her feet on a footstool.

"How many times do I have to remind you this is your party?" she said. "Meme will clean up later. Come over here and keep me company."

"This'll only take a minute. I'll just rinse the real dishes and put them in the dishwasher. Then we'll all be out of your hair that much sooner."

"*Uh-uh!* Get your little butt over here."

I set the dishes in the sink and went to sit with her.

"Normally, I'd be right in the middle of the action telling my own tall tales," she said, "but it can get a little tough when you're carrying around an extra forty pounds." She reached for an envelope sitting on the bookshelf next to her and handed it to me.

Inside was a card signed by all of them. There was a $50 Book Nook gift certificate inside the card. I bit my lip when my eyes started tearing up.

"No crying allowed," she said.

I knelt by her chair and hugged her. "It didn't take long for you all to figure me out."

* * *

Luckily, most of the guests had to be at work early the next day, so the party broke up soon afterward. Still, by the time Meme drove me home, it was eleven.

"Thanks for everything," I said when he dropped me off.

"Believe it or not, this was all Beto's idea," he said.

"You're joking."

"Just ask Guerrero. He was there when Beto suggested it. In fact, he wanted to have it at the restaurant."

"Maybe he just wanted to make sure I'd told them the truth about my age."

"Or maybe," Meme said, "he likes you."

※   ※   ※

Tuesday morning, I woke up with a smile on my face. As of that day, I was an adult with a real job, an apartment and, best of all, I was free.

I practically floated to the bathroom. The phone rang just as I was about to step into the shower. Pretty sure it was Patti, I picked it up after the first ring.

"I made you the cutest top for your birthday," she said, "but I don't have your address."

"Thanks. If it's not too fancy, I'll save it for when I start school."

I couldn't help but imagine what the top looked like. Our taste in clothes was as different as our figures, but that hadn't kept her from giving me fashion advice for as long as I could remember.

"I designed it with you in mind. It's just perfect for you. You'll have to take a selfie when you get it so I can post it on my Fashion Design by Patti Facebook Page."

After I gave Patti the restaurant's address, she was very quiet for a moment.

"I hate to spoil your birthday by mentioning this, but it's something you probably need to know."

I froze. "Is Mario okay?"

"He was the last time Fernando heard from him. It's not about Mario. . . . The witch showed up on our doorstep yesterday. She wanted to know if I'd heard from you. Said she's been looking for you all over the place, even called your aunt."

My breath stopped mid-inhale and my mind started racing.

"Of course, I said I hadn't. I don't think she believed me, but who cares?"

I let out my breath. "Thanks."

Patti's words increased my respect for Tía Delia. She would obviously never rat me out. *Had Sara actually remembered my birthday or was it just a coincidence that she'd waited until now to go to Patti?*

❧ ❧ ❧

After we hung up, I thought of Mario. Thinking about him took me back to our early years, to a day Sara let us play inside because it had been pouring all night and there was no sign the rain was going to stop anytime soon. We were in his room, where he was sorting his marbles while I played with my doll. He left to go to the bathroom and came back with the black velvet bag where Sara kept her cards. While he looked through one deck, I took a closer look at the red heart in front of the bag. It had an arrow running through the center with a couple of drops of blood dripping off its tip.

Mario held up a card so we could both see it: a picture of a green dragon with horns and wings and fire shooting out of its nostrils. He turned it sideways, and the dragon's eyeballs turned in the opposite direction. Our eyes were glued to the card as Mario turned it back and forth. Neither of us heard her footsteps until Sara was standing at the door. Before Mario had a chance to hide the evidence, she grabbed him by the arm, pulled him to his feet and shook him, sending cards flying all over the room.

"If you ever touch my things again, you'll be sorrier than the day you smashed your finger with the car door."

Mario sniffed. "I'm sorry, Momma. I . . ."

Sara cut him off. She turned to me, lifted me off the floor, then marched us both into the living room and pushed us outside, slamming the door behind us. Mario let out a big sob, grabbed my hand and half-dragged me to Nana's house.

"What are you doing out in this weather?" Nana asked when she opened her door.

We just stood there, rain, snot and tears dripping off our faces. Without waiting for an answer, she let us in, then disappeared for a quick minute and came back with two thick towels. While our clothes were in the dryer, we sat at her table eating toast with jam and drinking hot chocolate.

"Nana, is Momma a witch?" I asked. "Our neighbor Danny says—"

"It doesn't matter who says what," Nana said. "She's your mother. You should try not to upset her."

I quickly changed the channel in my head. I wasn't about to let bad memories spoil my independence day. Since Mr. and Mrs. Flores had insisted that I take the day off, I took the bus into Saguaro and spent it at the mall, mainly at the bookstore where I redeemed my gift certificate. I came home with a stack of new books and magazines.

CHAPTER EIGHT

A Love Story

"A check is fine," I said the following Friday when Mrs. Flores handed out paychecks and asked me if I preferred cash. "I need to open a bank account, anyway. Oh, and how much will my rent be?"

She wrinkled her brow. "I've heard or read somewhere that housing shouldn't cost more than a certain percentage of your income. I can't remember what the percentage was, though. Let's just make it $300."

"Three hundred?"

"Is that too much for one month?"

"Ah, per month! Sure. That sounds more than fair."

I filled out the paperwork under the name A. Lucía Sánchez and explained to the bank lady that I went by my middle name.

On my way back to the apartment, I made a few quick calculations. I'd be living in the place practically for free and eating most of my meals at the restaurant. Even working for minimum wage, and even after paying the rent, I couldn't believe how much money I'd have left. But then again, this wasn't LA.

Not wanting to show up at the Flores' empty-handed, I decided to take the bus to the Saguaro Shopping Mall, where I'd seen a florist shop. On my way to the bus stop, I dropped my two postcards in the mailbox. Now that I was eighteen and knew I could trust Delia not to tell Sara and Pedro anything about me, I felt better about sharing a few more details with her.

On her card I'd written: *You'll be happy to know I'm signing up for college classes. Although it's not exactly the plan I had in mind, it's a good start.*

I signed it, *Love, Lucy.* Maybe someday I'd be ready to tell her more. For now, I figured that would keep her from worrying about me. As I put the stamp on the card, I wondered if she ever used the recipes I'd left for her—some of the simpler ones she'd liked. I wanted to believe she was motivated enough to make them once in a while.

Patti's gift had arrived the day before. I was surprised to see it was exactly the kind of top I would've chosen for myself, a gauzy off-white peasant blouse with short puffy sleeves and delicate red flowers embroidered across the front.

On her postcard I'd written: *I love the blouse. I'll wear it on my next hot date,* and signed it, *Missing you, Lucy.*

After checking my e-mail and not finding a response from Mario, I bought a couple of magazines and headed to the florist's. Remembering the bubble bath I'd found in the apartment, I figured I couldn't go wrong with roses. I bought a dozen of them.

At six that evening, I arrived at a small brick house and was greeted by the sound of classical music streaming through the open window. Did I have the right house? At the restaurant, the only music I heard was the usual jukebox selections: *rancheras*, *cumbias* and mariachi. I checked the house number again to make sure this was their address. Yup! I knocked and waited. When there was no answer, I knocked a little harder. The door opened just as I was about to knock a third time.

"You found us," Mr. Flores said. "Come in."

I handed him the flowers and stepped into a bright living/dining area.

A loud "*¡Carambola, Lola!*" came from somewhere in the corner of the room.

Mr. Flores laughed. "This colorful fellow here is Nacho," he said, pointing at a cage hanging from the ceiling where a beautiful blue parrot with a yellow face and a white chest was grooming himself.

"Nacho, Nacho," the cage occupant said before letting loose a loud whistle.

"Watch out for him. He loves to flirt."

"He takes after his daddy," Mrs. Flores said from another part of the house. "Come on in, Lucy."

I followed her voice and found her in the kitchen. She stopped what she was doing and came to get a closer look at my blouse.

"You look lovely." She wiped her hands on her apron and gently caressed the fabric.

"It's a gift from a friend," I said. "She designs and makes her own clothes." I looked past her into the kitchen. "What can I do to help?"

"Not a thing," she said. "On Sundays, I do the cooking. It's a good thing Beto's not a picky eater because I've never been much of a cook." She held up a can of spaghetti sauce before she attached it to an electric opener. "I hope you're not too disappointed."

"I love spaghetti," I said.

"And I love those roses!" Mrs. Flores said, taking the bouquet from her husband and admiring them while he filled a vase with water.

In spite of the food, I really enjoyed the meal. It wasn't so much that my friends lavished attention on me. It was seeing the way they treated each other. I'd never seen people behave the way these two did. It had to be true love. But what did I know about love?

*** *** ***

After dinner, Mr. Flores carried a tres leches cake to their patio. His wife asked me to take some dishes and silverware while she brought out a pot of hot chocolate.

"We ordered the cake from the local bakery, especially for you," Mrs. Flores said as she poured the chocolate into colorful ceramic mugs.

"This tastes just like the chocolate my grandmother used to make," I said.

"Liliana Molina," Mr. Flores said. He turned to look at his wife. "I think we know everybody in town, but I don't remember any Molinas."

Mrs. Flores shook her head. "What about your grandfather? Where was he from?"

"I don't know much about him. He died before I was born." At least that much was true,

"What was his name?"

"Mario. Same as my brother."

"Oh, yes, Guerrero mentioned you have a brother." Mr. Flores said. "And where is he?"

"He's in the Navy, so I'm never really sure exactly where he is."

I suddenly felt sick, not because of the food but because of all the lies I'd told these people who'd been so good to me. It was time for me to come clean and hope they didn't fire me. I swallowed my fear and the truth started spilling out.

"I . . . uh . . . there's one thing I have to confess. My grandmother's name was Liliana Molina, but she never lived in Maguey. I grew up in Las Nubes, a little town in Texas. After Nana died, I couldn't stay in my parents' house. It was too dangerous. Too violent. Although I don't know anyone in California, I was on my way to LA when I saw your 'Help Wanted' sign and got off the bus. I'm sorry I couldn't tell you all this that day. I was desperate and scared. "I sniffled and stopped talking.

Mr. and Mrs. Flores looked at each other. Neither said a word for what seemed like a very long time.

Suddenly, Mr. Flores said, "Is there anything else we should know?"

"My father's sister lives in El Paso. I stayed with her for a little while before I came here."

"What about your run-ins with Berta?"

"I've never done any of the things she's accused me of doing, if that's what you mean."

"Thank you for your honesty, Lucy," Mrs. Flores said. "Families can be complicated. In Berta's case, you should know that she's not a bad person, but bad things have happened to her. Sometimes those things can make us bitter. They cause us to make bad choices. You seem to have chosen not to let the bad things in your life ruin your future. We'd like to see you succeed."

Mr. Flores was suddenly very quiet. I wondered if he felt the same way. I got my answer when he reached across the table and handed me his handkerchief.

I wiped my eyes and cleared my throat. "Enough about sad memories. I'm ready for a happy story. I'd love to hear how you two met.

Mr. Flores smiled but let his wife tell their story.

"Forty-nine years," she began. "Forty-nine short, wonderful years ago, my father hired Beto to work on his ranch. My parents had great expectations for me. Unfortunately, there was no room for Beto in those dreams. I was only seventeen and my passion in life was riding my horse every chance I got. I returned from one of those outings late one afternoon. Usually, I dropped my horse off at the stable, where one of the men would groom him. This time, though, I was met at the entrance by a new, and very handsome, young man."

She looked at her husband. He winked at her. I smiled, trying again to picture Mrs. Flores at seventeen. I couldn't even imagine her riding a horse.

"'You must be Gilberto,' I said. 'I heard Papá telling Mamá he just hired you.'

"'That's exactly who I am, young lady,' he said. 'And this is one beautiful horse you have here.'

"'Marinero!' I said. 'He's my favorite. Do you ride?'

"Always the charmer, he said, 'Not as well as you do, but I manage to stay in the saddle.'

"I invited him to meet me at my usual picnic spot, and we were soon meeting regularly. My parents became suspicious. When they found out about our rendezvouses, they fired Beto. I continued to ride, of course, but not for long because our poor cook, Lina, had to go with me as a chaperone, and I could see how unhappy it made her to tag along. After each short ride, I returned to mope around the house."

Mr. Flores was quiet, his head bowed. I thought maybe he'd dozed off, but then I noticed him nodding slowly.

"But true love always seems to find a way, dear. One day after our ride, Lina went to the house while I walked the horses to the stables. I turned them over to Andrés, one of the old ranch hands who'd worked for my father for years. That day I could tell he was a little nervous.

"'Señorita,' he said, 'I feel like I'm betraying your father and I certainly can't afford to lose my job, but Beto is like a son to me. He asked me to give you this letter.'

"I hurried home and locked myself in my room so I could read the letter without raising suspicions. As you know, dear, Beto is not one to beat around the bush. His note was short and to the point: *I have no more to offer you than my love. If you will have me, I will devote my life to making you happy.*"

She reached out and put her hand on his. "And you have, *cariño*. You have." He took her hand and brought it to his lips.

I felt like a peeping Tom watching the two old lovers.

"That's a beautiful love story," I said.

"Unfortunately, it doesn't have a happy-ever-after ending, dear," Mrs. Flores said. "We both knew my father would never approve of the marriage. Just the same, I wrote Beto back, assuring him that I felt the same way about him. I accepted his offer. With Andrés' help, we eloped. I wrote to my parents afterwards telling them how happy I was. But my letter was returned unopened.

"One day, I was thrilled to get a letter from my father. I missed my parents so much. I thought they were missing me too and were ready to forgive me and welcome Beto into the family. I was so excited, I could barely open the envelope. But he hadn't even bothered with a greeting. The letter simply said, *Do not contact us again. You are no longer welcome in this house.* I never saw either of them again."

Mr. Flores suddenly snapped out of his trance.

"You'll probably never want to visit us again," he said. "You must think all we do is sit around rehashing our youthful escapades. That could get pretty boring for someone who still has her whole life ahead."

"Oh no," I said. "Thank you for having me over and sharing your story with me. Why don't you come to my apartment for dinner next Sunday?"

From the amused look they exchanged, it was obvious the thought that I might know how to cook had never occurred to them. Heck, Mr. Flores hadn't even trusted me to wash the dishes.

"It'll be a belated wedding celebration," I added, hoping to convince them.

"Now, that's the best idea I've heard in years," Mr. Flores said. "How can we refuse that kind of offer?"

"I can cook at the restaurant, so you won't have to climb the stairs," I said to Mrs. Flores.

"It won't kill me to climb those stairs once more. We'd be honored to be your very first dinner guests."

"I'm glad I finally have a chance to thank you for all you've done for me."

🌸 🌸 🌸

I'd been in a panic ever since I'd blurted out the invitation. Sure, it wouldn't take much to top Mrs. Flores' canned spaghetti, but these were people I was really eager to please. Everything *had* to be perfect.

To make it seem like a real party, I decided to invite Guerrero, Meme and Elena. I didn't even think about inviting Berta. I wasn't about to let her ruin it for the rest of us.

"What are you doing next Sunday?" I asked Guerrero as soon as he walked in the next morning.

"Nothing special. I usually call Maricela around nine and then do laundry and a bit of house cleaning. Exciting stuff, eh?"

"Well, if you can tear yourself away from all that excitement, maybe you can come to my dinner party."

He looked at me with curiosity and amusement.

"It's kind of a wedding/anniversary celebration in honor of Mr. and Mrs. Flores."

"I wouldn't miss it, niña. How can I help?"

"You can help by bringing a big appetite."

"A party? At your place?" Meme said when I invited him a short time later.

❖ ❖ ❖

I hadn't noticed Berta standing behind him until she walked past us, adjusting her skimpy apron. I pretended not to have seen her, and she pretended she hadn't heard a word I'd said.

The following Friday, we were all in the dining room right after the last lunch customer had left.

"See you Monday," Berta said to Mrs. Flores as she sashayed her way to the door. "Me and Rigo are leaving as soon as I cash my check. You know, I can never pass up a chance to go to Vegas."

Perfect timing! And good riddance.

CHAPTER NINE

Celebration

I'd been planning this meal for weeks, but until now I hadn't figured out how to actually pull it off. Early Saturday morning, I took the bus into Saguaro and went to the farmers' market to buy the fruit and vegetables I needed. Besides the appetizers and desserts, I planned to serve tortilla soup, roasted root vegetables with fresh herbs and peppers stuffed with a mixture of wild rice, corn and black beans topped with jalapeño cheddar. Although I personally don't like okra, I added fried okra to the menu because I remembered hearing Mrs. Flores say she loved it. She compared it to tender young *nopalitos*. Maybe someday I'd learn to like okra the way I'd learned to love figs.

My fascination with gardening and food had begun in Nana's garden. Besides the fig tree, her backyard consisted of one row after another of all kinds of plants. The year Mario started school, I spent my days with her, pulling weeds and watering. We used to play a game where I'd close my eyes while she dropped a fruit or vegetable in my mouth and I had to guess what it was.

She even let me "help" in the kitchen. If she was baking cookies, she'd measure the ingredients and set them on the counter so I could add them to the bowl when she was ready for them. If she was making corn tortillas, she'd give me my own lump of dough to shape into a ball and flatten into a disk. No matter how much I practiced patting the dough between my hands as I'd watched her do so many times, it always ended up stuck between my fingers or on the floor. Still, she never failed to tell me I was a great helper and rewarded me with what I called a *hotilla* fresh off her griddle.

One day she gave me a slice of fig. I bit into it and spit it out. She normally didn't scold me when I did stuff that displeased her. That day, we had chili, cornbread and salad with her special sweet and sour dressing for lunch.

Afterward, she asked, "How did you like the salad?"

"It was yummy," I said.

"Remember the fig you spit out this morning?"

"Yeah!"

"It came from the same tree as the fig I put in your salad."

"I didn't see a fig."

"It was in the dressing. So don't ever turn up your nose at perfectly good food until you've tried it more than once."

After that, figs became one of my favorite fruits.

❋ ❋ ❋

The rest of Saturday, I alternated between my regular duties and helping Meme wait tables. As I worked, I went over my menu. If this went well maybe they'd let me cook some—*Oops! Better not get ahead of myself.* Nana had always encouraged me to dream big, but there seemed to be a very fine line between big dreams and fantasies.

On Sunday, I got up early to prepare the dough for my rosemary bread and bake miniature flans with thin hazelnut crusts. The aroma of the freshly baked goods and simmering soup filled the apartment. Meme had bought the wine I needed for the *sangría* I planned to serve. He'd stocked my refrigerator with beer the day before and he and Guerrero had carried up a couple of tables from the restaurant. Since the weather had been perfect lately, I'd asked them to set them up on the balcony.

Mr. and Mrs. Flores were the first to arrive that afternoon. I heard their voices in the backyard and went out to greet them. I froze halfway down the stairs when I saw them inspecting a corner of the backyard where I'd been weeding and digging and had started a compost pile.

"So this is where the coffee grinds, potato peels and whatnots end up," Mr. Flores said.

For a moment, I was afraid I might've offended them by digging around without their permission.

Mrs. Flores leaned over to inspect the little plot. "She's full of surprises, dear."

I hurried down the last few steps. "I was hoping to start a garden. If it's okay."

"Hey, you're doing us a favor by clearing away the weeds," Mr. Flores said. "You won't hear any complaints from me."

Meme, Elena and Guerrero arrived just as I was explaining that I was preparing the soil for an herb garden but was hoping to eventually grow fruit and vegetables too.

"As long as you're not growing any fancy weeds," Mr. Flores said. He gave me one of his sidelong glances. "Are you?"

"Don't listen to him, dear," his wife said. "This yard has never looked better."

"If you can make anything grow in this soil, you've got my respect," Guerrero said, tipping his hat and bowing dramatically. "You need anything, just let me know."

"I thought I'd plant a few seeds and see what pops up."

"I don't know where you find the time, Lucy," Meme said.

After everyone had a chance to admire my small future garden, I thanked them all and led them upstairs.

"If your dinner's half as good as it smells, you'll need to give me cooking lessons," Elena said as Meme helped her up the stairs.

"I sure hope you're not disappointed," I said.

Mrs. Flores was surprised to find the apartment exactly the same. I had changed nothing, except for the tablecloth, a bouquet of fresh flowers and the books I'd tried to arrange in a neat pile on the floor.

"I'd forgotten how gloomy it is in here," she said. "Some pretty curtains, a nice frilly bedspread and a bookcase would really brighten the place up."

"But I love it just the way it is," I said.

Elena wasn't much help when she suggested painting the walls a pale yellow.

"How long would it take you to paint this place, Meme?" she asked.

"I can't unload all my projects on you. I promise changes by the next time you come to visit," I said before Meme could answer.

That seemed to satisfy them.

I'd prepared *ceviche* as one of the appetizers. Since I knew Mr. Flores and Guerrero liked their food spicy, I placed it next to a large *molcajete* of *pico de gallo*. The *chiles* in the *pico* were so hot, it brought tears to my eyes when I tasted it. Although it was the Flores' party and I had made most of the meal with them in mind, I couldn't resist trying a new Thai roll recipe I'd seen in one of my cooking magazines. Mine didn't look as great as the ones in the picture, though.

I set out the appetizers and invited my guests to help themselves.

"I know you didn't have all this catered," Mr. Flores said. "But did you really cook it yourself?" Without waiting for an answer, he started in on the *ceviche*.

"We've always thought you were worth your weight in gold," Meme said. "Now we'll have to find a new way to measure it."

"Before you give me such high marks, try the food," I said.

Mrs. Flores walked around the table holding an empty plate. "It's such a feast for the eyes that eating it almost seems wrong,"

"Lucy, when you invited us over, I have to admit I wasn't expecting much," Elena said. "I figured we'd be dining on microwaved *enchiladas* or who knows what."

Mrs. Flores chuckled. "That must've been my cooking you were thinking of."

Everyone laughed. Mrs. Flores was the first to admit it wasn't through his stomach that she'd found her way to Mr. Flores' heart.

After Meme served everyone a beverage, the feast began.

"*Tamarindo*'s my favorite flavor in the world," Guerrero said when he tried the tamarind sauce I'd made for the Thai rolls, even though they'd started falling apart and he had to eat them with a spoon.

"My grandmother loved *tamarindo* too, but I guess I should've tested the recipe before today."

"That may be good, Guerrero, but nothing beats this *ceviche*," Mr. Flores said. "I think I've eaten most of it. If anyone wants a taste, you better be quick about it."

Mrs. Flores got an embarrassed look on her face. "You act as if I've been starving you this past week, Beto."

Mr. Flores turned to me. "I sure hope you're not planning to open a restaurant anywhere within fifty miles of here. If the word gets out that you're such a gourmet cook, we'll be out of business *en un dos por tres*."

Guerrero laughed. "We'll have to close shop and go work for you."

"Seriously, Lola," Mr. Flores said to his wife. "This could be the answer to our dilemma."

We all turned to look at them.

"I've been after Beto to cut down on his hours at the restaurant," Mrs. Flores said when she saw the blank look on our faces. "The older we get, the harder it is for us to continue the crazy schedule running a restaurant requires. Beto's been using the excuse that he can't dump the entire load on Guerrero's shoulders. If you're willing to assume some of the cooking responsibilities, Lucy, he won't have to."

"But . . ." I felt my throat tighten while I stared at her, like a dummy.

"Now that we know what you can do, we can't keep wasting your talents." She looked at her husband before she added, "Of course, it would also mean a raise in pay."

A raise wasn't that important to me, but the idea of a promotion to assistant cook was one of the fantasies I'd been trying not to dwell on. While cooking was what I loved more than anything, doing it so publicly, for strangers who'd be judging the results, scared the stuffing out of me. I looked at Guerrero.

He reached over and patted my hand. *"Niña,* I have to agree. You really must love to cook. Otherwise, you couldn't make food that tastes this good."

I turned to Meme. He winked and gave me thumbs up.

"Of course, that's going to take time away from your studies," Mr. Flores said, before my brain could absorb everything that was happening. "We may have to hang in there for a while so you can still go to school."

"I'll start with one or two classes once I get my GED," I said. "Now that I've passed probation as a dishwasher, I promise not to disappoint you as assistant cook."

"It's settled, then," Mrs. Flores said. "Starting tomorrow, the help wanted sign goes up for a new dishwasher."

After the meal, I suggested a game of Lotería. Guerrero had taught me how to play, and I'd become a big fan of the game. He shuffled and reshuffled the cards and, with a couple of beers under his belt, he called out each draw with much more flair than usual.

"¡El cotorro! ¡El soldado! ¡La luna!"

After Meme won the first two games, Guerrero asked him to entertain us with his guitar. Meme's face lit up. Since he sometimes practiced during his breaks and kept his guitar at the restaurant, he ran down to get it.

At eight o'clock, Mrs. Flores said, "Thank you, Lucy. This has been a perfect celebration but, at our age, Beto and I can only handle so much excitement in one day."

Elena insisted on cleaning up the kitchen. "I hear you're no longer a dishwasher. Besides, this is one thing I do well and it's the least I can do after that awesome meal." Her belly stuck out so much, she could barely reach the faucet.

Guerrero went to the sink and took her arm. "I'm a good dishwasher. I'll wash the dishes."

"And I'll rinse," I said.

"You two sit," Meme told Elena and me. "We can handle this."

After they left, I sat at the table and tried to absorb everything that had happened in the last few hours, especially the promotion part. If Berta didn't like me now, she was really going to flip when she heard the news. But that was her problem.

I was too excited to sleep or read. Every once in a while, especially when I had something to celebrate—hardly ever—I would take out the agate Nana had given me and hold it in my hands. Tonight was one of those special nights. I could hardly wait to share my good news with Delia and Patti. They'd be happy to hear I was getting closer to realizing my dream. I figured Patti was out with Fernando, so I sent her a short text. *Moving up in the world. Just got promoted to assistant cook.* Then, I called Delia and left the same message.

CHAPTER TEN

Changes

"How was your weekend?" Mr. Flores asked Berta the following Monday.

"I love Vegas . . . the shows, the boxing matches. Best of all, I love the slot machines. You and Lola should go there sometime."

"I'm glad you had a good vacation because you missed a great party. Now that we know Lucy's such a fine cook, we've decided to promote her."

Guerrero and Meme made a big show of acting surprised and congratulating me.

Berta's good mood leaked out of her like air out of a balloon. She stared blankly at Mr. Flores, the tension hanging in the air like skunk farts.

"She'll be helping Guerrero in the kitchen so me and Lola can cut back on our hours," Mr. Flores said.

"So you're rewarding her, even though she's a thief?"

"Berta!" Mrs. Flores said. "There was never any proof that Lucy took that money."

"That's right," her husband said. "Besides, we're trying to protect the business and having Lucy replace me in the kitchen makes sense. This way, me and Lola can take a break every once in a while. You might as well get used to the idea because I'll be breaking her in this week. . . . Not that she needs it." He turned to me and winked.

"Well then, what can I say? You certainly deserve a rest after all these years." She looked at me like she wanted to singe my eyebrows. "Boy! That must've been some party."

During my break, I checked my phone.

"I'm not one bit surprised," Delia said in her message. "I'm so proud of you. I really miss you and your good eats. Guess I'll just have to pop in and surprise you sometime."

Patti's text said: "Way cool, girlfriend! I want to hear all the juicy details. CALL ME." The rest of the text was full of hearts, kisses and hugs.

   ❀ ❀ ❀

Mr. Flores wasted no time "breaking me in" as he put it. "You already know your way pretty good around this kitchen. I'll just run you through our routine and you can always make changes later. Whatever works for you works for me as long as we keep the customers happy."

The real changes started later that week. When I wasn't bussing tables, loading the dishwasher or scrubbing pots and pans, I helped with the prepping and shadowed Mr. Flores and Guerrero as they picked up and filled each order.

Although the kitchen was already pretty clean, I spent the following Sunday scrubbing and cleaning counters, ovens, walls, under and behind appliances and finally the whole floor. If I was going to be feeding strangers in this place, everything had to be as perfect as I could make it. If inspectors ever dropped in, they'd find nothing to complain about. The place was spotless.

While they waited to fill the new vacancy, Mr. Flores started doing the dishes to give Guerrero and me a chance to work together. It didn't take me long to realize I had a lot to learn. Planning a meal and cooking for a few friends was way different from cooking for a string of customers when the orders were flying in, everybody wanting different things and expecting to be served within minutes.

My first day was nerve-wracking. I kept messing up, burning my fingers when I picked up a spoon I'd left inside one of the pots, and dropping a plateful of food on the floor as I hurried to place it on the counter.

"Whoa! Take it easy," Guerrero said. "Better to have customers complain about a long wait than about not getting their order at all."

The next day, he asked me to cook the rice while he diced, chopped and prepared other ingredients we'd be needing for lunch. Pretty soon the orders started coming. He took a pan of enchiladas out of the oven and added beans to the first plate he fixed.

"This rice isn't ready," he said when he got to the pot of rice.

I ran to the stove and stared in horror at all the water still bubbling on top.

"No wonder," he said when he saw I'd turned the heat to low. He turned it back to medium-high and handed me a basket of chips and a bowl of guacamole. "Take this out to table three. Tell them their order's going to be a few minutes late. And leave the settings alone from now on." He didn't sound angry or even upset, but I felt like everyone's eyes were on me as I walked to Berta's section and delivered the food and message to table three.

Berta watched me the whole time. "So now I'm not even trusted to serve my own customers?" she said as I walked back to the kitchen.

"Their order's going to take a little longer than usual," I said.

"What did you do, burn it? Aren't you supposed to be such a hot-shot cook?"

"I didn't burn it. . . ." What was I doing falling for her taunt? "It's just going to be a little late." Already, I felt like that day would never end.

"I'm sorry about the rice," I said to Guerrero at the end of the lunch shift.

"Hey, I've been doing this for years and I still mess up every once in a while. You're doing great."

"Are you sure you don't mind that I've been promoted so soon?"

He turned to face me. "Now, why would I mind? You're the best thing that's happened to us since the restaurant opened."

"Well, there's at least one person who would've preferred to see me disappear."

He frowned. "She may be disappearing herself if she doesn't change her ways."

❧   ❧   ❧

Once I felt more confident and started taking on more of the cooking responsibilities, our customers began noticing a difference, especially after Pepe, our new dishwasher, was hired and Mr. Flores began circulating among them, joking with the regulars.

I heard one of them kidding him one day, "Lola finally let you out of the kitchen, eh?"

"*Hombre*, I finally figured it out. I'm better at hosting than I am at cooking."

"I didn't know Guerrero was such a good cook."

"Actually, he and our dishwasher have taken over the cooking."

"Where did you find a dishwasher who can cook, man?"

"Luck landed her on our doorstep."

My feelings exactly. It had been my good luck to find them. I couldn't disappoint them now.

❧ ❧ ❧

The following Tuesday, we were getting ready to open for lunch when Meme called to say he wouldn't be in that day. He was at the hospital with Elena.

"I can fill in for him," I said.

"I guess I better go find my apron," Mr. Flores said.

I helped in the kitchen for the first half hour until Berta appeared at the pick-up window.

"I'm swamped out here, Beto," she said. "Where's Meme?"

"He's at the hospital with Elena," Mr. Flores said. "But help is on the way."

I washed my hands, took off my apron and went to help in the dining room.

Berta stared at me like I'd grown warts and horns when she saw me carrying two plates of food to the section Meme usually covered. I ignored her and tried to concentrate on keeping the orders straight. The last thing I wanted was to give her another reason to complain about me.

I'd heard that Berta and Meme usually split the tips. When I volunteered to fill in for Meme, I'd told Mrs. Flores I wanted him to still get his usual half.

"I'm sure he'll insist that you keep it. Why don't we compromise and split his half between the two of you."

"He and Elena have driven me around and done so much for me. With the new baby, they'll need the money more than I do."

She smiled and nodded. "I'll make sure he gets it."

At closing time that night, I saw Mrs. Flores standing by the cash register, putting some bills in an envelope. She had a puzzled look on her face.

"Everything okay?" I asked.

"I'm not sure. I don't usually get involved in the tip splitting, but something just doesn't add up. We were pretty busy for a Wednesday night and only have ninety-five dollars in tips? The Olsens alone leave about a third that much when the whole clan shows up for dinner. I know that because Meme loves to see them walk in the door."

"Berta probably thinks I'm getting Meme's half tonight and . . ."

Mrs. Flores shook her head. "I can't believe she would take more than her share, but we have no way to prove anything." She looked at me with that same sad expression she'd worn when Berta accused me of being a thief.

Berta was mean, but she wasn't that stupid. Even she wouldn't try accusing me of the same crime twice. Still, there was something fishy going on. I'd have to keep an even sharper eye on her from now on.

The following morning the proud new dad called to tell us the baby was a boy. Mr. Flores shared the news and pressed the speaker button so Meme could hear all our congratulations.

"If it's not too much trouble, I'd like to take another day off," Meme said.

"Take as much time as you need," Mr. Flores said. "We'll limp along until you get back."

"I'll be back Saturday, then."

❦   ❦   ❦

I was in the kitchen helping with the prep work just before we opened, when Berta popped her head in.

"Meme out again?"

"He called earlier to say Elena had a boy," Mr. Flores said. "Lucy will be covering his section again today. The tips Lucy gets will go to Meme, so make sure it's an even split."

"It's always a fifty-fifty split."

"I know."

Berta put her hands on her hips. "So, what are you really saying?"

"Exactly what I just said. Why are you all of a sudden having trouble understanding?"

Berta stood there for a moment staring at me, her nostrils flaring as if smoke was about to start streaming out of them.

"Look . . ." she started to say. She shot another fierce look in my direction before walking away. Her footsteps again echoed their guilty verdict but, this time, she didn't accuse me.

At closing time, she slapped the entire tip box on the counter next to the cash register and walked out without a word. Rigo followed her and, after the door slammed shut behind them, I heard Berta yelling at him. Although I couldn't hear the words, I heard them arguing in the parking lot until Rigo's truck sped off like a bat out of hell.

❦   ❦   ❦

I was setting the tables the next day when Berta came in. She whacked me with her purse as she walked past me, knocking me against the wall.

Before I could stop myself, I said, "What the hell's wrong with you now?"

She ignored me and kept going.

❧ ❧ ❧

After we closed for lunch that Friday, Guerrero drove the Floreses and me to meet Ricardo Ismael Hinojosa. Elena's mother answered the door. She let us in and rushed back into the living room to pick up little Ricky. She let Mrs. Flores hold him for about two minutes before taking him from her and offering him to me.

I shook my head. "Thanks, but I'm afraid to drop him."

To my relief, she said, "We wouldn't want you to do that." She handed him over to Mr. Flores, who sat stiffly, holding him at arm's length.

"Relax. Otherwise you'll make him cry!" she told him.

"What do I know about holding babies?" he said. "This little guy looks pretty tough and healthy to me, though." The baby yawned and fell asleep when Mr. Flores held him close to his chest.

We didn't stay long. Elena still looked pretty worn out.

On the way out, Mrs. Flores said to Meme, "Why don't you stay home tomorrow. Enjoy the weekend with your family."

"You sure it's okay?"

"We'll manage for one more day."

"Thanks. See you all Monday then."

After the shoving incident, Berta had been quieter than usual, and Rigo hadn't been showing up at night. Whatever had happened between them, I was glad he wasn't around.

❧ ❧ ❧

I spent all day Sunday experimenting with a new *mole* sauce recipe and brought it in the following morning for Guerrero, Meme and the Floreses to sample.

As soon as he saw me, Meme tried to return the tip money. "Lucy, we really appreciate what you've done, but this money belongs to you."

"How did you know it was from me?"

"Lola put a note inside the envelope."

"It's for Ricky's college fund."

Meme laughed. "I'll tell Elena to keep her hands off it then."

I set the sauce on the table. "If this passes the taste test, we can offer it as a special and, if the customers don't like it, we won't add it to the menu."

The tasting turned into a guessing game as the tasters tried to identify the different ingredients.

"Plenty of garlic," Mrs. Flores said. "I like that."

"It could use a little more fire," Mr. Flores said.

"I used three kinds of chilies," I said.

"I like the sweetness," Meme said. "What'd you use to sweeten it?"

"A little brown sugar and a few mashed raisins."

"Definitely a winner," Guerrero said. "And you all know how much I love winners."

"Sounds like you threw a little of everything you had in your pantry into this sauce," Mr. Flores said.

"Just about. Lots of spices, nuts, seeds and of course the main ingredient, *chocolate mexicano*."

"This is delicious," Mrs. Flores said, "but you shouldn't be spending your free time cooking."

"I love experimenting with new recipes. We'll see what the customers have to say."

"If they have any taste," Guerrero said. "They'll love it."

A month after my promotion, we started offering a new dish each week, gauging its popularity by the customers' response. I began crossing the less popular items off the menu and adding the new options that became a hit.

Mr. Flores picked up a menu and studied it for a moment.

"These menus are starting to look pretty shabby. We need to have new ones printed." He threw the menu on the counter. "Unfortunately, we'll also need to raise our prices. I just paid the bills and noticed that our food costs have gone up."

"I don't think people will mind paying an extra buck or two," I said. "After all, we're using more fresh produce."

Mrs. Flores came to put her arm around me. "The word is out, Lucy. People are even driving here from Saguaro. Where are we going to put them all?"

"Maybe someday we can add a patio," I said. "Of course, that means we'd need to shade it and cool it somehow."

"That's a great idea," Meme said.

"Whoa, there," Mr. Flores said. "You people deaf? I'm talking about raising our prices to cover our food costs and you're talking about expanding."

"I'm sure me and Guerrero can do the expansion work," Meme said. "We poured the concrete and laid the brick for the patio at my house three years ago and it's held up pretty well. We could have the patio done in . . . a week? We could even do the landscaping, all for our usual pay, plus the cost of materials." He looked at Guerrero, who nodded his agreement.

"Yeah, and who's gonna do your job while you're out there?" Mr. Flores asked.

"Beto," Mrs. Flores said. "If we close for a week, the money we save on operating expenses can go toward the project. Besides, we could all use a break."

"Aren't you forgetting a minor detail?" her husband said. "We won't have any money coming in either."

"Still, there's no question that we need to expand," she said. "The sooner, the better."

Mr. Flores rubbed his chin.

"It'll pay for itself in no time," Meme said.

"The extra business will help pay for it," Guerrero added.

"If you come up with an estimate and the bank will give us a loan, we've got a deal."

Suddenly everyone, except Berta, was caught up in the patio idea. Before the restaurant opened and during our afternoon break that day, we sat at the table drawing and redrawing our plans of what we thought the patio should look like. After we studied them all and discussed the pros and cons, we decided Meme's was the best. He had even included the landscaping and a canopy that would cover ten additional tables. It would be open on three sides during warm weather with fans at each corner, misters in the center and drop shades on the sides.

"In cooler weather, the fans can be replaced with heat lamps," he said.

I hadn't seen him so excited since Ricky was born. It made me wonder if he was wasting his talents by waiting tables instead of starting his own construction business.

"I'll draw up the estimate tonight and, as soon as the bank approves the loan, I'll order the building materials."

"Good," Mr. Flores said. "We'll close the restaurant and the rest of us can go on vacation while you two are hard at work."

"You're not fooling anybody, Beto," his wife said. "We know where you'll be spending your time while the work is in progress."

❊ ❊ ❊

I stayed awake that night thinking about the patio expansion and how we were going to need to hire more people. Berta was still riding her high horse, but she and Meme were already hustling to keep up with the new pace at the restaurant, and Guerrero and I were struggling to prepare the orders as fast as we could.

Although the thought of someday getting to LA popped up in the back of my mind every now and then, it still filled me with anxiety. I guess I wasn't as adventuresome as Ms. Svalinski after all. And I couldn't blame Sara for that. Deep down I knew it had been luck that made me stop here instead. Maybe someday I'd work up the courage to go all the way to LA.

With each passing day, the chances of me traveling anywhere while the remodeling was going on kept fading, until they disappeared altogether. I decided to play it safe by painting the apartment instead. I had to go to Saguaro to get the paint and figured I could stop by SCC first. Since I didn't know Prince Charming's work schedule, I tried to remember what day of the week I'd been there. It had been a couple of weeks before the surprise party, and I remembered Meme telling me what he and Elena had done that weekend, so it must've been a Monday. As for the time, Meme had dropped me off right after the lunch shift.

The next Monday, I took the bus to SCC. My heart started racing when I saw that the cutie was there. I took a deep breath and walked to the counter.

"Hi. My name's Lucy. I was here . . ."

"Hi, Lucy. I'm Jorge Chapa."

I stood there like a dope staring into his dreamy brown eyes. His long straight hair fell across his right eyebrow, making me want to reach out and brush it back. His smile got my heart thumping so loud, I was sure he could hear it.

"Have you decided what classes you want to take?"

"Not yet. I need to talk to Ms. Svalinski first, but I don't have an appointment."

He looked at the sign-in sheet. "There are a couple of students ahead of you. You can add your name to the list if you're not in a hurry."

"That's okay. I can come back another day."

"I'm here Mondays, Wednesdays and Fridays from one to three. Be sure to come one of those days."

I could feel my cheeks burning. Had I been that obvious?

I smiled, mumbled a quick thanks and headed for the door. I could've kicked myself as I walked back to the bus stop. I hadn't planned this very well. What had I expected? Well, at least I knew his name now and his work schedule. And had he actually flirted with me?

❧ ❧ ❧

At Tiny's Hardware I told the woman at the counter I needed some paint.

"Tiny, customer needs some paint," she yelled over her shoulder.

With a name like Tiny, I didn't know what to expect, but the man who came out to help me was just regular size. Since he was much younger than the woman, I assumed he was her son. Anyway, I wasn't there to figure out that puzzle.

"Paint's back here," Tiny said. "What'd you have in mind?"

"I want to paint my apartment," I said.

Tiny led me to a wall with a bunch of color charts. I went back and forth between sea-foam and cool mint before finally settling on the mint.

After I sort of answered Tiny's questions about the size of the area I'd be painting, he said, "One gallon might do it, then. You need a roller, brush, tape?"

"Yes, all of that."

I hurried home with the supplies and dropped them off at the apartment before running down to the restaurant a whole fifteen minutes before it opened for dinner.

"You fall asleep?" Guerrero asked with a smile.

He had already chopped a mountain of onions and was starting on the tomatoes. A pot of beans was bubbling on a back burner and rice was sizzling in a huge pan next to it.

"I'm thinking of painting the apartment while the patio's being built," I said.

"You need help?"

"No, thanks. I think I can do it."

"You're a stubborn one," he said.

I don't know about stubbornness, but showing up at SCC was pretty gutsy, almost as bold as leaving El Paso on my own. What did I really know about this guy? Was he like most people who only showed their good side before you really got to know them? And did I really believe he'd bother with someone like me? Had he really flirted with me, or had my imagination gone a little haywire? Either way, I couldn't stop thinking about him.

CHAPTER ELEVEN

An Intruder

My mind was so crowded the next morning—thinking about the coming changes, wondering why I hadn't heard back from Mario—that I didn't notice the truck creeping along behind me until the driver honked the horn.

"Hey, trouble," Rigo yelled out the open window. "I hear you're a big shot chef these days. What other talents you been hiding?"

I ignored him, hoping he'd give up and leave. Wishful thinking.

"What you running for anyway? You training for the Olympics or something?"

Thinking that one way to get rid of him might be to cut my run short, I headed back toward town. His truck tires crunched gravel as he shifted gears and tried to turn the truck around—back and forth, back and forth. Soon, he was right next to me again, like a persistent gnat.

"Sweet little bouncy buns you got there," he said. "Come on, I'll give you a ride back."

I slowed down and tried to catch my breath before I stopped to glare at him.

"I don't know what the hell Berta sees in you, but you deserve each other," I said before I sprinted off.

"Bet you never talk shit like that at the restaurant," he yelled. "Me and Berta, we're on to you. You better watch your ass, or you'll end up back where you came from."

He gunned the engine and tore off like a demon on wheels, pelting me with gravel.

Rigo's words shook me up. I didn't normally like to tattle, but this might be my chance to get rid of the creep. Of course, Berta might have to go, too. What a pity that would be!

I went home, showered and reported to work. While Guerrero and I did our prep work that morning, I mentioned the incident to him.

He stopped peeling the potato he was holding. "Have you told Beto?"

"No."

"Listen, Lucy, Beto needs to know and so do the local police. There's something about that guy that doesn't sit quite right with any of us. If Berta chooses to put up with his shenanigans it's her business, but . . ."

"What do you mean?"

"I don't like to gossip, especially about a co-worker, but you need to understand these are not reasonable people you're dealing with." He knitted his eyebrows. "A few weeks ago, I saw her walking home after work and stopped to offer her a ride. She just waved me on. When I asked her why she was walking, she said she needed the exercise. Since I've known her, she's never so much as mentioned exercise before. Rigo had probably left her stranded. It's sad that she sticks up for him, blames herself and then lies to save face."

I thought about Sara. Maybe she covered up for Pedro because she felt trapped. But Berta seemed like the type who didn't take crap from anybody.

"That must've been the night I heard them arguing outside the restaurant right after the tips went missing," I said. "Why does she put up with him?"

"Only she can answer that. There's no reason you should have to, though. You really need to talk to Beto."

I suddenly got really focused on my work, but Guerrero didn't buy it.

"Now!"

Mr. Flores got on the phone the minute I finished telling him my story.

"Officer Cano's going to stop by after the lunch shift," he said when he hung up. "I want you to drop whatever you're doing then and tell him everything you told me."

❦ ❦ ❦

Officer Cano was waiting for me when the restaurant closed after lunch. I repeated my story for the third time. He took notes while I talked.

"We'll keep an eye on him," he said, "but unless he actually threatens you or tries to harm you, we really don't have any reason to detain him. He won't be hanging around the restaurant anymore, though. If he shows up, we'll come in and remove him." He pulled a card out of his pocket and handed it to me. "You need to be careful when you're out there by yourself. Call us right away if he comes near you again."

When Berta walked in just before the dinner shift, Mr. Flores told her to follow him into his office. They weren't in there long, but she came out with a frightened look on her face. Other than when she came to the order counter, she kept her distance that whole evening. After their big fight outside the restaurant, Rigo had stayed away the following night. But they must've kissed and made up because he came back the next night. I was glad he wouldn't be hanging around anymore.

The next morning, I went for my run earlier than usual, thinking the lazy bum wouldn't be up that early. By varying my route and going out at different times, I managed to avoid running into him and soon put him out of my mind, like a bad dream.

After Mr. Flores got the loan approval for the patio, Meme ordered the materials. A week later the restaurant closed and the expansion work began.

While Meme and Guerrero worked on the patio project, Elena drove Mrs. Flores and me to the Saguaro Nursery in Guerrero's truck. We each had our own ideas of what we wanted to plant around the patio.

Elena picked out a ready-made miniature cactus garden in a huge Oaxacan pot, a spotted aloe, a few sedums and a variegated yucca.

We needed a second cart for the pair of sago palms and a hedgehog agave Mrs. Flores chose.

"I don't know if these will survive, but I couldn't resist them," she said, adding two climbing piñata roses to the cart.

"I need to replace some of the plants in my garden, since we've been using them at the restaurant," I said, putting pots of basil, chives, rosemary, cilantro and jalapeño in a shopping basket.

"You've already transformed the whole backyard," Mrs. Flores said. "You could probably even grow tropical plants if you wanted to."

I laughed. "I'm a gardener, not a magician."

"Some people are born with all the talent," Elena said.

※   ※   ※

The next day, I got up early, pulled the furniture away from the walls and spread newspapers on the floor. It wasn't until I tried to clean the cobwebs off the corners that I realized I wouldn't be able to reach the ceiling, even if I stood on a chair. Luckily, there was a step ladder at the restaurant.

By six that afternoon, after I'd painted the last wall, I went from room to room admiring my work. Not bad, except for the tiny dots splattered on the window in the living room and the drips on the sill. The gaps left behind after I peeled off the tape gave the corners a wavy look. Oh well. Overall, I'd done a good job. Besides, I wasn't planning to host more parties up there any time soon.

I'd just started cleaning up when my phone rang.

"Lulu?"

"Mario!" I started hopping around like a wound-up kangaroo. "I was afraid you hadn't gotten my message."

"I just got it. We're in Italy for a couple of days. You have no idea how glad I was to hear from you. I thought of you last night when I went to dinner with some buddies. You would love the food here."

We talked for forty minutes until he said he had to go. "Keep those e-mails coming, though. I'll call you again next chance I get."

That night I sent a quick text to Patti and lay awake replaying Mario's words in my head until I fell asleep.

※   ※   ※

I spent the rest of my free time experimenting with new recipes, redoing the menu and catching up on my reading, when I wasn't checking out progress on the patio. Just before the project was supposed to be completed, I handed the new menu to Mr. Flores so he could have copies printed.

He looked it over. "Fresh tortillas?"

"Why didn't I think of that?" Mrs. Flores said. "Tortillas always taste better when they're fresh and I know just the person for the job. Our neighbor Sofía makes the best because she makes them the old-fashioned way."

"I added them to the menu thinking we could just order them from the local *tortillería*, the way we order the packaged ones," I said to Mrs. Flores. "But your idea's even better."

"What's Sofía going to do when she's not making tortillas?" Mr. Flores asked.

"She's not much younger than me," his wife said. "I doubt she'll want to work more than a couple of hours per shift."

"You people don't seem to get it. We're trying to cut costs here." Mr. Flores walked away shaking his head. His wife winked at me and we burst out laughing.

❈ ❈ ❈

True to their word, Meme and Guerrero finished the job right on time. They'd removed part of the side cinderblock wall and replaced it with a fancy iron fence. A smaller fence was built between the patio and the rest of the backyard. The new design opened up the garden, while the fences gave it a feeling of privacy.

"It's amazing what young blood will do for a business," Mr. Flores said when he saw the completed space. "You got any to spare for a couple of tired old birds?"

"This calls for a grand *re-opening*," I said. "Do you think we could offer a half-off-on-a-second-dinner deal the first night as a way of thanking the community for their support?"

As soon as the words were out of my mouth, I remembered Mr. Flores' money worries and quickly added, "Or at least a ten percent discount on a second dinner."

"I swear, Lucy, you're full of good ideas," Mrs. Flores said.

"I'll think about it," her husband said. "They certainly deserve something after all these years."

"We'll have our own little celebration before we reopen," Meme said. "You're all coming over to my house for dinner tomorrow."

"But, Meme . . ." I started to say.

"No excuses. Six o'clock at my house. And, no, you're not bringing anything."

※   ※   ※

The following Monday we all went back to work, getting the restaurant ready for the re-opening the next day. Mr. Flores had put an ad in the paper for a new wait person and a bartender because Meme suggested we start serving mixed drinks. The applications had been pouring in.

"Looks like all of a sudden everybody wants to work here," Mr. Flores said. After he and Meme had gone through the applications, they came up with a list of five candidates.

"I'm scheduling interviews for Wednesday," he told Berta and Meme. "Since you'll be the ones working with these people, you need to sit in on them."

※   ※   ※

Wednesday morning, Guerrero, Mrs. Flores and I busied ourselves at the counter so we could check out the candidates as they arrived for their interviews. There were two women, one about Delia's age and one just a little older than me, from what I could tell. Two of the men were about Meme's age and the third more like Guerrero's age.

"How did it go?" Mrs. Flores asked after the interviews.

"They'll say anything on paper and interviews," Berta said. "But you can't tell for sure what you're getting until you actually see their work."

Meme scratched his head. "It's going to be a tough choice. They all seem like good candidates, but I'm leaning toward hiring Joel for the bartending job. He's also got waiter experience and offered to help wait tables when he's not busy tending bar."

"I vote for Joel, too," Berta said, to no one's surprise. Even Mrs. Flores had noticed him.

"¡Qué guapo!" she'd said.

I had to agree. He sure was good-looking.

"Hopefully he has more going for him than looks," Guerrero said.

"I also think Cristina would make a good waitress," Meme said.

Berta didn't agree, but she kept her mouth shut for once.

Even with Joel and Cristina on board, the night of the re-opening, we were all spinning like out-of-control tops, trying to serve the diners as quickly as possible to make room for the next wave. And, even with the patio expansion, the lines seemed longer than ever. Customers checked out the new menus, watched Sofía make tortillas or enjoyed a drink and appetizers at the bar while they waited.

Once they felt we had everything under control, Mr. and Mrs. Flores started coming in late most mornings. Some days, Mrs. Flores didn't come in at all. Mr. Flores usually replaced the cash drawer, picked up the mail and disappeared into his office. When she did come in, Mrs. Flores spent her time in the backyard. Her climbing roses were already starting to make their way up the patio columns and some of Elena's live forevers and hens and chicks were spilling out of blue, green, red and orange pots, while others crept along the rock garden and small stone wall Meme had built on one side of the patio. Mrs. Flores watered and puttered around in the garden until she tired herself out and came in to visit with the staff and customers.

I spent every waking moment focused on the restaurant. My bank account was growing quickly since I was no longer earning minimum wage and the only expenses I had, besides rent, were books and an occasional new outfit for work. If my employers still worried about me and my nonexistent social life, they never mentioned it. Other than the time I'd spent with Nana, I couldn't remember ever having been this happy.

❀ ❀ ❀

One Sunday night, while reading one of my new books, *Skies in Blossom: The Nature Poetry of Emily Dickinson*, I heard a noise outside, like someone climbing the steps to my door. They sounded unsteady. I didn't panic, until the banging started.

"Open up, baby girl. I got something I know you want."

Rigo! I hadn't seen him since the time he'd followed me on my run. How had he gotten into the backyard? I was sure I'd locked the side gate.

He yanked on the doorknob. Could he break the door down? If he did, what would I do? My mind raced through the options I had to defend myself: the mean-looking knives Delia had given me, several skewers and one or two heavy pans in the kitchen. Of course, I didn't for one minute believe I could fight off the husky six-footer, even if he was drunk . . . especially if he was drunk. Then I remembered the even huskier Officer Cano. I'd stuck the card he'd given me under the clock on my nightstand.

Rigo kept beating and kicking the door. "I know you're in there. Open the damn door."

As far as I knew, he had never been in the apartment. Thinking he'd have a hard time finding his way around in the dark, I unplugged my reading light, hopped on a kitchen chair and unscrewed the kitchen light bulb before rushing to the bedroom. I took the card from under the clock and tried to call the number, but my hands were shaking so much I kept pressing the wrong buttons. Rigo was now slamming his body against the door. I finally gave up and stuck the card and phone in my pocket before climbing on the bed. Realizing right away that I couldn't reach the ceiling bulb, I took off one of my slippers, jumped up once and smashed it. By then, my legs were so shaky I half-jumped, half-fell off the bed. I grabbed the bedside lamp and tiptoed to the door, feeling tiny shards of glass dig into my right foot.

I reached the bedroom entrance just as Rigo came crashing through the front door. My thoughts raced as I heard him stumbling around, cursing and running into the furniture. *If I can get outside, I can . . . what? I can't climb over the wall and . . .*

I held my breath when I heard him getting closer, then sensed him feeling around for the light switch. He flipped it. Nothing happened.

I lifted the lamp as high over my head as I could. If I missed his head and hit his shoulder or back, it would be like tapping an angry bull on the horns.

"You think you're so smart, you little shit. Well, I'll teach you a lesson. . . ."

The sound of his voice helped me direct my aim. I bashed him with the base of the lamp and heard a muffled "Oomph!" On his way down, I heard a thump and realized he'd hit the bed's footboard. Then, everything was quiet.

"Shit! Shit! Shit!" Although I couldn't see a thing in the dark, I kept imagining blood pooling all over the floor. *What if I killed him?*

I felt for my keys on the dresser, found them, tripped over Rigo and limped down the stairs, hardly feeling the glass in my foot anymore. I was shaking so badly it took about four tries before I could get the key in the lock to open the restaurant door. I slipped in and slammed the door shut behind me.

Still trembling while trying to pull my phone and Officer Cano's card out of my pocket, it took what seemed like forever for my fingers to find the right numbers.

A woman's voice answered, "Emergency Dispatch."

"I'm calling to report a crime in progress," I said, like I'd heard or read somewhere. "Can you please send Officer Cano?"

"Where are you?"

"At La Cocina Restaurant in Maguey." I gave the restaurant's address and phone number when prompted by the dispatcher.

She kept asking me questions. Trying to keep my voice calm and steady, I explained that an intruder had broken into my apartment, fallen and hit his head.

"Is he conscious?" she asked.

"No!" I screamed. "I don't know. I need someone to get here fast."

"An officer's on his way," she said. "Stay inside until he gets there."

I watched the front window, each second feeling like an hour, while I waited for the officer to arrive. But Maguey is small and Officer Cano could not have been far when he got the call, because I soon saw his car come to a screeching stop in front of the restaurant.

"He's upstairs," I said as I let him in the front door and out the back.

"Stay inside and lock the door," he whispered.

Apparently, Rigo had woken up and seen the flashing lights too. The head bashing must've sobered him up because I heard him stomping down the stairs and running toward the back wall when the officer yelled for him to stop. Even in his drunken, beat-up state, Rigo was too fast for the chunky policeman.

I watched from the back window as Officer Cano shone his flashlight up the stairs and around the yard before returning to the restaurant.

"Lucy, it's me," he said.

I let him in.

"Lock up until I get back." He ran out the front door, got in his car and raced away in one direction while Rigo's truck roared off in the opposite direction.

After a while, Officer Cano came back and knocked on the front door.

"You okay?"

"Yes, sir."

"Was it who I suspect?" he said.

"Yes. It was Rigo."

"As a precaution, I don't think you should stay in the apartment tonight. I can take you to the Floreses'."

"I can sleep in the office," I told him. "There's a couch I can use in there."

"Are you sure?"

"I'll call you if he comes back."

"Since it's pretty late, I'll wait until morning to call Mr. Flores. We'll be patrolling the area until then, but don't hesitate to call if you change your mind about staying here." He started out the door. "Now, are you sure you're going to be okay?"

"I'll be fine."

After Officer Cano left, I went to the kitchen, tore a strip off an old dishtowel, making a mental note to get an emergency kit for the restaurant. After picking the glass out of my foot, I tied the cloth around it and locked myself in the office. I sat in Mr. Flores' chair the rest of the night. There was no way I could sleep with my mind racing and my heart still thumping. At least I hadn't killed him. As much as I wanted him gone, making him disappear that way was too high a price to pay.

At seven I called Meme and told him what happened.

"That bastard! Berta sure doesn't have very good instincts when it comes to men. Where are you now?"

"In the office. I spent the night here."

"You need to come stay with us for a few days."

"Thanks for the offer, but I really didn't want to involve you in any of this. I'm sure we won't be seeing the idiot for a while. At least not until he gets rid of the black eyes he must've gotten from bouncing around on his head."

"Serves him right. He is an idiot, a dangerous one, so don't be so sure he's learned his lesson."

"I know. The day he followed me wasn't the first time he'd harassed me."

"What? What else has he done and when?"

I'd been pacing back and forth the whole time we'd been talking, but Meme's question stopped me in my tracks.

"Lucy?"

"He . . . he grabbed me once at the restaurant."

"Why hadn't you said anything before now?"

"I didn't want the Floreses to worry."

"Look, I know you're not stupid, but you did a stupid thing by not telling us sooner. I think you should stop your daily runs for a while. And, if anything ever happens again, I want you to call me right away, no matter what time of day or night."

A sob of frustration escaped from my throat. "I shouldn't have to change my life because of that lunatic!"

"Now you're just being stubborn. Look, the Floreses can't stand Rigo any more than I can, and Berta's been skating on very thin ice at the restaurant. Even though she's been around since the restaurant first opened, I'm sure Beto will fire her after this."

Great! Just what I need. If Berta gets fired, they'll both be out to get me. What am I going to do? I love my job, my apartment, my friends. Did Sara put a curse on me after all?

⁂   ⁂   ⁂

At eight, Meme showed up with a locksmith and Officer Cano. I followed them to the apartment. While the locksmith replaced the lock and put in a deadbolt, Officer Cano questioned me and filled out his report. Afterward, Meme and I went around checking things out. He replaced the light bulbs while I swept up the glass.

"Somebody's been busy," he said when he saw the paint job.

"Don't look too closely," I said.

He scratched at the specks of paint on the window with his thumbnail. "No biggie. This can easily be cleaned up."

Officer Cano waited for us at the bottom of the stairs. "I've been looking around to see if I could find any clues as to how this guy got in. He must've parked right next to the wall and climbed on his truck to hoist himself over."

"How did he get out?" I asked.

"Adrenaline." Officer Cano turned to me. "I'll make sure Rigo knows we're watching him, but you still need to take precautions. I don't normally do this, but this might come in handy."

He handed me a small cylinder and explained how it worked. The spray was only to be used to give me time to call for help. "Carry it and your cell with you at all times."

The Floreses didn't normally come in on Mondays, but Meme had called them and told them there was a break-in without giving them any details.

Mr. and Mrs. Flores and Guerrero were already there when we walked back to the restaurant.

"We didn't want to alarm you," Officer Cano said, "but the break-in was actually into Lucy's apartment."

"Rigo?" Mr. Flores said.

Meme nodded. "The day he followed her wasn't the first time he'd harassed her either."

I jumped when Mr. Flores slammed his fist on the counter. "What else has he done to you and why didn't you tell us? I knew that guy was nothing but trouble. But you, young lady," he pointed his finger at me, "if he so much as looks at you again, you will call one of us. Is that understood?"

"I'm sorry. I was scared. I . . ."

"Cano says you called him from the restaurant. Why didn't you call him the minute you heard the rat prowling around your place?"

"I tried," I said, "but I kept hitting the wrong keys."

"Before you start work today, you're going to put Cano's number on direct dial so you don't have to fumble around if you ever need to call him again."

All I could do was nod. I'd never seen him so angry.

Mrs. Flores put her arm around me. "Oh, dear! What a horrible experience. You need to come stay with us."

"I've already invited her to stay with us," Meme said. "She's a stubborn one, though. Anyway, Officer Cano will be keeping an eye on her."

"I don't want to intrude on anyone," I said. "There's a deadbolt on the door now, and it's not like I'm out looking for trouble."

"But trouble came looking for you," Guerrero said.

"I'll have a couple of motion detector lights installed in the backyard," Mr. Flores said. "You can be sure we won't be seeing that fool's mug in the restaurant again."

"But you know how Berta feels about me. She's going to—"

"If she wants to hang out with riffraff like that, it's her business," Mr. Flores said, "but I've had enough."

I knew there was nothing more to say. He was right, of course. They all were. Still, I couldn't shake the guilt that hung over me like a thunderhead.

Berta walked in just then. "Hey, Cano, what're you doing here this time of day? Did someone break-in?"

"We need to talk to you," Mr. Flores said.

He headed toward his office. Officer Cano looked at Berta and gestured for her to follow.

"What's going on?" She gave Mrs. Flores and Meme a puzzled look.

"They need to talk to you," Mrs. Flores said.

A few minutes later, we heard Berta whimpering. After a while, all three of them came out of the office.

"Berta has some explaining to do," Mr. Flores said. "Go ahead. Tell them what you just told us."

Berta closed her eyes and pursed her lips for a moment. "It was Rigo who took the tip money I accused Lucy of stealing when she first got here. He started taking money from the tables before we had a chance to pick it up." She sniffled. "I swear I didn't know at first. When I caught him in the act, we got into a big fight. I tried to cover up by leaving my tips for Meme."

"Why didn't you report him?" Meme asked.

"He threatened me. He gets so angry sometimes, I just . . ."

"We'll issue a restraining order against him," Officer Cano said, "but if he tries to contact you, you need to call us immediately."

I almost felt sorry for Berta. She looked so scared and, for the first time, I noticed she also looked old.

"Please, Beto," she said. "Give me another chance. I promise you'll never see him around here again."

"I have no complaints about your work. If you're willing to make an attitude adjustment and stay away from that loser, I suppose you deserve a second chance, just like any-body else. But aren't you forgetting something?"

"Thanks," Berta said. She turned to me and mumbled a quick "Sorry" before she disappeared behind the counter.

Mr. Flores turned to me. "Remember that from now on, you'll carry your phone with you wherever you go."

I suddenly felt like I was in the witness protection program.

❧ ❧ ❧

That whole day, Berta scurried around like a scared mouse.

When Officer Cano stopped by that evening, I said, "Dinner's on me tonight. What can I get for you?"

"Thanks, Lucy," he said. "I was just doing my job. I'm only here to see how you're doing."

"Fine. I'm taking your advice and carrying my weapons with me everywhere I go."

He laughed. "Good girl. I can see you're busier than ever tonight, so I won't keep you. We still haven't been able to track down that weasel. He could be anywhere. You'll need to keep your guard up at all times."

Meme walked by and overheard the officer. "I told Lucy she should keep a low profile for a while."

"It's sad when the victim ends up paying for a crime committed against her," Officer Cano said, "but it's better to play it safe."

He looked down at his uniform. His shirt buttons looked ready to pop off. Then he turned to me. "My doctor's been after me to lose a few pounds. I should offer to join you on your runs."

"Good idea," said Meme. "Heck, we should all be out there, with Lucy leading the pack, whipping us all into shape. Of course, it may take a year before we're in good enough shape to keep up with her." They both laughed.

After work, Guerrero and Meme walked me to my door. They stood at the bottom of the stairs watching me until I went inside. I lay awake that night listening to noises I'd never noticed before creaks and cracks the place made as it settled, sounding like a tired giant grunting with relief as it cooled off after standing in the scorching sun all day. I pictured Rigo with a big black bruise in the middle of his forehead. Even he wasn't stupid enough to come back again. I hoped.

I finally dozed off only to find myself free-falling through the sky, arms and legs flailing helplessly until I woke up with a jolt.

Despite the dread of falling into another nightmare, I was so tired I drifted off again. This time I was tied to a chair while piles of rags smoldered around me and blue flames burned in the center of each pile, growing bigger and hotter by the second. I sputtered and choked as smoke began to fill the room and the intense heat made my lungs feel like they were on fire. Cold sweat ran off my chest and back when I jumped out of bed and ran to the bathroom to grab a towel.

I changed into a dry T-Shirt, propped myself up with all the pillows I owned and managed to get in a few winks before the phone woke me up.

"Hey, girl, I've left so many messages, I was starting to wonder if you were trying to tell me something by ignoring my calls," Patti said.

"It's been a little wild around here lately." I told her about the break-in.

"Freakin' freak!" she said. "That totally sucks. Pretty soon you'll need to start packing a gun!"

"No way! I'd probably end up shooting myself in the foot."

After she got over being indignant about all my troubles, Patti started telling me the latest about her own life.

"I guess you haven't noticed that I've left a few messages of my own," I said when she stopped to catch her breath.

"Sorry. Since Fernando left for UT, we've been spending hours on the phone almost every day. I went with him when he left and then drove back with his parents. I wish you'd been with us. Austin's way cool. But then I cried all the way back."

I tried to think of something comforting to say. All I could manage was a lame, "Why don't you apply there too?"

"You kidding? I'll be lucky to get into the local community college. Besides, Mom can't afford the tuition. Anyway, I'll go there to see him every other month, and he'll come home for the holidays and maybe . . . oh, sorry to be going on and on about myself as usual. Even though I miss you, I was glad you finally got away from your nutty parents. Glad your friends are watching out for you."

After we hung up, I thought that I'd be missing Fernando too if he were my boyfriend. *But Jorge is much cuter. I just hope he's as nice as Fernando.* I sighed. *What difference does it make? He probably has as many girls hanging around him as Art does.*

CHAPTER TWELVE

Small World

Next to Mexican, Italian's my favorite cuisine. After Mario's phone call, I started fantasizing about the food in Italy. Now that I had a posse of bodyguards watching my every move, I didn't have a chance to get away very often. But the following Saturday, I took the bus into Saguaro and went straight to The Book Nook to look for an Italian cookbook.

"Sorry," the clerk said after I told her what I was looking for. "Our cookbook section's kind of limited. If you had a title, I might be able to order it for you. Have you tried The Cellar? You never know what you might find there."

"The Cellar?"

"It's not far—kind of hidden at the end of Arenas Street. Right around the corner from the Lizard Lounge."

When she saw the blank look on my face, she drew a detailed map and handed it to me. I still didn't know my way around Saguaro very well. But the hand-drawn map helped me find it easily.

My reaction when I first saw it was that I'd been sent on a wild goose chase. The small sign on the door was turned to OPEN, even though it looked dark inside. I turned the doorknob, sending a tinkling warning of intrusion from the string of bells attached to it. Inside, it was like stepping into a dream. This was definitely not a place for claustrophobics. The walls were lined floor to ceiling with books. They seemed to sprout from shelves, from piles on the floor, from the counter. I stood there for a minute taking it all in, not sure what to do next.

Then I heard shuffling footsteps approaching and was glad to still be standing by the door, in case I needed to make a quick exit.

"Heh, just in time for a nice cup of tea," said the rumpled figure that appeared from the shadows.

"Oh, sorry. I didn't mean to interrupt your break," I mumbled.

"My life is one long break, young lady. You're welcome to come by and interrupt it any time."

I started to ask where the cookbook section was, but it was obvious this wasn't a typical bookstore.

"I'm looking for a book on *trattoria* cooking," I said.

The man held up a finger and slowly disappeared as he made his way back in the direction he'd come from. I waited, wondering if I should leave. Maybe The Book Nook clerk had made a mistake. Maybe this was a private collection and nothing was for sale. I was still trying to decide what to do, when he reappeared holding exactly what I'd been looking for although I hadn't known it until I saw it.

"How much is it?" I asked.

"Consider it a gift," he said.

"A gift? But isn't this a bookstore, sir?"

"Book storage is more like it."

"How can you afford to stay in business if you give your books away?"

"This is no business, sweet. Books are my passion."

"They're a passion of mine too, one of them anyway. I will accept your gift, but only if I can give you something in return. Stop by the restaurant where I work whenever you're in Maguey. Dinner will be on me."

"Not necessary, but if it makes you happy, then we'll come."

Before I had a chance to wonder who "we" meant, he said, "Now, how about that cup of tea?"

I hesitated, but only for a moment, before following him into a small, cluttered kitchenette.

"I know you!" The voice sounded familiar.

I turned in the direction that it came from. Small world, I thought when I saw Ms. Svalinski sitting there with a cat on her lap and an open book in front of her.

"It's good to see you again," I said, surprised that she even remembered me, especially since she hadn't really seemed to take much notice of me when I first met her.

"No need for introductions then," the old man said, forgetting that he hadn't yet introduced himself. "Anne is my chauffeur, a fellow booklover and a nag, hee, hee!"

"And you're lucky to have me around, you old coot!" Ms. Svalinski told him before she turned back to me. "If it weren't for me, he wouldn't even remember to eat. He's pretty *loco*, if you ask me."

"Nobody's asking, sweet. Nobody cares."

"Well, I care," I said to Ms. Svalinski. "I just invited him to La Cocina in Maguey. You're welcome, too, of course."

"Did you hear that, Fred? Maybe there you'll get a decent meal for a change."

She turned to me again. "What kind of food, dear?"

"Mexican, but I offered . . ."

Ms. Svalinski slapped her forehead. "Well, of course. With a name like that, what else could it be? Anything's an improvement over the swill he gets next door."

"The Lizard Lounge? I didn't know they served food."

"If you can call it food," she said.

"That, to answer your question, is how I stay in business as you say," Fred said. Noticing the look on my face, he added, "It pays me rent, which in turn pays for the books and keeps me in swill up to my eyeballs."

"Oh?" I didn't even try to figure it all out. "So, you just keep adding to your collection?"

"I sell a few books every now and then, mail-order mainly. It's hard to part with any of them. They're like my children. Not a good practice, selling your children. I do it only to make room for more. I see it as emancipating those I sell and adopting more."

"That makes perfect sense, I think," I said, turning to Ms. Svalinski, who was pouring a cup of tea for me. "I've been thinking of signing up for a class or two next fall. When can I take my GED? And what should I study to prepare for it?"

"You look like a smart cookie. I wouldn't worry about it."

Easy for her to say, but I couldn't help worrying. Had I learned enough to pass this test before I dropped out of school?

"If it'll make you feel better, you can take a practice test online. That'll give you an idea of what to expect on the real one. I can call you as soon as I have a test date for you."

She hovered over Fred like a mother hen, dropping two cubes of sugar in his tea and stirring it for him after adding cream. He drank it without bothering to thank her.

❊   ❊   ❊

Before I left, I wrote the restaurant's name and address and my phone number on a piece of paper I found in my pocket. *Time to order business cards. After all, we're getting more and more popular every day.*

"Consider this an IOU," I said to Fred as I tried to hand him the note.

Like a rattlesnake striking out of nowhere, Ms. Svalinski's bony hand reached out and snatched it from me. "I'll take that if you don't mind," she said. "Otherwise, we may never see it again. Fred can never keep track of anything unless it's one of his precious books."

On my way to the bus stop, I wondered if Jorge ever shopped at The Cellar. Although I was happy to have discovered it, I soon put it out of my mind once I returned to my crazy schedule at the restaurant.

❊   ❊   ❊

We had just opened the following Friday night, when Meme came to the order window and held up the paper I'd given Fred and Anne.

"Looks like you got some visitors," he said. "They were the first in line, so I let them choose their table."

They were sitting at a table that looked out on the patio.

"We're here early because Anne's blind as a bat at night," Fred said.

"I only wish I could get around as well as a bat at night," Ms. Svalinski said.

As I handed them menus, I realized I'd never introduced myself to Fred.

I smiled. "By the way, my name is Lucy Sánchez. I'm glad you could join us tonight."

"See, I told you it was Lucy!" Ms. Svalinski shouted, as if Fred had a hearing problem. "I told him it was Lucy," she said to me a little more quietly.

"It's amazing that you remember me," I said. "You must see so many students."

"I never forget a face and, for some reason, I remembered your name, too. You must've made quite an impression on me the day you came to my office."

"She's funny that way," Fred said.

I laughed. "What can I get you to drink while you check out the menu?"

"*Una Bohemia para mí y para Anne un vaso grande de horchata*," Fred said in flawless Spanish.

"What the heck is that?" Anne asked suspiciously.

"Just try it, sweet. Trust me this once. You'll like it."

"Where did you learn such perfect Spanish?" I asked Fred.

"In Nicaragua. I spent a couple of years there with the Peace Corps."

"He also happens to speak French and Portuguese," Anne said. "He's just a natural linguist, aren't you, Frederico?"

I tried not to laugh. She obviously was no linguist.

🌸　🌸　🌸

I brought them the drinks, *pico de gallo*, chips and guacamole. "Any questions about the menu?"

"No questions," Fred said. "This is one heck of a menu you got here, though. I'll have the *pozole* and Annie will have the green enchiladas.

I hadn't yet figured out their relationship, but whatever they were, it was obvious they were perfect for each other.

I brought them fresh mangos and blueberries with a dash of tequila syrup for dessert. At the end of their meal, Anne asked for the check. I assumed that, besides being his chauffeur, she was also his personal accountant.

"As I said at the bookstore, since Fred wouldn't let me pay for the book, the meal is my way of saying thanks."

"No need for that," Fred said.

"Okay, then," Anne said. "I have to say this whole experience has been pretty special. I can't remember eating so well since I was in Santa Fe."

"Thank you. I'll have to remember that, if I ever get to Santa Fe."

After they left, the busboy came to the kitchen and handed me an envelope with a fifty-dollar bill inside.

"Where did that come from?" I asked.

"The old couple," he said.

I thanked him and stuck the money in my pocket, thinking about what I would say the next time I saw them.

⁂

I was just starting my run the next morning when a police car pulled up next to me.

"You Lucy?" the officer said.

I stopped, suddenly wide awake and fully alert. "Yes, sir."

"Morning, Lucy. I'm Sergeant Grant. How ya doin' today?"

"Okay."

"Good. You keepin' your eyes open out here?"

"Yes, sir."

"Remember, we're never far away. Call us at the first sign of trouble."

"Thanks, I will."

I pulled my cell out of my pocket and flashed it at him before I took off again.

On my way back, I saw the car again as I got close to the restaurant. Officer Cano must've told the whole Maguey Police Department, all two or three of them, to keep an eye on me. Would anyone even have noticed if I'd gone missing in LA? Another reason to be glad I'd landed in this little town.

Although there had been no more Rigo sightings, Berta was still keeping her distance, which suited me fine.

I continued to keep the little canister on my nightstand when I slept and in my pocket when I ran. During my run I usually picked apart recipes I'd read about or dreamed up the night before. One morning, I was thinking about a Middle Eastern dish made with fava beans that I'd read about in one of the cooking magazines I subscribed to. I was wondering where I'd find the ingredients, when I saw him. A puppy.

He was standing on the side of the road a few feet away. I stopped to watch. He watched me back. He couldn't have been more than a few weeks old, but instead of bouncing and playing as puppies do, he cowered in fear. I took a few steps toward him and stopped again, when he ran to hide behind a desert broom. He kept watching me from behind the shrub.

"It's okay, pup. I'm not going to hurt you." I knelt and held out my hand. He took a couple of steps toward me and swished his tail once.

"Come," I said.

He stayed put.

Forgetting about my new recipe and the changes I was planning for the menu, I ran back to the restaurant and rummaged through the fridge, finding a hunk of cheese and a couple of tortillas left over from the day before. I put them in the microwave just long enough to melt the cheese, filled a jar with water, grabbed a bowl and a take-out container and stuck everything in a bag before I ran back out.

The puppy watched my every move as I tore the food into bite-size pieces and set it and the water on the ground. I backed away slowly and watched him walk to the food, gulp down every bite and lick the container. As he lapped up the water, his tail gave an occasional swish.

I looked at the spot of shade behind the shrub—no bigger than what a kid's umbrella would provide. If the puppy was going to stay cool, he'd have to move at least every hour.

"Try to stay in the shade, if you can," I told him. "I'll be back later."

I ran back to the apartment, took a quicker than usual shower and hurried to the restaurant.

As soon as Meme and Guerrero walked in, I told them about the pup. "Do you think the Floreses will mind if I bring him here?"

"Girl, you know they're like your private genies waiting to grant your every wish," Meme said.

I looked at him for any hint of jealousy or sarcasm, but he was smiling.

"I can always say I need a guard dog."

Guerrero laughed. "A guard puppy."

"I need help catching him, though. He looks like he's had it pretty rough already, and it's hard to get near him."

"Does he have a collar?" Meme asked.

"No."

"I'm sure I've seen some rope around here. It'll do until we can get him a proper collar and leash."

That whole morning I thought about the puppy, worrying that he might not be staying in the shade, wondering if he had enough water, plotting what I would do with him. After lunch, Guerrero, Meme and I jumped in Guerrero's truck and went back to look for him.

"That's the spot," I said when I saw the bowl. "He was behind that shrub."

Guerrero pulled as far off the road as he could without driving into the ditch. Part of the puppy was in the shade, but most of him was slow cooking in the hot mid-afternoon sun.

I'd brought along a bowl of rice, beans and odds and ends left over from lunch.

"Wait here until I grab hold of him," I said. "If he sees us all at once, we'll never catch him."

"I'll catch him," Meme said. "He looks scared. He may try to bite."

"But he already kind of trusts me," I said. "Let me have the rope."

Meme opened the door. I slid out and made my way toward the pup. He lifted his head and watched me, ready to jump up and run. I crouched down as far as I could without touching the hot ground with my hands or knees and crept toward the shrub like a timid ghost. The puppy stood up, but he didn't run off.

"Hey, I'm back," I whispered. I slid the food toward him. This time he ate a little more slowly, raising his head to look at me every once in a while.

I kept cooing, whispering and creeping a little closer. When I was close enough to touch him, I petted his head and knew I had him when his tail started wagging wildly and he looked up at me with more trust than fear. I scooped him up and held him close, trying to keep his head facing away from the truck.

Guerrero had opened the tail-gate and put his seat cushion back there for me to sit on.

Meme took the rope, which was still hanging around my own neck, and tied it around the puppy's.

"What breed do you think it is?" he asked.

"Because of his coloring and the shape of his head, I'd say he's part Airedale. But I also see some Black Lab in him. Whatever else he is, he's a perfect mutt, my favorite breed."

"You're one lucky pup," Meme told him. "What are you going to name him?"

"You just did. Lucky."

That afternoon, Meme showed up with a collar, a leash and a flea comb. Guerrero brought a bag of puppy kibble, a chew bone and a red ball. I'd already given Lucky a bath, brushed him with my own hairbrush and made a bed for him out of a box top and a towel. I set his bed with his new toys on the shady side of the restaurant and laid him in it. He immediately jumped out and followed me to the restaurant door. I closed the door and ran to a side window from where I could see his bed. After a while he came around the corner, curled up in it and fell asleep.

Chapter Thirteen

Ghosts

It was hard to tell who was more excited our first night together. After Lucky got tired of gnawing on his new bone and chasing after the ball, I read to him from *To Kill a Mockingbird*. "Well sir, I was on the porch and—and he came along and, you see, there was this old chiffarobe . . ."

I leaned over to look at my pup. "Isn't that a beautiful word, Lucky?"

It hadn't taken him long to learn his name. He jumped up to lick my face, and I petted him until he settled down a bit.

I'd once asked Nana if she had a chiffarobe.

"If I do, I don't call it that," she'd said. "What is it?"

"Not sure, but I like the sound of it."

"Look it up. Then we'll both know."

I got the dictionary from her bookshelf and looked up the word. "It's spelled with an o here instead of an a, but this says it's a combination wardrobe and chest of drawers."

"Well, then, I do have one. I call it a *ropero*," she said.

When Lucky fell asleep, I picked him up and lay him on my chest, tucking his head under my chin, holding him the way I imagined Atticus would've held Scout, the way Meme held Ricky, the way any normal father would hold his child.

I watched Lucky sleep for a few more minutes, wondering what his life might've been like until now. Whatever troubles he'd known were forgotten, and I was determined to make sure he never had a reason to be afraid again.

"Never again, Lucky. Never again."

I squeezed him gently and kissed the top of his head before I set him on a blanket next to my bed. As soon as I lay down, he leaped up on the bed and snuggled next to me.

Lucky, Lucky . . . I fell asleep with his name on my lips and a smile on my face.

The next thing I knew, I was pressed against the wall like a squashed bug against a windshield. A heavy weight kept me pinned to the wall. My mouth opened and a silent scream escaped from it before a great beefy hand clamped it shut. I tried to push the weight off me and run, but my legs collapsed under me.

I sat up with a start and sent Lucky tumbling off my chest. The covers were tangled around my legs, my nightgown soaked with sweat. I pulled up my knees, buried my face in my hands and sobbed—great, big, snotty sobs. Though I knew Pedro wasn't much of a threat anymore, the unpredictable Rigo was still a very real danger. Together they continued to haunt my dreams.

After Lucky disentangled himself from the covers, he ran back to me, poked his head through the space between my left arm and leg, and licked away my tears.

"I'm sorry, Lucky. It didn't take me long to break my promise. It was the ghosts' fault. I thought I'd left them behind forever."

Lucky crawled under the covers and licked my toes.

I pulled him out and held him. He wiggled and shook, his tail slapping my side as I leaned over to pick up his blanket. I wrapped him in it, lay back down and held him close until we both fell asleep.

⁂   ⁂   ⁂

Fred and Anne showed up again at five the following Friday. They seated themselves at the same table. When I took their order, they asked for the exact same meal. After they ate, instead of a check, I put the fifty on the table.

"You seem to have left this behind last time."

Neither Fred nor Anne would take it.

"That was your tip," Anne said. "I've never seen Fred actually enjoy a meal before. Did you notice he ate every last bite?"

Of course, I'd noticed they had both cleaned their plates.

She pulled me close and whispered, "Just take it easy on the beans from now on. Otherwise, he'll be tootin' his horn all night."

When they were gone, the busboy brought me a book they'd left behind: *Where I Come From* by Aarón Sánchez. There was a note inside the cover. *Any chance you could be related?* it read. As I leafed through it, the fifty-dollar bill fell out.

I stayed up all night reading the book. Was Fred kidding? This guy came from culinary royalty as far as I was concerned. It made me wonder if Nana had ever dreamed of having her own restaurant.

I called The Cellar the next day and was about to hang up after the ninth ring, when I heard Fred's voice.

"I will continue to accept your books on one condition only," I said. "No more outrageous tips or gifts if I can't pay for the books."

"And who, may I ask, is calling?" he said.

I giggled. "Thanks for the book. Unfortunately, no relation, but I am one of his biggest fans."

Once we reached an understanding, I became a regular at The Cellar and they at La Cocina. We agreed on a kind of bartering system that worked well for all of us. They were the first at the restaurant every Friday night, sat at the same table each time and, no matter how much I tried to entice them with new menu items, they stuck with the same choices they'd made on their first visit.

CHAPTER FOURTEEN

Growing Pains

"See what you've done, young lady," Mr. Flores said the next time he and Mrs. Flores showed up at the restaurant. "Just yesterday I was talking to a long-distance trucker who said he drove one hour out of his way to eat here, because somebody told him he had to try the best Mexican food this side of the border."

"Thanks, but I can't take all the credit," I said. "I only do part of the cooking. The rest of you do all the work. I have to admit that we make a great team, though. Of course, I can always move out of the apartment so we can expand upstairs."

"I knew we could count on you to come up with the perfect solution," Mrs. Flores said. "Just the other day I was saying to Beto that we should consider renovating the storage area upstairs, but we didn't want you to think we were kicking you out. Since you're okay with the idea, why don't you move in with us?"

Oops! I should've seen that coming.

"Thank you, but I don't want to impose on you any more than I already have. Besides, now I have a roommate."

Although they'd both fallen in love with Lucky the moment they saw him, I wasn't sure Mr. Flores would be open to his wife's idea.

"I have to admit that business has really picked up since you took my place in the kitchen," he said, "but we haven't even paid off the loan for the patio, and I'm sure this is one job Meme and Guerrero can't do. It's the kind of growing pains every business dreams of. Still, I need time to think about it."

"Maybe the contractor will hire us to work with his crew," Meme said. "We'll make sure to keep things on schedule."

"You're young," Guerrero said. "You work if you want. I might go spend some time with Maricela."

"You in New York?" Meme said.

"Why not?" Guerrero looked insulted.

"You'll be like a fish out of water," Mr. Flores said.

Guerrero laughed, "Only until Maricela shows up to rescue me."

Mrs. Flores seemed more interested in getting me to move in with them than in the restaurant's finances.

"Lucy, you can see for yourself there are no decent rentals in town. We never use our spare bedroom, and our backyard is plenty big for Lucky to run around in."

"I have a better idea," I said. "Why don't we convert half of the apartment, along with the storage room into an upstairs dining area? Most of our customers will want to sit where they'll have a view of the garden. Lucky and I can manage with just the bedroom and bathroom."

"Lucy needs her privacy," Mr. Flores said. "She sees enough of us as it is."

"Oh, I didn't mean it that way," I said.

"If we can afford to expand, we don't really need to use up any of your space," Mr. Flores said. "We can convert half of the storage area and add an upstairs balcony. That should be big enough for a few more tables." He leaned back in his chair and looked at all of us. "This job will take longer than the patio job, though."

"It would be a perfect time for you to take a vacation, Lucy," Mrs. Flores said. "Go on a cruise. Enjoy yourself. You work too hard."

"Actually, I'm getting ready to take my GED exam. I'm thinking of taking a computer class and see what else sounds interesting."

"Speaking of computers," Mrs. Flores said, "We wouldn't know what to do with one, but I've been trying to convince Beto it's time to hire an office manager."

"Great idea!" I said. *Free Wi-Fi!* I thought.

"Guerrero and Lucy are also going to need help in the kitchen," Meme said. "And we'll need to hire at least one more waitperson."

Mr. Flores held up his hands. "*¡Basta!* All these changes will add up to big bucks. Once we know how much the expansion is going to cost, I'll go see what the bank has to say. We may have to limp along without extra help for a while longer."

❊   ❊   ❊

Mr. Flores seemed to have worried unnecessarily about the loan approval. The bids started coming in a week later and the contractor he hired confirmed that the storage area would be big enough for eight more tables, if they extended it by adding a small balcony. They wouldn't even have to touch my apartment.

❧ ❧ ❧

Mrs. Flores gave Meme and me the job of picking out the furniture for the new space. Meme picked me up one morning and we drove into Saguaro to see what we could find at International Furniture Station.

"I was just thinking that the renovation will be finished right around the Floreses' anniversary," he said on the way there. "It'll be a great anniversary gift for them."

"Let's plan a party," I said. "We'll make it a surprise this time."

"Great idea. We'll limit it to fifty of their closest friends and best customers. I'll help Elena prepare the guest list. She's good at that kind of thing."

International Furniture Station was like a Toys R Us to me.

"Whoever does your buying has great taste and a good sense of color," I said to the salesman.

"Thanks, I'll be sure to pass that on to my wife," he said. "She orders most of our inventory. I'll let you look around. Let me know if you have any questions."

Although my taste in clothes ran toward plain and boring, this furniture was anything but plain and far from boring. Everything was bright yellow, green, red, blue and dozens of other eye-popping colors—perfect for a Mexican restaurant. I went from one set to another, sitting on chairs, running my hands over the tabletops.

"Look at the prices, I said to Meme. "I thought they'd be more expensive. But what do I know? I've never bought furniture before."

Meme checked the table legs, put his hands on one of the tabletops and pushed his weight onto it. He turned a chair on its side, before sitting in it and tilting it back.

"They feel pretty sturdy," he said. "Looks like they're made of pine, but La Cocina's not the kind of place where people expect fancy wood we can't afford anyway. These look like they were custom-made for us. I'm sure whatever you choose will be great." He walked to a rocking chair, sat in it, closed his eyes and laughed. "If our customers don't like the new furniture, we'll say you chose it."

❦ ❦ ❦

After looking at everything in the showroom, I kept going back to the first one I'd liked. It was one of the simpler styles.

"Good choice," Meme said when he saw the price.

We bought eight square tables, each with four matching chairs. Meme paid the deposit and agreed to call the store to set a date for delivery once the remodeling was finished.

"Lunch-time," Meme said on our way out of the store. "My treat. There's a deli I like on Arenas."

"The Lizard Lounge?"

"How do you know about the Lizard Lounge?"

I told him about The Cellar and how I'd met Fred. I found it so easy to be around Meme. He never probed into my life and never offered advice, unless I asked for it.

"Hello, handsome," the woman at the deli counter said to Meme. Tattoos covered the exposed parts of her body: neck, shoulders, arms and much of her chest. "Haven't seen you in a while. What you been up to?"

"Hey, Candy. I've been working at getting used to being a dad."

"Congratulations! Bring junior and mom in next time."

Meme introduced me as the chef at La Cocina.

"I keep hearing great things about the place. Me and Buster need to get our butts out there one of these days."

"Better make it soon. We keep having to expand because the place hasn't been the same since Lucy took over the cooking."

All through lunch Meme talked about his favorite topic these days.

"I swear Ricky said 'Pa' today. Elena didn't believe me because when I tried to get him to say it again, he just laughed in my face, so young and already disrespecting his old man."

We both laughed.

I talked about *my* favorite topic. "Do you know anything about dog training?" I asked. "Lucky's such a good boy, but I'd like to teach him a few tricks."

"What he needs is obedience training," Meme said. "I don't know that you'd even find a trainer in this neck of the wilderness. The dogs in Maguey aren't the academic type."

"Lucky's an exception," I said.

⚅ ⚅ ⚅

Lucky and I had started running together a week after we found each other. I'd started him out slowly, one mile each way, increasing the distance by half a mile each week. Although no one had seen hide nor hair of Rigo since the break-in, Officer Cano and Officer Grant were still keeping an eye on me. I continued to carry my phone and pepper spray with me, just as I'd promised them I would.

Because of all the sawing and hammering going on at the restaurant during the remodeling, I'd agreed to drop Lucky off at the Floreses' when I went to SCC. They were excited to have him and ready to spoil him. Nacho had other ideas.

The first time they met, Nacho shrieked while Lucky stood on his hind legs, barking and lunging at the cage.

I grabbed Lucky's collar and tried to pull him away, but the screeching and barking continued until Mr. Flores took the cage, with Nacho in it, into the spare bedroom.

"We didn't know he was so territorial," Mrs. Flores said.

Although he could no longer see us, Nacho kept up his end of the ruckus, and Lucky ran to the bedroom door the second I let go of his collar.

I led him to the back porch, got him to sit and left him there.

"I'll be back around three," I said. "Call me if Lucky gets to be too much trouble."

"Have fun, Lucy. Don't worry about Lucky."

"Remember, I'm bringing dinner," I yelled on my way out, not giving them a chance to protest.

I'd arranged to take the practice test at the campus library Wednesday afternoon at one. That morning I dressed in my newest pair of jeans and the blouse Patti had made for me. On the way to SCC, I began to worry. I should've at least brushed up on my math skills or reviewed some world geography. Too late now.

As soon as I started the test, I realized Anne was right. I breezed through science, social studies, language arts and even the math problems. Afterward, I checked out the library and found at least ten books I wanted to get my hands on as soon as I got my student ID. I sat in a sunny spot by a window, looking out on a quad where students sat at tables or hurried from one building to another, talking and laughing. Soon I'd be one of them. Or at least pretend to be.

I stood in front of a library shelf and took a selfie. I texted it to Delia, Patti and Mario. *Feeling good about taking my GED test. The practice test was a breeze.* After I sent it, I felt like a braggart. Now I had to make sure I passed the real test.

At two forty-five, I made my way to Admissions.

Jorge's face lit up when he saw me. "Hi, Lucy. Ms. Svalinski called in sick today, but I'll tell her you stopped by." He looked at his watch. "I get off in ten minutes and my next class doesn't start until three-thirty. Do you have time for a smoothie?"

"Sure. I'll wait for you." I walked into the waiting area and pretended to check out a catalog. A few minutes later, he was standing at the entrance.

"JC!" Jorge's friends yelled from a corner table, temporarily drowning out Lady Gaga when we walked into the student union.

"Your fan club, JC?" I said.

Jorge laughed. He took my arm and led me toward a table where a group of three guys and two girls were waiting for him.

He introduced me to all five, their names going in one ear and out the other.

"You new here?" the prettier of the girls asked.

"I'm not really a student," I said.

"Not yet," Jorge said. I was glad when he added, "See you guys later."

We ordered a couple of smoothies and went outside to find a table.

"Hey, Sheba," Jorge said to a beautiful Persian cat sitting under the table.

"One of the campus cats," he said when she disappeared into the bushes. "I hope this table's okay? If we sit with my friends, we'll have to yell over one another and we only have a few minutes as it is."

"They seem nice."

"I've known them all since elementary school. Some of them still act the same way they did then."

I laughed.

"What classes are you thinking of taking?"

"A computer class that I can fit into my schedule. I've been thinking of buying a computer."

"I can help you with that."

We talked easily for about fifteen minutes. I asked as many questions about SCC as I could think of to keep the focus off me. Then Jorge checked his watch again.

"I hate to go, but I've got a chemistry test next period. When will you be back on campus?"

"Not sure. I need to call and make an appointment with Ms. Svalinksi."

"Well, you don't need an appointment with me. You can always just walk in."

"Thanks." I practically floated to the bus stop.

※ ※ ※

The renovation went pretty fast with a whole crew working on it. Once it was finished, we all went to work cleaning up the interior and arranging the new furniture. Four of the tables were set up inside and the rest on the balcony. What was left of the old cinder block wall had been expanded, coated with stucco and painted terracotta to match the restaurant's exterior walls. I'd ordered several lanterns from the same ironworks shop Meme had used before. The result exceeded my dream of the perfect restaurant.

※ ※ ※

Lucky and I were heading home after our run one morning, when we saw Mr. Flores standing across the street from the restaurant. *I hope he's not having second thoughts about all the changes,* I thought to myself.

Lucky barked. Mr. Flores knelt down and called to him. I let Lucky off his leash and he ran straight to his friend.

"Looks beautiful, doesn't it?" I said, turning to look at the new, bigger sign.

"This place has come a long way these past few months. Maybe we should change the name to La Hacienda."

"I still think La Cocina is perfect."

"It was Lola's idea. She'll be happy to hear you like it and want to keep it."

❧ ❧ ❧

Mr. and Mrs. Flores were asked to arrive at six on the night they thought was our official grand re-opening. Since the entire staff was in on the surprise, we spent the day cooking, decorating the main dining room and rearranging the tables. At four, we all went home to shower and change.

The previous Sunday, I'd gone to The Fashion Spot to look for a dress for the party. Ignoring Elena's advice about bright colors and short hemlines, I'd bought a knee-length white linen dress. Since it had a red sash around the waist, I'd gotten red sandals with two-inch heels to go with it. Feeling like I was crossing over to the wild side, I also bought red nail polish for my toenails. I hadn't worn a dress since Nana's funeral, and this would probably be the only time I'd wear this one.

My only accessory was the agate, still hidden in the bag. It was time to have it made into a pendant so I could show it off, now that I was getting so daring, wearing heels, nail polish and eye make-up. Patti would think it was all way too tame. I thought it was a step in the right direction. As I checked myself out in the mirror, I pretended to be standing in front of Jorge, wishing he was coming to the party.

He was still practically a stranger, though, and my friends were sure to have lots of questions I wouldn't be able to answer. Besides, that night the spotlight should be on the Floreses.

🎔   🎔   🎔

We were all back at the restaurant by five, making the last-minute preparations, except for Berta, who managed to make herself scarce until just before the guests started to arrive.

"Anything I can do to help?" she asked Meme when she finally showed up.

He put her to work setting out the appetizers.

A few minutes before six, Elena shooed me out of the kitchen. "We'll take care of serving the guests, Lucy. You belong out there."

I grabbed Guerrero's arm. "I need an escort."

"Con gusto, Niña Lucía," he said.

When Mr. and Mrs. Flores walked in, the guests formed a circle around them and the mariachi band began to sing "Toda una vida." Elena had selected the song. It was a perfect choice for a couple who had devoted a lifetime to each other.

"Where are all the customers?" Mr. Flores said after the serenade. "I thought they'd be breaking down the door for the grand re-opening."

I planted a kiss on his cheek. "The customers can wait a few more nights. This is a private party, and you two are the special guests."

I hugged Mrs. Flores and whispered, "Happy Anniversary!"

She kissed my cheek. "We're so fortunate to have you, Lucy."

"I'm the fortunate one," I said. *You have no idea just how fortunate,* I added to myself as I thought about the day I'd arrived with nothing but a clean slate.

For once, I didn't care who saw me or what they thought as I kicked up my heels, dancing first with Mr. Flores, then with Guerrero, who soon had me shimmying and shaking the way Lucky liked to do after a bath. I saw Berta watching us when Meme asked me to dance.

Sulk all you want, Berta. Tonight is not about you. I smiled in her direction before Meme twirled me around and I almost lost my footing. Meme caught me and dipped me back, turning the room upside down.

I couldn't help smiling every time I caught a glimpse of Mr. and Mrs. Flores. It was like giving myself a gift to finally be able to do something for them in return for the new life they'd given me.

Only one thing would've made the celebration even more perfect—having Delia, Patti and Mario there. And Jorge, of course.

CHAPTER FIFTEEN

On the Map

The following week, we re-opened for business. Although we'd expected a bigger than ever crowd, we were blown away by the line that started forming a half hour before we opened. Mr. Flores had kept his word about hiring extra help for the kitchen and the dining area, but he was still interviewing people for the office manager job. Even with the extra help, we had to stay open two hours later than usual to serve those who'd waited up to forty minutes for a table.

I was up to my elbows in soggy cornhusks for tamales the following day, when Mr. Flores came into the kitchen.

"We're famous," he said. "Or at least we will be pretty soon. I just got off the phone with a reporter from *The Desert News* in Saguaro. She wants to drop by to interview you for an article she's writing on local restaurants. I told her Tuesday at two would be a good time."

I dried my hands on my apron. "Why me? It's your restaurant. You and Mrs. Flores and Guerrero should talk to her."

"Lucy, we were here for almost twenty years before you came along, and nobody has ever wanted to interview us until now."

I gave Guerrero a hopeful look. He was no help.

"I knew someday you'd put Maguey on the map," he said. "You're the star of the show, and this is your chance to shine."

"Will you be there for the interview?" I asked Mr. Flores.

"If you want me to, I'll sit there and hold your hand." He laughed. "Don't worry. Just give the reporter a beer and a sampler platter. That should keep her happy." I must've still looked worried because he added, "You just keep doing what you do best and let me worry about the rest." He patted my shoulder and disappeared into his office.

I immediately started obsessing about the interview. What kind of questions would the reporter ask? That night, I pretended to be the reporter and tried to interview Lucky. His response was to drop the ball at my feet, tilt his head to one side and wag his tail, waiting for me to get down to the serious business of playing with him.

Although the restaurant staff raved about the new dishes I'd been introducing, I only kept the real crowd-pleasers. I'd recently added tortilla soup to the menu as our Saturday night soup of the day. When customers started asking for it every day of the week, it became a regular menu item. Then I started experimenting with *envueltos*, and they soon became another customer favorite. I'd make sure the reporter tried both.

❦ ❦ ❦

"Hey, Lucy, your coffee's getting cold," Meme said as soon as I walked in the day of the interview. "We're already on our second cup."

"Did Mr. Flores tell you we're in the spotlight today?"

"We've been in the spotlight since you put us there." He poured a fresh cup of coffee for me while Guerrero slid the pastry plate toward me.

"This is different. Everybody will hear about us this time."

"More business," Guerrero said.

"And more work. But I'm not complaining," I said, thinking of how my savings account kept growing since I wasn't spending much of the money I earned.

❧   ❧   ❧

Tori blew in like a sirocco wind, sweeping us all off our feet. She was tall, thin and as bubbly as the glass of champagne I'd tried at the anniversary party—the kind of girl Elena would love to fatten up.

"I've been hearing about this place for months and can't believe it's taken me so long to get here. How long you all been open?"

"My wife and I opened the original version almost twenty years ago," Mr. Flores said, "but it wasn't until Lucy came along that anybody really noticed. Once the word got out about her cooking, we've had to expand twice and, by the looks of it, may have to open a second restaurant before long."

A second restaurant? News to me. Hopefully Mr. Flores was just taking advantage of the chance to brag a little.

"Sounds like you've got a gold mine here." Tori winked at me. "And you must be the head prospector."

"I'm just one of the cooks," I said.

"Don't let her fool you," Mr. Flores said. "There are cooks and then there are chefs. In my book, she's a chef."

"Hmmm!" Tori said. "You look pretty young. A cooking prodigy, maybe?"

"I've always been interested in food. My grandmother was a great cook. I learned the basics from her and have been experimenting with different recipes. Since Mr. and Mrs. Flores let me into their kitchen, it's kind of taken off."

"I'll say! Everybody seems to have heard about you already. Even my boss kept asking when I was going to do a write-up on y'all."

"We're glad you're here." I handed her a menu. "I hope you're hungry."

She closed her eyes and took a deep breath. "I skipped lunch, and the aroma alone is making me drool. I should try a little of this and a bit of that, so I'll know what I'm talking about when I write the article.

"What may I get you to drink while you decide?" Mr. Flores said.

"I've heard about your kick-ass sangria. I'll have a glass of that."

"Our ranchero salsa is a customer favorite too," I said.

"Corn, avocado, onion, jalapeño, mango . . ." she read off the menu. "Interesting combination."

"The fruit cuts down on the heat," I said. "Even kids like it."

"Heck, yeah, that sounds good. I was also told I had to try your tortilla soup. How about a cup of that. And, although I don't know how I'm going to fit it all in, let me try an *enchilada de hongos* and one of those great wraps I've heard so much about."

Mr. Flores served her the drink and salsa while I prepared a sampler platter. Then, we sat around watching her eat, like Mrs. Flores had watched me the day I came in asking for a job.

"Mmm, do you have a cookbook? Mom's birthday is coming up. She's the cook in the family. All I have is good intentions, which don't translate into good results when I try to cook."

"No cookbook," I said. "But that's a good idea. I made a special dessert for you, though."

"I wasn't planning to eat so much," she said. "Is your dessert something I can take with me, along with the rest of my leftovers?"

"Sure. It's called '*Trufa Azteca*'—salted caramel balls rolled in peppery chocolate powder and pecan bits." I packed a half dozen *trufas* and a copy of the takeout menu for her.

"Everything was incredible, but I have to say those little wraps were my favorite. I've never had anything like them before. What do you call them again?"

"*Envueltos*. We just added them to the menu. Mr. Flores doesn't consider them traditional Mexican food and he's right, although they're not a new concept either. Most cultures have some form of wrap . . . any flat bread will do when you stuff it with all kinds of savory fillings."

"What's in the ones I had?"

"The 'Jardinero' is made with grilled seasonal vegetables, sunflower and pumpkin seed paté, bits of serrano pepper, all topped with our secret sauce."

"*Jar-dinero*? Does that mean pot of money?"

We laughed.

"We wish," Mr. Flores said.

"Most of its ingredients come from the garden, or *jardín*," I said.

"Oh, right. I need to revisit my Spanish. So, are you also a *har-DEEN-ero*?"

"I do a little gardening, mostly herbs, peppers and a few easy-to-grow vegetables."

"I'm telling you, you need to write a cookbook." She was starting to sound a little tipsy after her second glass of sangria. "You could have a whole section on *en-voo-el-toes* alone. By the way, the article will be out this weekend. You'll need to require reservations from now on if you don't want a line going around the block."

"Another good idea," Mr. Flores said. "So far, we haven't had any complaints, even though the wait keeps getting longer."

"Well, thanks for the eats. I won't take up more of your time except for a quick shot or two," she said, holding up her camera.

"Why don't you take a picture of the front of the restaurant so people will recognize it when they drive by," I suggested.

"How about one of you two, and then one of the building itself?"

A smiling Mr. Flores came to stand next to me and put his arm around me, leaving me no choice but to grin and pose.

After she left, Mr. Flores said, "That was pretty painless."

"And cheaper than putting an ad in the paper," I said.

❦ ❦ ❦

Sunday morning, I raced out the door and down the stairs in a hurry to get to the local market and buy a copy of the paper. At the bottom of the stairs, I found three. One of them had been opened to the page with the restaurant article. A note from Meme was attached.

I smiled when I read it. *Elena wants you to autograph her copy.*

Monday morning, Meme showed up with five more copies. "Just in case somebody hasn't seen it."

"I clipped the article and I'm posting it right at the entrance where no one can possibly miss it," Mrs. Flores said.

"I'm sending a copy to Maricela," Guerrero said.

"Thanks, Meme," I said. "I'm going to frame a copy and keep it on my nightstand,"

"I thought you'd be a little more excited," Meme said.

"I am. It's just kind of bittersweet. I wish my grandmother were alive so I could send it to her." I didn't tell them that was the sweet part.

That afternoon I sent copies to Patti and Delia with a short note to each.

Chapter Sixteen

Macho Dog

Expecting a larger than usual crowd Saturday night, Guerrero, our new helper, Joaquín, and I started prepping at three. As soon as we opened, we began to sweat buckets as we zipped around the hot kitchen filling the nonstop orders. Around eight-thirty, we noticed that the steaming plates were starting to back up at the order window.

"What's going on?" I asked Meme when he stopped to pick up a couple of plates.

"Berta took off," he said with a frazzled look on his face. "Cristina and I are doing our best to cover her section."

"What happened?" I asked, feeling my own brow knotting up.

"I'll tell you later," Meme said as he hurried away with a tray full of glasses and a pitcher of beer.

He seemed more put out than angry, so I dismissed the thought that Rigo had shown up and forced Berta to leave with him. *Apparently she has her secrets*, I thought, *and from what I can see, she's guarding them as closely as I am mine.*

Mr. Flores had called early in the afternoon to tell us his wife wasn't feeling well and they wouldn't be in that day, so we limped along the rest of the night with Joaquín and me taking turns helping carry food to the tables.

At one table I noticed a man I'd never seen in the restaurant before. He probably caught my attention because he was with a woman less than half his age. They were so absorbed in each other; they didn't even notice me when I dropped off their orders.

"Enjoy!" I said before I hustled back to the kitchen.

After we'd closed, cleaned up and everyone, including Guerrero, Joaquín and Pepe had left, Meme sat down at the counter and motioned for me to join him.

"You asked why Berta split when we most needed her?"

"Yeah?"

"You were probably too busy to notice an old guy with a young chick who looks like she could be his granddaughter."

"I did, unless there was more than one old guy with . . ."

"Tall, gray hair, western look. He owns half of Saguaro and most of Maguey. Berta was his second wife before he traded her in for a newer model. The chick he was with tonight must be wife number four or five. Berta had everything she wanted while she was married to him. Can't really blame her for not wanting to wait on him or even let him see her working here."

"He was so focused on his, uh, woman that he didn't seem to notice anything or anyone else. But what's that got to do with the way Berta treats me? I wouldn't touch her old goats with—"

"It's got nothing to do with you. She just can't handle being yesterday's darling, seeing someone younger getting the attention she thinks she deserves. You wouldn't believe how she trashed Cristina when she applied for the hostess job. When you first showed up, she probably figured you'd be stealing her thunder. Then, after you caught Rigo's eye . . . well, you know the rest of that story."

"That's crazy. For one thing, nobody saw me then because I spent my time washing dishes in the kitchen. For another, even if they did see me, who'd look at me twice when she's around? I look like a stick next to her."

"You're young, Lucy, and you're no stick. You're much prettier, even with all the tricks she uses to make herself look better."

I felt myself blush at the compliment. Elena and I were such opposites that it had never occurred to me Meme would find me attractive.

"You once asked me how old I thought she was. She looks like she could be number four's older sister."

"Try number four's mother," Meme said.

I'd never gotten close enough to Berta to see if she really looked as old as Meme made her sound. I'd have to pay more attention from now on. Who knows what else I might learn by paying closer attention to my surroundings.

✦ ✦ ✦

Monday morning Meme and I were on our way to Saguaro to drop Lucky off at the vet's. Lucky's whole body wiggled and his tail slapped the seat when he stuck his head out the window, letting the wind blow his ears and tongue every which way.

"I didn't tell him he's being neutered today," I whispered to Meme.

"Ouch!" he said. "You're a real macho dog, Lucky."

"Hey, it's nothing compared to what females of all species have to go through."

"Can't argue with that. Don't tell Elena I said so, but I'm glad it was her and not me who had to carry Ricky around for nine months. I almost passed out when she was in labor."

"Well, just make sure you're around to help carry him from now on."

"No way am I going to skip out on him. I love that kid, and Elena's the best."

My phone rang.

Meme turned toward the back seat. "Maybe it's Dr. Spook calling to cancel your appointment, Lucky."

"I've got a test date for you, Missy."

"Hi, Anne. When?"

"Saturday, the eighth, at nine in the morning."

"I'll have to ask for time off," I said.

"To do what?" Meme asked.

I covered the phone with my hand. "Take an exam."

Meme took the phone from me. "She'll be there," he told her before he hung up.

The phone rang again. It was Anne again. "That your boyfriend, hon?"

"No."

"Well, whoever he is, make sure you're here for the test a week from Saturday. I'll drop off the information and forms you need next time we come in for dinner. You can fill them out and bring them with you the day of the test."

I looked at Meme. He gave me a raised eyebrow.

"Sure. See you then."

"I'm glad you're taking this college idea so seriously," Meme said.

"I'm trying to make one more dream come true." I didn't mention the other part of my SCC dream, the one with the shiny brown eyes and the smile that made my heart melt.

❧   ❧   ❧

The next day, I happened to glance out the window on my way to the ice machine behind the bar. Berta was sitting on the little stool where I kept the garden tools and plant food. Lucky seemed to have forgotten all about his vet experience the previous day. He was lying on his side next to her while she rubbed his belly. I set my water bottle on the counter and hurried outside.

"He never gets tired of being petted," I said. "I'll take him inside so you can enjoy your break without him pestering you."

Without turning around, Berta said, "I used to have dogs a long time ago. I kind of miss them."

I went to stand next to her. "Lucky's the first pet I've ever had."

Still staring at Lucky, she said, "I heard about how you found him."

Since she wouldn't look at me, I had a chance to take a close look at her. Meme was right. From a distance she looked much younger, much prettier. Up close in bright sunlight, it was hard to miss the tired look, and for the first time, I noticed a deep sadness in her voice.

"Well, back to work," she said. She got up and walked away without another word. Lucky ran to pick up a new chew bone. Guerrero and Meme still brought him gifts every now and then, but this bone hadn't been here when I'd let Lucky out that morning.

Chapter Seventeen

Back to School

Anne called me with the results the day after I took the real GED. She said I could now sign up for classes. Since the new quarter would start a week later, I went in that same afternoon and signed up for a computer class I could easily squeeze into my work schedule. If I was ever going to write a cookbook, as Tori had suggested, it was time to start keeping track of my new recipes and do research on the competition. Back-to-school time.

I decided on a class that started at nine in the morning so I could leave the restaurant at eight-thirty and get back just in time to start prepping for lunch.

※ ※ ※

I wiped my sweaty hands on my jeans, my new note-books, pens and pencils bouncing around in my backpack, as I walked across the campus to my first class. *What's there to be nervous about? It's not like I've never been to school. I have as much right to be here as anybody.*

I found the classroom and started to take a seat in the back row, changing my mind at the last minute. I hadn't come this far to hide in the back. But I wasn't brave enough to sit in the front either, so I compromised and sat in the middle. This proved to be a good place from which to check out the other students as they filed in. A young woman I thought was just another student walked to the front and introduced herself.

"Welcome to Introduction to Word Processing. I'm Lily Lane." She held up a stack of papers before handing them to a student sitting in the front row. "I'm sending around copies of the syllabus."

Ms. Lane explained what would be covered in class and told us what text we'd be using. Before dismissing us, she gave us our first reading assignment.

After class, on my way out of the building, I heard my name, followed by the sound of running feet.

I turned and found myself face to face with Jorge.

"Hi," he said. "I'm headed to the student union to meet my friends. Want to join us?"

"I'd love to but, after I pick up my textbook, I have to go to work."

"Maybe next time, then. Uh, could I call you sometime?"

"Sure." I could barely breathe as I pulled one of the restaurant's new cards out of my backpack and scribbled my number on the back.

"Thanks. Talk to you soon." He waved and disappeared in the direction of the student union.

That was enough to spin me around. I waved back and hurried away, not realizing I was headed in the wrong direction.

That night I told Lucky about Jorge. "I can't believe he even talks to me."

Lucky jumped up and licked my face. I tried reading to him from my new textbook. He must've thought it was a bedtime story because he was soon snoring softly at my feet. I never finished reading the assigned pages because my mind kept drifting back to Jorge.

It was almost midnight when I fell into bed, my mind still processing the day's events, Jorge's image reflected in the dark walls and ceiling. I closed my eyes and breathed deeply. *Stop mooning over him,* I told myself. *He probably has a girlfriend.* That thought didn't make his image any less sharp in my mind. *If he did have a girlfriend, he wouldn't be wasting his time with me. Would he?*

The minute I awoke, I jumped out of bed and started going through my dresser drawers. I'd been wearing jeans and T-shirts ever since I could remember, whether I was going to work or school or just hanging out at home. Suddenly, the stuff I wore just didn't seem good enough. It was time to make some wardrobe changes.

Right after the lunch rush, I caught the bus and headed for the mall. On the way there, I checked out all the female passengers, especially the younger ones, to see what they were wearing and how I might look in something similar. Most of the girls that looked like students were wearing jeans. They wore them with cute sexy tops. Cute I could handle. Sexy? Not!

I stood outside the Desert Loft trying to decide if this was the kind of place that would have something I'd like. The outfits in the window looked great on the mannequins, but how would they look on me? There was only one way to find out. With the salesgirl's help I found a denim skirt, a pair of blue Capri pants and a pair of black chinos to try on. I bought all three.

At The Fashion Spot I bought a red and blue utility blouse, a silky green top and a couple of fancy boatneck tees. The new clothes didn't look that great with my tennis shoes, so I stopped at Robyn's Nest and told Lisa, who looked about my age, that I needed something comfortable but with a little height. She brought out a stack of boxes. I tried on the first pair of clogs she showed me.

"These are very popular with people who spend a lot of time on their feet," she said.

I walked around the store in them for a few minutes. They were perfect for work, but not exactly the look I was after.

I put the clogs on the counter and, as I started to pull out my wallet, I saw a pair of black ankle boots with a low heel that looked like it wouldn't turn my ankle. I bought them too.

Still dreaming about Jorge while I waited for the bus, I didn't see Rigo until he pulled up and parked right in front of me.

"I see you're out spending Berta's hard-earned tips."

I ignored him and turned to look for the bus, trying to figure out how to get my phone out of my pocket without dropping my packages.

"Hop in. I'll give you a ride."

Just then, I noticed a woman and her teenage daughter walking towards me. I waited until they were close enough to hear me.

"Go away, you pervert!" I yelled.

He glanced at the pair who were now standing next to me. The mother started to say something, but her words were drowned out by the screech of tires as Rigo raced away, cutting off a car that was just about to pass him. The driver honked his horn and swerved into the wrong lane to avoid hitting him.

"Are you okay?" the woman asked.

"Yes, thanks. I'm glad you came along when you did."

"I got a good look at him," she said.

"I didn't get his license plate number, but he was driving a dark blue . . . uh, truck," the daughter added.

She sure wouldn't make a very good witness. Rigo drove a green Dodge Ram pickup.

I immediately called Officer Cano to report the incident and repeated it to Meme and Guerrero when I got to the restaurant.

"That bastard never gives up," Meme said. "From now on, I'll drive you to SCC."

"And I'll pick you up," Guerrero said.

"Thanks, but there's no need. Officer Cano said he was contacting campus security and the Saguaro police to keep an eye out in case he shows up there."

❄ ❄ ❄

The next class day I wore one of my new tops with the denim skirt and the ankle boots.

Jorge was waiting for me outside my classroom.

"Hi, Jorge." I pretended I hadn't been dreaming about him since the last time I'd seen him.

He gave me a big smile. "I hadn't put two and two together until you gave me your card. You're the Lucy from La Cocina. My mom told me about the article when it came out."

"I'm surprised you remember. It's been a while since that interview."

"Yeah, well, I even went to the restaurant for lunch a week later, but I don't remember seeing you there. Do they ever let you out of the kitchen?"

"I'm here, aren't I?"

The teacher walked into the classroom just then.

"I have to go."

He followed me in. "So, would you like to see a movie or something this weekend?"

"I work weekends," I said.

"On Sunday?"

"Sunday's my only chance to come to the lab."

"Mind if I meet you there, then?"

"That would be great." If he only knew I'd be counting the seconds until then.

❦ ❦ ❦

"So, you must really be burning the midnight oil now that you've got all that homework," Meme said the next day.

"What makes you think so?"

He put an order I'd just filled on the counter. "First time I've seen you get an order wrong. This guy wanted black beans and he got refried instead. Of course, it could've been Joaquín who filled the order."

"Oops! I'll fix it. Tell the customer lunch is on me today."

❦ ❦ ❦

Jorge beat me to the lab that Sunday. "I should've offered to bring my laptop to your place and save you a trip, at least until you get your own computer."

What do I really know about this guy? Sure, he's cute, but . . . .

He must've read my thoughts. "We can also meet at the Student Union."

"How about the library?"

"Why didn't I think of that?"

With him explaining what we'd covered in class, I had no trouble completing the class assignment.

"Why are you in this class, anyway?" he said. "You already seem to know all this stuff."

"It's a prerequisite. Besides, I thought it might help me sharpen my skills since I haven't used a computer in a while."

"You should talk to Anne. She can probably help you transfer to a more advanced class."

"I'll see if I can fit it into my schedule first. So, is your offer to help me find a computer still good?"

I could almost feel myself melt when he grinned and said, "Sure."

That night, I lay awake thinking about shopping for my computer with Jorge. Who knew what else I could learn from him.

The following Sunday we met at the library.

"I'll have to stick with the class I'm in," I said. "The other class I was considering won't really work for me right now."

"No problem. We can start by going over whatever you've covered in class so far. You'll be ahead of everybody else before you know it."

It was hard to concentrate with him sitting so close to me. Each time his hand brushed mine, his touch sent thrilling little shocks up my arm. He was right, of course, about me learning things much faster with him tutoring me. I started sopping up the information so fast, I was sure I'd soon be bored sitting in class listening to things he'd already taught me.

"You're a great teacher," I told him. "Are you a computer science major?"

"Uh, I'm still undecided about my major, but I love computers and figure I'll be using one no matter what field I go into." He looked into my eyes. "Everyone needs a computer. Look at you. You're already getting to be a real geek, the prettiest one I've ever seen."

Flustered by the unexpected compliment, I looked down at my notes for a moment. "Listen, I'd like to repay you somehow since I'm taking up so much of your time." When I'd steadied my nerves, I added, "Why don't you come by the restaurant and let me feed you at least once for each lesson."

"Mmmm! Of course, I'll let you feed me. Even better would be to alternate one dinner or lunch and one date, dinner/date, dinner/date."

I smiled. "Deal!"

"You're beautiful when you smile."

Me beautiful? I felt the blood rush to my face again. *And you're beautiful even when you don't.*

"So, about going out with me." He put his elbow on the table and rested his cheek on his fist. "I know you're busy, but how long will you need to know me before you trust me enough to go to a movie with me or for a motorcycle ride?"

The silence between us grew heavier with each passing second.

"I've never ridden a motorcycle." Realizing how lame that sounded, I added, "Sounds like fun."

"I promise you'll love it. How about next Sunday? I'll bring along an extra helmet."

I closed my eyes. Just thinking of us roaring off on his motorcycle took my breath away.

"Next Sunday, then."

That night I had to call Patti three times since her line was busy the first two.

"It's finally happened," I said. "I've met someone."

"Ooh!" Patti said. "I can tell it's not just any old someone. I'm all ears."

"I just met him. We're going on our first date next Sunday."

"Is he gorgeous?"

"Gorgeous, smart, sweet, you name it."

"¡Ay, cosita linda, Mamá! Where are you going?"

"For a motorcycle ride, not sure where. I'm thinking of taking a picnic lunch."

"You'll have him eating out of your hand, licking your fingers and—"

"Stop already!"

"I want to hear every little detail Sunday night."

She then started giving me a detailed update of who was doing what at Las Nubes High and who was dating whom. She kept it up for another half hour.

"I'll call you back soon," I finally said when she stopped to yell at Luis to turn down the volume on the TV. "I've got some planning to do."

❄ ❄ ❄

Lucky's cold nose on my neck woke me up the next day. I threw off the covers, slid to the floor and nuzzled his neck.

"I've got loads of energy to burn and I see you do too. Go get your leash."

He ran off to find his leash and followed me around until I was ready to go. The sun seemed much brighter, the air much cleaner and my heart much fuller as we ran. I waved to Officer Grant, who was making his first rounds of the morning. He honked the horn in response.

"I think your not-so-secret admirer is here," Meme said around six that evening. "Now I know why you've become such a fashionista all of a sudden."

I made a face at him, wishing I had a mirror to make sure I didn't have flecks of food or grease spots on my face and clothes.

"You look great," Jorge said when I went out to see him. "But then again, you always do."

"Thanks, you look pretty great yourself."

He shrugged. "I wasn't fishing for compliments. I'm glad you think so, though." He turned back to the menu. "What do you recommend? I've heard everything here is good."

"Try the sampler. That's what got us that great review your mom saw in the paper."

"Can't go wrong with something that's been taste-tested by the experts. Uh, I know you're pretty busy, but can you take a little break?"

"Maybe. I'll be right out with your dinner."

As I carried a sampler plate to Jorge's table, I noticed Meme, Joel and Berta scurrying around with plates of food and trays of drinks.

"Wow! Is this place always so crowded on weeknights?" Jorge said.

"Yeah. We stay pretty busy in the kitchen every night. What time should I expect you on Sunday?"

"Will ten work for you?"

"Perfectly! I'll pack a picnic lunch."

"So where should I pick you up?

"Here."

"You live here . . . at the restaurant?"

"I have a little bed in the kitchen, next to my ball and chain."

"Very funny."

I laughed. "I have a little apartment upstairs."

"Must be nice."

"The apartment's nothing much, but the location is pretty convenient. See you Sunday. Hope you still have my number."

He patted his back pocket.

"Call me when you get here."

He winked at me. "Can't wait."

"Remember to put this on my tab," I said to Meme on my way back to the kitchen.

"These classes are really perking you up," he said. "Or maybe it's a certain classmate?"

I smiled. "He's tutoring me, and I offered to feed him in exchange for each session."

"Good. We'll do a background check on him and . . ."

"Meme! Please don't scare him off."

"Just kidding! I'm glad you're meeting kids your age."

"We're going for a motorcycle ride on Sunday."

"Whoa! He doesn't waste any time, does he?"

Sunday morning, I took a long soak after my run, packed our lunch and checked for messages every few minutes, even though I'd been carrying my phone around with me all morning. At ten, I heard the roar of the motorcycle. When the call finally came, I let the phone ring three times before answering.

"I'm in the parking lot."

"Come around to the side gate. There's someone here who wants to meet you."

Lucky ran out the door, darting here and there as if he'd never been in the backyard before. When he saw me heading toward the gate he raced past me, stood on his hind legs and barked a few times, a warning kind of bark.

"You didn't tell me you had a guard dog," Jorge said as I fumbled with the latch.

"Now you know."

"Some guard dog," he said when Lucky jumped up and began to lick his face. Jorge knelt down to play with him.

"He'll be guarding the backyard while we're gone."

"Next time, I'll borrow my dad's truck so he can come along."

I was already flipping over this guy, but when he said that, his rating shot up a few notches on my scale.

"Thanks. He doesn't get many chances to go for a ride."

I pulled Lucky back into the yard before following Jorge to where he'd parked his shiny burgundy Honda with silver lightning bolts running along the sides.

"Flashy!" I said.

"You think that's flashy. You should see my friend Buster's ride. Neon green, black and yellow, a little too cool for me."

He handed me a red helmet and helped me onto the bike. "Don't be afraid to hold onto me," he said as he revved the engine a couple of times and gave me a jolt as we peeled off, tires squealing and my heart singing for the first time since I couldn't remember when.

"Show-off!" I yelled, but whatever sound made it through my visor was swallowed by the wind.

I put my arms around his waist, closed my eyes and let the wind blow away any lingering doubts.

After we roared past Maguey and Saguaro, we started gaining elevation.

Not much of a desert girl, I'd always dreamed of little farms with ponds and streams, gardens and fruit. Now, as I gazed out at the mesas and distant mountain slopes, I began to appreciate its stark beauty. I noticed that, along with the shrubs, saguaros, barrel cactus and pipe organs, beautiful wildflowers filled the desert floor with brilliant red, orange and purple flowers. A coyote made his way along a dry gully. Lizards and rabbits darted about as we invaded their territory.

After about an hour, Jorge pulled off the road at what looked like a popular gathering place for bikers. It was a scenic lookout point with one of those telescopes that only work when you put in a quarter. There were picnic tables on each side, some partially shaded by mountain laurels and pepper trees.

Jorge dismounted and took off his helmet. "First impressions?"

"Of your bike or your driving?"

He grinned. "Of just being out on the open road. I always feel so light and free whenever I come out here. But with you along . . . I'm glad you agreed to come with me."

"Hey, Georgie Boy!" someone yelled.

Jorge and I both turned toward the voice.

"Hey, Buster. Hey, Candy," Jorge said to a huge hulk and his skinny companion.

As they got closer, I recognized her from the deli where Meme and I had eaten lunch the day we'd gone furniture shopping.

"Hello," I said.

"Hey, there. I thought you looked familiar," Candy said. Noticing the puzzled look on Jorge and Buster's faces, she added, "We met at the deli when she came in with Meme."

🐾 🐾 🐾

Buster wore leather pants and a sleeveless black shirt to show off the tattoos running down both arms all the way to his wrists. Candy was dressed in tight jeans and a low-cut tee, her boobs threatening to spill out over the top.

"Hey, sweet thing," Buster said to me. He laughed and added, "Glad to see Georgie's found himself a girlfriend."

"Lucy, this is Buster," Jorge said. "He owns the motor-cycle shop in Saguaro and drives the flashy bike I told you about. And sounds like you already know Candy."

"Hi," I said.

They looked friendly enough, but I sure hoped we weren't going to be spending the rest of the day with them.

"Well, you kids have fun," Candy said. "We're starting our vacation today and have miles to go before we sleep." She giggled and headed toward the women's restroom.

"Nice meeting you, missy," Buster said. "Don't take no sass from Georgie." He laughed as he headed off to catch up with Candy.

"Don't let their façade fool you," Jorge said. "They'd both give you the shirts off their backs if you needed them."

"They seem nice," I said. "Is this our picnic spot?"

"It could be if you're hungry. If you can wait another hour or so, I know a cool little spot by a lake. It's probably crowded by now because it's not a very well-kept secret.

"Sounds great. I need to make a quick visit to the most popular room in this place before we go, though."

"I'll stand guard over our picnic lunch."

※   ※   ※

Tuna Lake wasn't that big, but it was even more crowd-ed than I'd imagined. All the shady spots were taken by peo-ple who'd obviously been there before and had come pre-pared with little tents and beach umbrellas.

We left the main road and drove along a narrow path until we found a mesquite that offered a bit of spotty shade. Jorge pulled up under it.

"It isn't much, but at least it's away from the crowd. It'll save us from burning our butts when we're ready to leave,"

Jorge said, patting the motorcycle seat. "Oh, dang! I forgot to bring a blanket."

"I brought a towel. It's not very big, but it'll do."

I pulled out the towel and handed it to him. While Jorge spread it on the ground, I unpacked the food.

"By the way, I never did get a chance to thank you for dinner Friday night. Good thing you told me to show up early. On my way out, I heard somebody say, 'It's a thirty-minute wait for a table.'"

"You'll be glad to hear, there's no wait today. But you'll have to settle for sandwiches, fruit and a thermos full of ice-cold lemonade."

"Killer sandwiches!" he said when he saw them. "I'm not that hungry yet. You go ahead. I had a huge breakfast."

"I'm just thirsty." I poured lemonade into one of the small cups I'd brought along. "Nice place. How'd you find it?"

"I've been coming here with my parents for as long as I can remember. There aren't too many lakes around this area, so everybody comes here on weekends, especially this time of year. My dad used to bring my brother Jaime and me fishing. Mom doesn't fish. She would walk along the shore and sometimes just lay in the sun and read."

"Nice." Before he could ask about my family, I said, "I'm finally ready to buy a computer."

"Great! Let me know when. I'll borrow my mom's car, so we can haul it back to your place."

"Thanks. I will."

I hugged my knees and looked at the lake, surrounded by people and their stuff. Jorge took my hand and traced the lines across my palm with one finger.

"I'm glad you brought me here," I said. "You picked a perfect spot."

"Just watch out for the rattlesnakes."

"What?" I tried to scramble to my feet.

"Relax. I'm kidding." He pulled me down next to him and ran his thumb across my lips. His kiss was so light and tender it made me tremble. He brushed my hair behind my ear and let the back of his hand slide down my cheek.

"You have such soft hair. Ever think about letting it grow long?"

"I used to wear it in braids when I was little. And it's been a while since I last got a haircut."

"I'd love to see a picture of you as a kid. You're beautiful with short hair, but . . ."

I closed my eyes. This was the second time he'd called me beautiful. If he kept saying it, he'd soon have me believing it.

"Is something wrong?"

"I'm so happy to be here with you. I just want to . . ."

He waited for me to finish, the silence hanging between us like suspended question marks.

"It's nice to know this place is here. I just want to relax and enjoy it."

Jorge smiled. "In other words, slow down. I'm fine with that."

I took his hand and willed away the negative thoughts that tried to squeeze into my brain.

"You like games?" he said after a while. "My family's always been into games."

"Depends. What kind of game did you have in mind?"

"My favorite one is something like charades."

"I'll give it a try," I said, even though I had no idea what I was getting myself into.

"Mind if I go first?"

"It's your game."

"I don't know about that, but here goes." He put both hands on top of his head with his fingers raised all around it.

I looked at him and kept on looking, wondering what he was doing.

"You're supposed to guess what I am."

"A . . . a . . . an elk?"

"Not a bad guess. Try again."

"A peacock?"

"What? I'm a king with a crown on my head. Your turn."

"That'll be hard to top."

It took me a while to come up with my own idea. When I did, he guessed it right away.

"A barber. I mean a hairdresser," he said when I pretended to snip away at my hair.

I got better at the game with each turn until, after a while, we ran out of ideas.

"So where are you hiding *your* tattoos?" I asked, lifting his T-shirt sleeve.

"I'm not telling. You're welcome to search me." He made as if he was about to pull his shirt over his head.

I put my hand on his arm. "Maybe next time we can bring our swimsuits. Then I won't have to search for them."

"Mmm! You plan ahead. I like that."

I blushed.

Jorge took a grape and popped it in his mouth. "Okay, I'm ready for one of those mega sandwiches."

I watched him eat as I nibbled at my own sandwich and followed his gaze when he turned to look at the lake. Families had started packing up their stuff and heading out.

"We should get going," Jorge said. "Traffic will only get worse the longer we stay, and I've got one more surprise for you. It's waiting for us just down the road."

It didn't take us long to pack up, and we soon found ourselves sandwiched between cars heading back toward the main road. About halfway to Saguaro we slowed down. I noticed that many cars were pulling off the road and people were making their way toward a railing. Jorge maneuvered the motorcycle between parked cars and stopped close to the overlook where the crowd was already lined up three layers deep.

We dismounted and he pointed in the direction of the crowd.

"The icing on the cake," he said. "Desert sunsets are the best you'll ever see."

"How are we going to see it with all those people standing in front of us?"

"I know a secret spot. Jaime and I found it the first time our parents brought us here."

He took my hand and led me up a steep path on one side of the overlook. We had to walk through weeds and brush for a few minutes until we reached a small clearing. By then, the sun had begun to drop behind the distant mountains, setting the sky on fire with bright orange, red and yellow hues. Thin, hazy clouds performed a smoky dance around it. Jorge stood behind me, his arms around my waist, his chin resting on my head as if we were both worshipping at nature's altar. We stayed that way until all that was left was a soft orange glow.

Jorge turned me around to face him. "Well?"

"You were so right. I've never seen anything like it. It's been a perfect day. Thanks."

He kissed me again before leading me back toward the parking lot. When we reached the motorcycle, our helmets were gone.

"Damn!" he said. "I always leave my helmet with the bike when I come here. This is not the kind of crowd that steals stuff like that."

"Will we get a ticket for not wearing them?"

He shrugged. "We'll just have to be extra careful."

We hopped on and, as Jorge eased the bike onto the road, we noticed a truck following so closely it felt like it was going to run into us. I turned around and saw Rigo illuminated by the other cars' headlights. He was holding up a helmet.

I gasped, but Jorge was already accelerating, wedging us into the bumper-to-bumper mess. To our left, a driver blasted his horn when Rigo forced his way in behind us. Most of the traffic was going in our direction, snaking its way down toward Saguaro.

Jorge kept checking his rearview mirror when Rigo started flashing his bright lights and tapping his horn. He seemed to be two inches behind us. This was a winding road and, with no shoulder or passing lane in sight, we had nowhere to go. If Rigo got any closer . . . I didn't want to even think about that.

Suddenly, Jorge pulled into the oncoming lane. He sped up until we'd passed about eight cars, then slowed down and straddled the middle of the road, staying on the double yellow line. The car coming toward us was still a distance away, but I wasn't sure it would see us in time to avoid hitting us.

The drivers in the cars we'd passed were shouting and honking their horns. As the oncoming car got closer, Jorge slowed down even more and put on his turn signal to show he wanted back into the right lane. I turned to the driver next to us and put my hands together in a pleading gesture.

"Someone's trying to drive us off the road," I yelled.

The driver looked at me as if I'd lost my mind and I realized he probably couldn't hear me. I could see his wife next to him in front and two children sleeping in the back seat. I pointed toward myself and Jorge and then toward the front of his car.

"Please! Please!" I yelled.

The car coming toward us was getting so close, the driver had turned on his bright lights and started moving as far to the outer edge of his lane as he dared.

Finally, the man I'd been pleading with put on his brakes, and Jorge pulled into the space he created. I turned around and waved at the couple. We were safe . . . for the moment. Rigo was stupid, but not stupid enough to try to pass and get stuck when no one would let him back in.

It seemed like hours later that we finally reached the stretch where the road turned into four lanes. As soon as it did, Rigo was right beside us, taunting and yelling. The cars behind him kept honking for him to get out of the way. He ignored them. When the first Saguaro exit appeared, the man in front of us signaled his intention to exit, and Jorge turned on his signal too.

"Keep going," I yelled.

"Why?" Jorge yelled back.

"We'll be safer in Maguey."

"I've got to lose this nut," Jorge said.

I reached back, pulled my phone out of my pack and pressed the number at the very top of the list. While I waited for an answer, I saw Rigo flipping us a bird before he sped up and disappeared down the next exit. I canceled the call.

Jorge turned his head to one side. "Who did you call?"

"The police. Listen, instead of driving to the restaurant, take the Maguey exit and turn right on Llano Street."

"Why? Where are you taking me?"

"You'll see."

Jorge did as I asked and a block later, I pointed toward the police station. He pulled into the parking lot. What had I been thinking? The building was dark. Of course they'd be closed at this time.

"What's your backup plan?" Jorge asked.

Just then, a car turned the corner and headed in our direction. I froze. When I saw it was a police car, I jumped off the bike and started waving my arms like a lunatic. The officer pulled over and I ran to his car.

"What the heck are you doing here?" Officer Cano asked. Then he saw Jorge. "What are you kids up to?"

"Officer Cano, this is Jorge."

The officer got out of his car and walked toward the motorcycle.

"This yours, Jorge?"

"Yes, sir."

"Where are your helmets?"

"They were stolen," Jorge said.

"We went to Tuna Lake and stopped to watch the sunset on the way back," I said. "By the time we got back to the bike, Rigo had taken the helmets. We didn't know he was there until he tried to run us off the road."

"Where'd he go?"

"We last saw him taking the exit just this side of the SCC campus."

"Why didn't you call as soon as you saw him? We could've had the Saguaro police waiting for him."

"I did, but as soon as he saw the phone, he disappeared and I hung up."

The officer shook his head. "You know I can't let you to go home now. Your boss will have a bigger fit than he did last time if he finds out we left you alone after another brush with that guy."

"I don't want to worry them. If I can't go home, I'd rather go to Meme's."

Officer Cano nodded and turned to Jorge. "Where do you live, son?"

"In Saguaro."

"I'll follow you home after I drop Lucy off."

"I'll be okay," Jorge said.

"Jorge, Rigo's pretty crazy," I said. "I'd feel better if you let Officer Cano follow you home."

"You sound like my mom," he whispered before he turned to the cop. "Okay, Officer. Thanks."

"I'll call Meme," I said.

Meme let out a string of expletives I'd never heard him use before when I told him what had happened.

"Sorry," he said. "I'll be right there."

Officer Cano went to his car and started talking on his radio.

"Who's this Rigo character and what does he want with you?" Jorge asked.

"His girlfriend's a waitress at the restaurant. He's followed me in the past and they've both accused me of taking tips from the tables."

"Were you ever planning to tell me about him if this hadn't happened?"

"Why would I ruin such a perfect day by talking about him? Too bad it had to end this way. I'll call you in the morning."

I kissed him lightly on the lips and ran to Meme's car.

❦   ❦   ❦

We stopped by the apartment on the way to Meme's. While he took Lucky for a walk to help calm him down a bit, I packed my bag and some food for Lucky.

After he gulped down his dinner, Lucky followed me around the house, not letting me out of his sight for a second. Although he now weighed forty-five pounds, he acted like he was still a puppy. As soon as I sat down on the couch, he plopped himself on my lap and fell asleep.

Elena, Meme and I stayed up talking. They wanted to hear all about Jorge.

"Where do I start? He's . . . he's special."

Meme winked at Elena. "I told you she was in love."

I just smiled. No sense in denying it.

"We're so happy for you, Lucy," Elena said. "Did you have a good time today, before that scumbag came along and ruined everything?"

"It was perfect. The ride to Tuna Lake was great, but half the population of Maguey and Saguaro got there before us. The best part was the sunset."

"Tuna Lake's no secret, that's for sure," Meme said. "And we know just the spot you're talking about. The sunsets are spectacular."

"So, when do we get to meet this mystery man?" Elena said.

"Meme's already met him."

"Not really," Meme said. "I've seen him, but you haven't actually introduced us."

"You're right. Sorry. I still get a little flustered when I'm around him."

"You'll have to invite him over one of these Sundays," Elena said.

"Yes, one of these Sundays," Meme said, "but right now it's time to go to bed. Otherwise, Guerrero's going to wonder what happened to us if we don't show up for work in the morning."

"You sure you want to sleep on the couch?" Elena asked. "The bed in the spare bedroom would be much more comfortable."

"I'm sure." I figured if I had to get up and pace during the night, at least I'd be far enough away from their bedroom that I wouldn't disturb them.

Patti had sent me a couple of messages. I sent her a quick text telling her I'd call her later. I eased Lucky off my lap and stretched out beside him, replaying the day in my head, unable to even savor Jorge's kiss without Rigo's ugly face popping up to ruin the memory.

My worries about Jorge had been fading little by little until they disappeared altogether, like snowflakes melting before they reached the ground. I held on to that thought until I drifted off, only to wake up to a strange sensation of flying off a cliff while angry drivers yelled out threats and sounded their horns.

Lucky let out a whimper. I sank to the floor where he was now standing and hugged him.

"Let's try this again," I whispered.

I grabbed the pillow and blanket and lay down on the floor. My ever-trusting pup curled up beside me. His regular breathing soon lulled me to sleep.

Chapter Eighteen

A Normal Family

Mr. and Mrs. Flores were waiting for Meme and me when we got to the restaurant. Mrs. Flores started fussing over me right away, brushing my hair away from my face as if to reassure herself that I was still in one piece. Mr. Flores came around the counter and asked me to follow him into his office. He asked me to sit in his chair while he paced around the small room. I knew his anger wasn't directed at me, but it still scared me to see him so unsettled that he couldn't seem to find the words he wanted to say.

"I'm glad you're okay," he finally said, "but this incident just goes to show that we can't let our guard down."

"I'm starting to feel like I'm the bad guy," I said. "When I finally have a chance to go out and have a little fun, he shows up again. Why is he targeting me? I've never done anything to him or Berta. Or anybody else."

"By now you should know you're not dealing with a rational person. As slippery as this thug is, the police can only do so much. We'll all have to be on constant alert, you in particular. Cano and his men will keep patrolling the area. Rigo knows that, so you have to be extra careful when you go to Saguaro or any place where he feels he can get away with harassing you."

My phone rang.

"That must be your friend," Mr. Flores said. "Go ahead and answer it. Make sure he understands he could be in danger, too."

After he left the room, I answered the phone.

"I hope you got some sleep last night," Jorge said.

"A little. What about you?"

"I stayed awake for a long time thinking about that creep and what he's done to you. It was also kind of embarrassing to have the police escort me home."

"Did anyone actually see him following you?"

"No, when I turned into our driveway, he drove off. That's good. I don't usually keep stuff from my family, but Mom's such a worrier, I don't think I'll mention anything to them this time."

"I'm sorry I put you in danger."

"Don't start playing the guilt game, Lucy. That's what the jerk wants you to think. You and your friends and the police are doing all you can. I just felt like I was the only one who didn't know what was going on yesterday."

I took a deep breath. "You were, and I apologize."

"You weren't kidding when you said the guy's crazy."

"Crazier than anyone realized. I had a great time yesterday, though, before he showed up. By the way, I want to pay for the helmets."

"It wasn't your fault he stole them."

"Still, I'd like to replace them."

"I'll get new ones when Buster gets back. He has the best prices in town. That should save you a few bucks. You can apply the savings toward your computer. Do you want to go shopping for it next Sunday? Mom said we could use her car. She also asked me to invite you over for lunch."

Uh-oh! My mind and heart started racing with excitement and worry. Would I pass the parent test?

"Hello? They don't bite. I promise."

"Sorry, it's just . . . what should I bring?"

"Nothing. My parents always cook enough for a small army. Good thing since Jaime eats like a small army. I know you need to get back to work, so I'll see you tomorrow."

"Wait!" I said, but he'd already hung up.

That day, I caught Berta watching me a couple of times, as if she wanted to say something but couldn't quite make up her mind. I knew Meme had told her about the latest incident. I wasn't sure if she was mad at Rigo, at me, or at both of us.

❧ ❧ ❧

I always knew when Fred and Anne were in the restaurant because their order and table number never varied. That Friday, before the dinner rush started, I had time to carry out their orders and chat for a few minutes. Anne was so excited, she was practically bouncing out of her seat.

"Tomorrow, we set off on our next adventure," she said as soon as I set their food on the table.

"Where you headed this time, the wilds of the Amazon?"

"Guess again," Fred said. "Guess wilder."

"You're going on Safari?"

"Close. We're going to DC," Anne said.

"You must be planning to give your politicians a piece of your mind, straighten them all out."

"I got better things to do with my time than waste it on hopeless causes," Fred said. "We're going to the Smithsonian and the Museum of African American History."

"This is our third trip there," Anne said. "We can't get enough of DC."

"I want to hear all about it when you get back. I'd love to go there someday."

"If we'd known that, you could've come with us. Fred loves to play tour guide."

"I'll settle for a postcard this time," I said. "Have fun!"

❈ ❈ ❈

"What? You're a kook magnet!" Patti said when I told her the latest about Rigo. But she forgot all about him as soon as I mentioned Jorge wanted me to meet his parents.

"That's a great sign, Lucy. I didn't get to meet Fernando's parents until we'd been dating for six months or so."

"Just because I'm meeting them doesn't mean they're going to like me."

"Shut up! They're going to love you."

❈ ❈ ❈

Sunday morning, Jorge picked me up in his mother's car.

"I thought I asked you not to bring anything," he said when he saw the almond torte I'd made.

"I don't like to show up empty-handed."

"You're really something." He lifted my chin and kissed me before opening the door for me.

"I hope you don't mind if we make a quick stop along the way," he said as we took the first Saguaro exit. "It'll only take ten minutes."

I couldn't believe it when he pulled up in front of The Cellar a few minutes later.

"It's closed this week," I said. "The owner's on vacation."

"That's exactly why we're here. I pet sit the cats. So, you know Fred?"

"I met him when I came here looking for a book. Anne was here, too. Since then, we've become each other's best customers.

"You know their cats King Tut and Queen Nef then."

"I've met one of them, not sure which."

We went inside, and the cat I usually saw when I visited the store came running out to greet us.

"Hey, Nef. Where's Tut?" Jorge turned to me. "Tut's kind of shy. He has to know you pretty well before he trusts you. Can you play with Nef while I clean up after them and fill their food and water bowls?"

I picked up the cat and carried her around while looking through the book stacks. She jumped out of my arms and headed toward the kitchen when Jorge rang a bell.

"Come in and meet Tut," he called from the kitchen.

I tiptoed in and saw a striped blur as the cat ran out of the room.

"Told you," Jorge said.

❧   ❧   ❧

At the Computer Station Jorge asked, "Any idea what kind of computer you'd like to buy?"

"I like the one you have. I've kind of gotten used to it."

"What about a printer? You may as well get one while we're here."

"You're the expert. Pick one out for me."

"I don't know about that."

He took my hand and led me down the aisle to the printer section, stopping in front of one that looked just like all the others to me.

"This is a newer model of the one we have at home. Ours is two years old, but it's been pretty good so far."

"I'll take it," I said, without looking at the price tag.

"Great! That makes this whole process a lot easier."

He called over a saleswoman to show her the printer we wanted and tell her I was looking for a specific computer.

"We have a floor model right over here, if you'd like to try it," she said.

"I'm already familiar with it." I turned and winked at Jorge.

"I'll be right back, then."

I paid for the computer and printer and Jorge put them in his mom's car.

"Are you always this easy to please?" he asked before starting the car.

"Only when it comes to electronics."

"Well, I'm not just a one-trick pony, you know. It may not look like it, but I do have other skills."

"I don't doubt it. And I'm sure you're just as good at all of them."

Before I could fasten my seatbelt, he leaned over and kissed me right there in the parking lot. I kissed him back. This was our first real kiss and it was softer, sweeter and much more tender than I'd imagined it in my dreams. It left me hungry for more, but I noticed two kids in the car next to us pointing at us and laughing.

"We seem to be the main attraction," I said, blowing a kiss at the kids.

Jorge waved at them and started the engine.

❧ ❧ ❧

We arrived at Jorge's house to find his brother washing a car in the driveway, music blaring from the car stereo. He was scrubbing the front wheel on the driver's side. When Jorge stepped out of the car, his brother turned the hose on him.

"Ma said you've got to wash her car if you want to eat today." Then he saw me. "Whoa! Where did you come from?"

Jorge shook the water off his arms. "Lucy, this lazy bum who's always trying to get me to do his work is Jaime. He can't even do his own laundry . . . brings it home once a month for Mom to do."

Jaime stood up. "Hey, Lucy. What are you doing hanging out with the neighborhood cat lady? Don't believe a word he says, by the way."

"Hi, Jaime."

Jorge put his arm around me and led me toward the house. "Don't encourage him. He'll go away if you just ignore him."

"Wishful thinking," Jaime said. He threw the hose in the grass, followed us inside and walked into the kitchen. "Ma, you trying to starve us or what?"

"Almost ready," a woman answered, "but we need to wait for Jorge."

Jorge pulled me into the kitchen. "We're here."

"Oh, hello, Lucy," Mrs. Chapa said. "I'm so happy to meet you. After reading the restaurant review, I was a little nervous about inviting you over. I'm Julia."

"She's the Julia Child of the Southwest," Jaime said.

"Oh, stop," Mrs. Chapa said. "Go get your dad."

A man came in the back door just then. "Somebody call me?"

"Julián, this is Lucy," Mrs. Chapa said.

"Well, I can see why Jorge's smitten!"

"Dad!" Jorge rolled his eyes.

"Good to meet you, Lucy." He shook my hand, then turned to his wife. "Everything's ready out there."

Mrs. Chapa handed Jaime a tray with five glasses and a pitcher of iced tea.

"Here, hon, make yourself useful for a change."

Jaime started to walk off, stopped and turned around. "So now you've met the JC family. What are the odds of two people with Mom and Dad's names meeting, marrying and having two little Js?"

Mrs. Chapa laughed and gave him a playful push. "I wouldn't exactly call you little."

I set the torte on the counter. "Is there anything I can do to help?"

"You're our guest," Jorge said. "Today we get to serve you."

"Go make yourselves comfortable," Mrs. Chapa said. "We'll be right out."

"Has Lucy met your kits?" Mr. Chapa asked.

"Oh, yeah." Jorge took my hand and led me toward the backyard. "Come out and meet them. They're only allowed outside when we're out here to keep them out of trouble. Hey! See what I mean?"

A fat black cat hopped off the chair he'd been standing on, checking out the table where Jaime was making room for the tray. At the sound of Jorge's voice two more showed up.

"Did you continue the J tradition when you named your cats?" I whispered, so Jaime couldn't hear me.

"Not me," Jorge said. "This fat guy here is Sancho, the long-legged calico is Don Quijote." He picked up a beautiful chimera with a green eye on the black side of her face and a blue one on the orange side. "And this little beauty is Dulcinea, Dulce for short."

"They're all gorgeous." I petted Dulce while Sancho and Don Quijote lay on their sides and purred.

"They all came from the SCC campus colony, same as Nef and Tut. I help Anne trap them, fix them, feed them and find homes for them."

"That's why he's the cat lady," Jaime said. "He ends up bringing most of them home."

I squeezed Jorge's arm. He turned around to kiss me.

"Uh-hmm!" Mr. Chapa said. "Sorry to interrupt the love fest, but it's time to eat."

❈ ❈ ❈

So this is what a normal family is like? I thought as Mr. and Mrs. Chapa told stories about when the boys were little.

"Jaime was always getting into fights at school," Mrs. Chapa said. "Thank goodness he came to his senses when he was about thirteen."

"That's when he discovered girls," Mr. Chapa said.

"And Jorge . . ."

"Jorge's always been a mama's boy," Jaime said.

Jorge threw a piece of carrot at him and caught him on the side of the head.

"Come on," Mr. Chapa said. "You're acting like babies now."

"They'll always be my babies, no matter how old they are," Mrs. Chapa said.

✹ ✹ ✹

I was ready when the question I knew would come up finally did. It was Mrs. Chapa who asked it in a roundabout way.

"The newspaper article said you inherited your love of cooking from your grandmother."

"Yes, cooking and gardening. When she died, I moved to Maguey."

"It must've been hard to leave your family behind," Jaime said.

"Just an aunt in El Paso and an older brother. He's in the Navy."

"So, your aunt raised you?" Jaime asked.

"No, I just stayed with her for a while after my grandmother died."

There it was: Not the whole truth, but not exactly a lie either. Now that I was among normal people, I wouldn't let myself dwell on my past.

Jorge saved me from more questions by telling his family that I was writing a cookbook.

They all turned to look at me.

"I don't know about a 'cookbook,'" I said, "but now that I have a computer, I'll be able to keep track of new recipes, at least the ones that our customers like."

"Now I know what to get you for Christmas," Jaime said to Jorge. "Lucy's cookbook."

He ducked just in time to dodge a cherry tomato.

CHAPTER NINETEEN

A Pilgrimage

The postcard I got from Fred and Anne started me thinking again about going to LA. I still felt a need to satisfy my curiosity about what my life there would've been like if I hadn't stopped in Maguey instead. After I met Jorge, I tried putting the thought out of my mind, but it kept hounding me like an unsatisfied craving. Now that I could afford it, it was time to complete that trip.

The following afternoon, Jorge came over to set up my computer and printer.

"You're kidding!" he said when I shared my plan with him.

"This'll be my first real vacation," I said.

"And you're taking the bus? You must be planning to walk your feet off once you get there."

I closed my eyes and shook my head. "They have city buses, you know. Besides, there are only a few places I want to visit. I'll go on a bus tour when I get there and take the regular bus the rest of the time."

"If you wait a few weeks, I'll drive you in Mom's car. Her family lives in Pasadena. We visit them every year, it's like my second home."

"Thanks, but this is something I need to do on my own."

"Is it like a pilgrimage or something?"

"I guess that's one way to look at it."

"Another way to look at it is it's crazy, Lucy." He leaned one elbow on the printer box and turned to me. "Look, let's make a deal. We'll drive there together. I'll drop you off at your hotel and then go stay with my aunt and her family. I'll be your private chauffeur and guide, and you don't even have to tip me."

I put my arms around him and kissed the tip of his nose. "I'll be fine. Really. If you must know, I just want to see what the city's like, what I might've missed by stopping here instead. I was headed there when I . . . when I first came to Maguey."

He nuzzled my neck. "If you'd kept going, we never would've met." In a serious voice he added, "Why were you going to LA in the first place?"

"I wanted to find a job and eventually enroll in a cooking program."

"What did your aunt have to say about that?"

I dropped my arms, walked to the balcony and stood looking out at the garden.

Jorge came to stand beside me and put his arm around me.

"Sorry. I didn't mean to be so nosey."

"She didn't want me to leave, but there was nothing for me in El Paso."

"Whatever it was that landed you here, I'm glad, and I'm sure all your other friends are too."

I turned to face him. "Nobody's gladder than me."

"There you go. Look, I can tell you what LA's like, but I'd rather show you."

"I'd like that. This time, though, you can be my long-distance guide. I'll call you every day, several times a day."

He lifted my chin and looked into my eyes. "How long will you be gone, anyway?"

"Four days. Here, let me show you where I want to go, and you can help me plan the trip."

I brought out the tour books I'd been studying and spread them out on the kitchen table. I'd flagged the pages that covered the sites I wanted to visit. Jorge flipped through the flagged pages and found my short list.

"Day tour of LA and Hollywood, The Getty Center, the LA County Museum, the Farmer's Market, Olvera Street, a culinary school. You still think you need to go to culinary school?"

"I've always dreamed of learning from the pros."

"You're already a pro. Are you thinking of moving to New York or San Francisco or . . . LA to work in some fancy restaurant?"

"My resume wouldn't get me very far in any of those places, and I can't imagine working anywhere else but here."

Jorge looked at me as if trying to figure me out all over again.

"I'll bet if the owners of restaurants in any of those cities ever ate your food, they'd be falling all over themselves trying to hire you. You're a cooking prodigy."

"Ha! Have you been talking to Tori?" Seeing the puzzled look on his face, I added, "Never mind. I may not even be able to visit a cooking school while I'm there. I've been meaning to call and see if I can schedule a visit. I just haven't gotten around to it."

"You could teach your own cooking classes. Talk to Anne. She'll set you up to teach a PEP class or two at SCC."

"Wait!" I shook my head. "First you think I should write a cookbook and now you want me to teach cooking classes. Where am I going to find the time to do all that?"

"Well, running off to LA is just going to take time away from your cookbook project. That's too bad. If you assign homework to your class using recipes from your book, you'd sell a ton of books."

"I'm glad you've got my future all figured out."

"Always happy to help." He took a strand of my hair and pushed it behind my ear. "So that's it . . . museums, shopping and maybe a cooking school? What about Disneyland, Universal Studios, the Santa Monica Pier . . ."

"In four days? Anyway, I don't want to go to those places by myself."

"That's why you should let me come with you. Otherwise, you'll miss all the good stuff."

"That's okay. I'll have done what I needed to do."

"Which is?"

"We've already been through that, Jorge. I've done my homework, most of it anyway. After the trip, I'll be able to say I was there and I'll have a clearer picture of what my life would've been like if I hadn't ended up in Maguey."

He looked a little hurt. "You're not really happy here?"

I kissed his chin. "I've never been happier, especially since I met you."

"It's a scary thought that you might've gone to LA and we'd never had a chance to meet." He slapped the tour book shut and drew me to him. "Okay. I can't stop you from doing what you need to do. But promise me you'll call me if you run into any problems."

"I'm calling you even if I don't."

❧ ❧ ❧

Mr. and Mrs. Flores, Meme and Guerrero couldn't make up their mind about whether to be happy for me or worried about me.

"I'll take Lucky home with me at night and bring him back during the day," Meme said.

"And I'll water your garden," Guerrero offered.

Mrs. Flores looked worried. "We'll miss you, Lucy."

I told them I'd be fine.

❧ ❧ ❧

Two days later, Jorge stood with me across the street from the restaurant waiting for the bus.

"Oh, I almost forgot." He ran to his mother's car and came back carrying a paper sack. "Mom packed a lunch for you."

"That's sweet. Why don't you bring your parents to the restaurant for dinner when I get back."

He squeezed my hand. "Can't you just accept a gift without always wanting to pay for it somehow?"

The bus pulled up just then and the driver hopped off to load my bag.

"I'll call you when I get there."

I gave him a quick kiss before boarding, found a window seat near the front and waved. Jorge waved back and gestured that he'd be waiting for my call.

This trip was much less scary than the one that had brought me to Maguey. For one thing, I had a clearer idea of where I was going and why. I had friends who knew where I was going this time. And, I didn't have a drunk leaning on me, snoring my ear off.

I'd brought along Fred's latest gift, *The Fall of the House of Dixie*. I'd flipped through the first couple of pages when he gave it to me. *Decades after the Civil War ended . . .*

"Thanks, Fred," I'd told him. "This will help me brush up on that part of the country's history. How did you get to know me so well so soon?"

"People are like books to me. Once I read the title and a paragraph or two, it doesn't take me long to size them up. Anne and I recently watched the movie *Lincoln* and it re-ignited my passion for history. I hope you like it."

As usual, he'd made a good choice for me. I was drawn in right away, but I stopped reading every once in a while to look out the window.

Around one in the afternoon I opened the lunch bag Jorge's mom had packed for me and found a sandwich, granola bars, fruit, juice, and a card with the names and telephone numbers of her relatives. I put the card in my backpack and, after eating half the grilled veggie sandwich, drank from my water bottle and saved the juice for later.

Afterward, I looked out the window at the blue sky, the silhouette of mountain slopes in the distance and the road signs that started to pop up. The sound of the bus tires rolling along the highway soon lulled me to sleep.

I woke up as we were approaching LA. A chill ran up and down my spine. *What would've become of me if I'd landed here instead of Maguey? Where would I be now?*

The other passengers seemed to have come alive, too. I heard snatches of excited conversations and saw fingers pointing at billboards, road signs or whatever caught their owner's attention as we made our way to the magical city.

Finally, we arrived at the bus station. I waited for the other passengers to exit the bus and took a deep breath before walking toward the door. By then, my bag was the only one left to be claimed. I picked it up and, although my mini-tour didn't start for another couple of hours, I showed the driver the address where I was supposed to board the tour bus. He went out of his way to point me in the right direction, even walking to the curb so I could see where he was pointing. I gave him five dollars for his trouble and headed in the direction he'd told me to go.

I found LA a great place to people watch while I waited for the tour bus. When it arrived, it was already crowded with tourists. I was the only one with a bag.

"I just need to get to Hollywood," I said to the guide.

"Maybe you should take a city bus or shuttle then," she said. "It'll be cheaper."

"But I'll get to see more this way. I'm staying at the Star Dust Inn. Can you drop me off somewhere near there?"

"No problem, hon. We'll be going right by it. If you want to miss half the tour, it's your choice and your money."

"Thanks." I took a seat next to a lady in a ruffled skirt and patent leather tap-dancing shoes.

"You running away to Hollywood?" she asked when she saw my bag.

I laughed. "Nah. I'm just a regular tourist."

"No such thing as regular 'round here," she said. "Name's Daisy McPherson. Remember that name. Next time you see me, I'll be on the big screen. I'm still waiting to be discovered, so I'm always prepared, all set to audition at the drop of a hat." She kept yammering on and on in her Texas drawl until the people sitting in front of us turned around.

"Do you mind? We can't hear the tour guide."

"Hmph!" Daisy closed her eyes and stuck her chin out at them before turning to look out the window.

Like everyone else, I looked toward the sights the guide pointed out, paying particular attention when we drove along museum row, the Original Farmer's Market and the other destinations I intended to come back to. Who cared if I missed Rodeo Drive and the mansions of the rich and famous?

"I'll remember your name and be on the lookout for it," I said to Daisy when the bus stopped to drop me off near my hotel.

"You won't be disappointed, darlin'."

※ ※ ※

After checking in and taking a few brochures from the lobby, I headed to my room, dumped all of my stuff on the floor and called Jorge. When he didn't answer, I left a message.

"Just got to my hotel. I'm already missing you and wishing I'd taken you up on your offer. Call me."

I'd been too excited to sleep the night before, and the naps I'd taken on the bus had just tired me out. I decided to take a shower and another quick nap before going out to explore and get dinner. After my shower, I checked for messages. Still no call from Jorge.

I set the phone on the pillow next to me and lay down. It felt good to stretch out. Before I knew it, I was asleep.

I didn't wake up until nine the next morning. After checking for messages and seeing there weren't any, I tried Jorge's number again. Still no answer. I left another message.

Thinking that my friends were probably worried about me, I called the restaurant. The line was busy. I tried Meme's number hoping that, by some slim chance, he'd heard from Jorge. I forgot that he muted his cell during work hours and checked it every half hour or so. I left a short message saying I was okay and would call back later.

❀ ❀ ❀

I had my first and best crepe ever at The French Crepe Company, then wandered around the market, stopping to gawk at mouth-watering pastries, candy and nut displays. I bought some tea for the Floreses, fancy lavender soap for Elena, a small stuffed panda for Ricky and a recycled shopping bag to carry it all in. I kept checking my phone every few minutes and started to worry. Had I offended Jorge more than he'd let on? It just wasn't like him to not return my calls or at least send a quick text.

❀ ❀ ❀

I was eager to see as much of the Getty Center as I could, but the gardens drew me like magnets from the moment I arrived there. The architecture and gardens alone would make my first trip worthwhile, even if I never stepped inside the buildings to see the art.

As I made my way through the tree-lined walkway leading to the Central Garden, I was transported to another world, one in which Nana's spirit guided me along the stream that wound around the various plants and down to the plaza, where I could almost see her moving gracefully behind the bougainvillea. I stepped to the side and stopped to listen to the water flowing down to the pool. The other visitors walking past me disappeared when I closed my eyes and breathed in the calm and beauty that surrounded me. Even then, the image of flowers, shrubs, grasses and water stayed in my mind's eye like a photograph.

As much as I wanted to stay there, I forced myself to move on, stopping only long enough to admire the views of the city, mountains, and ocean. I lost track of time until I noticed a small group eating a picnic lunch in the courtyard. I stopped at the café and bought a sandwich and iced tea, then found an outdoor table where I let myself be hypnotized again by the magic of the place. If I hadn't stopped in Maguey, would I eventually have found my way here to work in the restaurant or café just so I'd be surrounded by such beauty?

As I was making my way to the West Pavilion, my phone finally rang.

"Jorge," I said. "Where have you been?"

"Lucy, it's me, Meme." The strain in his voice caught me off guard.

"Is everything okay?"

He didn't answer.

"Meme, what's wrong?" A group of school children walking behind me bumped into me.

"You need to get back here as soon as you can."

"What happened?" I felt my hands go cold.

"Jorge's been injured."

"How?" I yelled into the phone.

"All I know is that he crashed his motorcycle."

I started sobbing. Everything was suddenly spinning around me.

"Lucy!"

"I'm leaving right now," I whispered.

"Call me when you get here. I'll drive you to the hospital."

"Can you pick me up in Saguaro?"

"Sure. Call me before you get there. I'll be waiting for you."

I somehow managed to stumble to the tram and find my way back to the bus station. The whole time, I kept replaying Meme's words in my head. Did he not want to tell me, or did he really not know how badly Jorge had been hurt? My heart was racing as the bus crept along mile after painful mile. If only I hadn't gone to LA. What had I been looking for anyway, when everything that mattered to me was in Maguey?

I asked the bus driver where the bus stopped in Saguaro and started trying to call Meme when we were still thirty miles from town, until I was able to get through. He was waiting for me when I arrived. I ran into his arms and started to cry again.

He held me close for a moment. "I don't have Jorge's parents' phone number, and the hospital wouldn't give me any information on him. I'll drive you there now." He helped me into his car. "Where's your luggage?"

Until then, I hadn't given my bag a moment's thought. "I left it behind. Tell me what happened."

"I didn't want to upset you any more than necessary," Meme said. "It was Rigo who forced him off the road."

I started sobbing uncontrollably. "It's all my fault."

"Lucy, don't even think that."

"How can he keep getting away with his crimes?"

"This time he was caught in the act, at least on video. A guy was driving behind them, watching Rigo trying to force Jorge off the road, until Jorge lost control of his bike. The driver's girlfriend videotaped it. It's been in the news all day. Rigo's face, truck description and license plate number have been plastered all over the TV screen. The policeman who talked to the reporter said they think he's in Mexico."

I dried my eyes with the tissues Meme handed me and tried to calm down as we drove into the hospital parking lot.

Meme went with me as far as the waiting room. "I'll wait here for you. Stay as long as you need to."

I hesitated for a second or two before opening the door to Jorge's hospital room. Jaime was standing at the window. He came and put his arms around me and we both broke down.

"How is he?" I asked between sobs.

Jaime wiped his eyes with the back of his hand. "He has a broken nose, jaw, collarbone, several shattered bones in his right leg from the bike falling on him and there's some internal bleeding." He started to cry again. "He's been unconscious the whole time."

I hugged him again. "How are your parents?"

"They've been by his side since he was admitted. I finally convinced them to go home and rest."

I went to stand by the bed. If I hadn't known it was Jorge, I wouldn't have recognized him. His handsome face was bruised and swollen, and there was a bandage across his nose.

I leaned over to kiss his cheek. "I'm so sorry," I whispered.

Jaime put his hand on my shoulder. I turned to face him.

"I love your brother." It was the first time I'd said it to anyone. "If it weren't for me, this wouldn't have happened to him. It's all my fault."

Jaime wrinkled his brow. "I don't see how this could be your fault. I've never seen Jorge as happy as he's been since he met you." He tried to smile despite his bloodshot eyes. "Our parents thought you were the best thing that ever happened to him. Mom kind of lost it, though, when she heard that guy had harassed you in the past."

"How did she know? Jorge said he didn't tell her."

"Apparently, he mentioned it to Buster. When Buster saw the video, he went berserk. That's when he told Mom

and Dad about the other incidents. I guess Mom just needed someone to blame. Unfortunately, she's blaming you."

I put my hand on Jorge's shoulder and said to Jaime,
"Believe me, I'd give anything to undo this. Jorge wanted to
go to LA with me. If I hadn't been so stubborn about needing to go by myself . . ."

"Stop blaming yourself, Lucy. It sounds like this guy was
determined to hurt you any way he could, even if it was
through Jorge. It would've happened sooner or later and, if
you'd been with him, you might be lying in a hospital bed
too." He shot a nervous look at the door. "Look, Mom and
Dad will be here any minute. It might be better for you to go
downstairs and wait for me. I'll drive you home."

"Thanks, Jaime. My friend Meme drove me here. He's in
the lobby waiting for me."

"Go home, then. Get some rest. I'll call you the minute
Jorge wakes up."

I looked back at Jorge and started to cry again.

Jaime hugged me. "He's going to be okay. He's a fighter
and now that he's got you, he has an even bigger reason to
fight. I'll let you know when the coast is clear."

I nodded and made my way back to Meme.

❧   ❧   ❧

"I'll take you to your apartment to pick up whatever you
need," Meme said. "While you're doing that, I'll get Lucky
and then drive you both to my house. Beto's orders."

"I'll just be a minute," I said when we reached the
restaurant.

Lucky acted like he hadn't seen me in years. I played
with him for a while until he calmed down a bit. Meme took
the rest of the day off and, after he took me to his house, he
went out to pick up a pizza. Elena insisted I eat a slice. After

we ate, I gave them their gifts and watched Ricky play with his stuffed toy.

"I didn't have a chance to get any more gifts. Not even for Jorge."

"We don't need gifts," Meme said. "And you're the only gift Jorge needs."

Elena was quiet for a change. At ten, she said, "Meme put your stuff in the spare bedroom. You may not be able to sleep but try to get some rest. I'll drive you to the hospital in the morning."

"Jorge's mother doesn't want me to see him," I said. "She thinks it's my fault this happened."

Elena came to put her arms around me. "Of course, she's got to be out of her mind with worry, but everyone knows it's not your fault. Try to get some sleep. We'll figure something out. Even if we have to sneak you in when she's not there."

Elena's words kept going through my mind as I lay staring at the darkness, seeing Jorge's bruised face and broken body. Each time I closed my eyes, I was drawn into a kaleidoscope of colors exploding before my eyes like shooting stars, filling the darkness with their brightness, each one carrying off bits of me and scattering me throughout the universe. Here I thought I'd left all this violence behind when I left Las Nubes. But angry nuts like Pedro and Rigo seemed to be everywhere. At some point, I fell asleep listening to Lucky snoring peacefully on the floor next to the bed.

I awoke to Ricky's cries and got up to let Lucky out in the backyard.

"Good morning," Elena called from the kitchen where she was feeding Ricky his breakfast. "I was just going to have a second cup of coffee. Would you like some?"

"Thanks," I said. "I'll get it." I refilled her cup and served myself my usual half cup.

Ricky clapped his hands and spit out his cereal.

"Watching Ricky eat will probably spoil your appetite, but you really should eat something."

"Coffee's fine for now. I'll eat later if I get hungry."

⁂ ⁂ ⁂

I was wracking my brain, trying to figure out a way to see Jorge again. I didn't have Jaime's number and I hadn't thought of giving him mine. When he said he'd call me, I assumed he'd call the restaurant. Then it dawned on me that Anne and Fred would be back by now and might be visiting Jorge. I'd ask them to give Jaime my number.

I felt Elena watching me as I ran to the bedroom to get my phone.

"Are you okay?" she yelled after me.

"Yeah," I yelled back. "I just need to make a call."

When Anne didn't answer, I left a short message asking her to call me. Then I tried The Cellar.

"We were there last night," Fred said. "We're going back as soon as Anne gets home. Can we give you a ride?"

"I'm not allowed to visit him," I said. "His mother doesn't want me there."

"¡Ay, caramba! What's her problem?"

Exactly! Whether his mother liked it or not, I had every right to be there, for Jorge's sake and mine.

"Hello? You still there?"

"Uh, I'm here."

"We'll see what we can do about this nonsense with his mother. Call you later."

"Thanks, Fred."

❋ ❋ ❋

Elena and I stopped by the restaurant just after the lunch rush. Berta was clearing the table closest to the entrance.

"Hi, Berta," Elena said as she walked past her.

"Hello," Berta answered without looking at her. Her eyes were focused on me.

Instead of following Elena to the counter, I walked up to Berta. She'd been keeping her distance since Rigo had broken into my place, but she and Lucky had become friends in the last few weeks.

"I've never done anything to you or Rigo," I said. "Maybe I was just an easy target, but what gives you the right to hurt people you don't even know?"

Berta closed her eyes and took a deep breath, as if bracing herself. "You probably won't believe me, but I had nothing to do with Jorge's accident. He—"

"It was no accident."

"You're right." She put her hand on my arm. "This whole thing makes me sick. I thought I knew Rigo. It was one thing for him to take his anger out on me, but I never imagined he'd sink so low. After he took the tips, we started fighting all the time. Then he broke into your place and it just kept getting worse." She gave my arm a little squeeze. "I'm really sorry."

"If you're truly sorry, you'll help the police catch him."

She nodded and gave me such a sad look, as if her eyes had run out of tears.

"I know this is of little comfort to you, but it's been fear that's caused me to cover up for him and a whole string of losers like him." Her eyes started clouding up. I've been fighting that fear, putting up with things no one should have to endure, just to keep from being alone."

I stared at her, but instead of Berta, I saw Sara's face before me and wondered if she had similar reasons for staying with Pedro.

"I resented you when you first got here, not so much because you're young and beautiful, but because you had the guts to leave whatever drove you away, to set out on your own."

"You don't know anything about me."

"I don't know the details, but I've seen the signs so many times before."

I didn't realize I was crying until Berta reached up and wiped away my tears. She opened her arms and I collapsed into them.

"I should've spoken up when he broke into your place. I just couldn't find the courage. I'm not afraid anymore. This time he's gone too far. He has to be stopped. I've got Cano's number and will call him as soon as Rigo comes around again."

I stepped back and looked at her. "How do you know he'll be back?"

"He's a coward. He'll be back when he runs out of places to hide."

Guerrero, Meme and the rest of the crew had gathered around Elena and little Ricky, but they were all watching Berta and me.

"Thanks," I said to Berta before I went to join the others.

They all took turns hugging me, telling me to let them know if there was anything they could do to help.

☙ ☙ ☙

Patti called me at ten that night. I started crying as soon as I heard her voice.

"What's wrong, Lucy? I expected you to be excited about being in LA."

I told her what Rigo had done to Jorge.

"The freak's a psycho. He's not going to stop until he's caught and put away for good."

"There's a posse on his tail here in Maguey and another in Saguaro," I said between sniffles. "I'm sure it's just a matter of time before he's caught. I'm focusing all my energy on Jorge right now, except his mom won't let me see him."

"Forget her. I'd like to see Fernando's mom try to stop me if that ever happened to him."

Her words kept echoing in my ears and brain. "You're right. I have to find a way to convince her that I need to be there for him."

❦   ❦   ❦

"There's been no change," Anne said when she called. "Jaime and his dad asked about you. They've tried to talk some sense into the mom, but she won't listen. Fred and I also put in a good word for you. Maybe with all of us working on her, we can change her mind."

"Thanks, Anne."

"I've gotten to know Jorge pretty well, and it's obvious he's crazy about you. Believe me, he could've had his pick of the litter, and I'm not just talking about the felines."

Of course, the girls would like him but, crazy as it seemed, he'd picked me.

"We haven't known each other that long," I said, "but I feel the same way about him."

"Course you do," Anne said. "By the way, some guy named Buster stopped by while we were there. He asked about you too. I asked how he knew you. 'You kidding me?' he said. 'The kid can't stop talking about her. I only met her once, but that was enough to convince me he'd picked a winner. Even Candy thinks so,' whoever Candy is."

"They're both good friends of Jorge's."

"I'll tell you one thing," Anne said. "If Buster gets a hold of that sleazebag before the police do, he'll wish his mother had hung him out to dry before he was born."

I had no doubt Rigo would regret it if he ever ran into Buster. I didn't care what happened to him, as long as he was caught and put away before he hurt anyone else.

※ ※ ※

Jaime called me later that day. "I hope you don't mind that Anne gave me your number."

"I can't believe I forgot to give it to you. When are you going back to Tucson?"

"Not until I know that Jorge's going to be okay. Mom, Dad and I are taking turns staying with him. We want to be there when he wakes up."

"I'd like to be there too," I said.

"If it makes you feel any better, Dad and I are working on Mom."

"Thanks, Jaime."

※ ※ ※

After reassuring everyone at the restaurant that I'd call Officer Cano if I so much as got a whiff of Rigo, they allowed Lucky and me to go back to the apartment. I spent the morning working on soup and smoothie recipes for when Jorge came out of his coma. While printing them, it occurred to me I was trying to mend him with food, the same way I've been trying to fix everything wrong in my life. In the meantime, I'd been letting everyone else fight my battles.

Even Berta had finally found the courage to face her fears, so why was I letting mine keep me from what I wanted more than anything? Now that I knew there were people like my friends and men like Jorge, I needed to put my past behind me for good.

I dropped everything right then, took the bus to Saguaro and went straight to the hospital.

I knocked before I let myself into Jorge's room. His mother was sitting by his bed. She stood when she saw me, blocking my view of her son.

"Don't you think you've done enough harm already?"

The words I wanted to say had been running through my head like a catchy jingle since she'd first decided I was to blame for Rigo's actions. Now, I took a deep breath before I spoke to them.

"Mrs. Chapa, I would never do anything to hurt Jorge."

"Apparently you didn't have to." She folded her arms over her chest.

"I don't know why Rigo did this. He's just evil." My voice came out shakier than I would've liked. "It's true he went after Jorge because of me, but I'd trade places with Jorge right now if I could."

She turned to look at her son and started to cry.

I walked toward her and put a hand on her shoulder. "I want to help take care of him. Please."

She caressed Jorge's cheek. "He never gets up before eight unless he has to, but the day you left, he woke up at six to see you off. I knew then how much he cares about you."

Tears welled up in my eyes. "I should never have gone to LA. Everything I care about is here. I love your son very much."

She finally turned to look at me, the last of the animosity fading from her face.

"Julián, Jaime, Anne and even Buster have been telling me that all along." She held me at arms' length and looked at me. "I'll go home now and give you some time with him. Call us when you're ready to leave. One of us will come by to drive you home."

❁   ❁   ❁

The following week I went back to work.

"I'm here physically," I said to Guerrero and Joaquín, "but I think I'll take a back seat for a while since you know where my mind is these days."

We were busier than ever a couple of days later, when Jaime called to tell me Jorge was awake and asking for me.

"When can you get here?" he said.

"I'm leaving right now."

"Jorge needs me," I told Guerrero. "I'm taking the bus to the hospital."

"Wait just one minute," he said. He took his keys from the hook where he kept them and tossed them to Pepe. "Why don't you drive Lucy to Saguaro."

As we were walking out the door, he yelled, "Call us when you're ready to come home."

Jorge was sitting up in bed when I arrived. I kissed his cheek and held his swollen hand.

Jaime stepped out of the room. "I'll be out here if you need me."

"I'm so sorry," I said to Jorge, my tears spilling out, although I'd told myself I wouldn't cry in front of him.

His jaw had been wired shut, and he could only blink. When he did, a tear ran down his cheek. I wiped it away and leaned over to kiss his swollen lips.

"I love you. I'm sorry I went to LA without you. I'm going to help you recover as quickly as you can so I can make it up to you."

He swallowed and tried to squeeze my hand.

"Jaime says you've already started physical therapy and should be going home before long. I've been working on recipes for food you can eat until you're able to chew again."

He said something that sounded like, "Mmm."

There was a light knock on the door before Fred and Anne walked in and came to stand next to me.

"Now we know you're in good hands," Fred said.

Jorge blinked and tried to smile.

Anne took Jorge's hand. "The campus kitties say hello. They miss you as much as the rest of us in the office."

Jorge nodded slightly.

Jaime came back in a few minutes later. While he gave us the latest details about the new treatment plan, Jorge drifted off to sleep.

"He's been a real trooper," Jaime said. "Although he's still heavily sedated, I can see that every little movement causes him pain."

"Sounds like he's on his way to recovery," Fred said.

"It's good to know he's going to be okay," Anne said. "We're headed out for a bite to eat. Anybody else hungry?"

"I just ate," Jaime said. "I'm leaving for Tucson in the morning, so I need to go home and pack."

"What about you, missy?" Anne said. "We can drive you home after dinner."

"Thanks. I need to stay with him in case he wakes up again before his parents get here."

Chapter Twenty

News Flash

The phone was ringing when I stepped out of the shower. I ran to the living room to answer it.

"News flash!" Meme said.

"You're pregnant again?"

"Would I be calling you at this time to tell you that? Too bad you don't have a TV. But don't worry, I'm taping the whole thing for you."

My ears perked up.

"They finally got the SOB."

"How? Where?"

"Berta got home and found him passed out on her couch. She called the police right away. They just picked him up and dragged his ass to jail."

I could almost see Rigo trying to hide his ugly head from the cameras as he was hauled away. But the idea that Berta had kept her word and finally helped trap the rat was also great news. This was the new Berta, the one who'd been changing right before my eyes—evolving into a tamer, humbler version of the old witch who'd made my life so miserable when I first arrived in Maguey.

"Hello? Lucy? You still there?"

"I'm here. I'm just . . . I just can't believe it. I mean . . . that it was actually Berta who turned him in."

"Well, remember you heard it here first," Meme said. "Now you won't have to look over your shoulder every time you go out."

"Thanks, Meme. You've made my day."

❧   ❧   ❧

I called Jaime as soon as Meme hung up.

"I just tried to call you, but your line was busy," he said.

"You've heard the news?"

"Mom called me. She and Jorge saw it on TV. She wants to come to the restaurant and personally thank your friend for getting that menace—that's what she called him—off the road. She also wants to apologize to you for . . . well . . . for everything."

My "friend." As I thought back on the times Berta had talked to me the past few weeks, I realized that's exactly what she had been trying to do, make nice with me. I'd grown so distrustful of her, I'd ignored, or at least misread her when she'd raised her white flag: the times she'd gone out to play with Lucky, the day she apologized for Rigo's actions.

"Your mom doesn't owe me an apology. I'm sure most mothers would do anything to protect their kids. As for Berta, she's come a long way since we first met."

We all showed up at the restaurant earlier than usual that morning. The Floreses were there when I walked in, and even Berta appeared a few minutes later.

Mr. Flores raised his cup in a toast. "To Officer Cano and his men for putting that fugitive away where he can't cause any more trouble."

I turned toward the bar where Berta was pretending to look through her purse for who knows what.

"Of course, he'd still be on the loose if it weren't for Berta's courage and quick thinking," I said.

Meme let out a loud whistle. "Berta, get in here so we can pin a red badge of courage on that microscopic apron your wear."

Berta came to stand next to me. "If I was really brave, I would've turned him in a long time ago." She looked directly at me. "He never would've broken into your place and never would've hurt Jorge."

There was no question that this was a very different Berta. It must've been tough for her to go from a man who gave her everything to one who took what little she had. Yet, here she was, a hero in our eyes. If she could go through such a huge transformation, maybe . . . maybe there was still hope for Sara.

"I wish neither of those things had happened," I said, "especially Jorge's injuries. At least Rigo won't be hurting anyone else, thanks to you."

Jorge was released from the hospital the following Monday. Meme dropped me off at his house that afternoon. His mom led me to his room, closing the door behind her when she left.

Jorge held out his good hand to me. I rushed to his side and hugged and kissed him. He patted the bed, and I snuggled in beside him, taking his face in my hands and kissing him again and again. As we lay next to each other, I kept imagining the look on Pedro's face if he could see me at that moment.

"Hope I don't gross you out," Jorge said. "The first thing I'm going to do when I can get out of this bed on my own is take a long, hot shower."

"I've been meaning to talk to you about your personal hygiene." I laughed and kissed him again.

Jorge tried to wrinkle his nose and winced.

"Just kidding," I said. "I love you. And I'd love you even if you did stink." I started to get out of bed. "I brought you some goodies."

He pulled me close. "I'll try them later. You're all I need right now."

I put my head on his pillow and snuggled into his side. We lay there, neither of us feeling the need to say anything more.

CHAPTER TWENTY-ONE

A Visitor

In response to requests from our regular customers, we'd started serving breakfast right after the second expansion. At first, we just offered basics like juices, coffee, pastry, any style *huevos*, potatoes and choice of tortillas. Even with the limited options, our breakfast business took off from day one. It wasn't unusual to see our customers come in for both breakfast and lunch or dinner.

The breakfast crowd had just left and we were starting the lunch preparations one day when Meme walked into the kitchen.

"You have a visitor."

I gave him a puzzled look.

"There's a guy out there asking for you. He wouldn't tell me his name. Said he wanted to surprise you."

I wiped my hands on a dishtowel and followed Meme to the dining area. He gestured toward the entrance and walked off to clear a table.

Although I could only see his profile, I recognized him right away and, letting out a small cry, ran toward him and threw my arms around him.

"Mario! I can't believe it!"

"Lu." Mario held me gently with one arm while patting my head and back as if he were trying to calm a crying baby. "It's been so long."

He kept holding me while I soaked his shoulder with my tears. I finally managed to stop bawling long enough to let go of him.

Keeping my hands on his broad shoulders, I stood there gawking at him. He wasn't much taller than me, but the skinny kid I'd grown up with was nowhere in sight. His scrawny neck had thickened, his shoulders had broadened and his arm muscles rippled under his clingy shirt every time he moved. His voice had also changed to match the rest of him. It was now deep and rich and music to my ears.

"It's so good to see you," he said. "You look great. You've always had such great hair, but it looks even better now that it's longer."

"Thanks. You look great yourself." I tried to squeeze his thick biceps. "Lifting weights professionally these days?"

He laughed. "Not hardly. I work out a little, just to stay in shape."

"You hungry? *Huevos con chorizo*'s our most popular breakfast special."

"My favorite," he said, "but without the *chorizo*. I'll take some *picante* instead if you have some."

"What kind of Mexican restaurant would we be if we didn't?" I signaled to Meme, who was hovering nearby.

"Meme, this is my brother Mario."

"You've got one amazing sister," Meme said as he shook Mario's hand.

"I've always known that," Mario said. "I'm glad to hear other people think so." He turned to me and put his arm around my waist.

"One order of scrambled eggs, *papas con queso*, salsa, flour tortillas and a pot of coffee," I said to Meme.

"On its way."

I took Mario's hand, led him to a booth and sat across from him.

"I was so scared when you left," I said. "I kept hoping you'd come back for me. It took me a while to realize there was nothing you could've done for me then. Now that you're here, I want to hear everything you've been up to since I last saw you."

"You have no idea how tough it was for me to leave you, Lulu. Not a single day's gone by that I haven't thought about you. I didn't know how, when, or where we'd see each other again, but I always hoped it would be as far from Las Nubes as possible."

"Maguey turned out to be far enough for me."

"With my work schedule, it was hard to stay in touch regularly. As soon as I found out I'd be going to San Diego, I requested a week's leave so I could come see you."

"I'm so glad you're here."

He squeezed my hands and looked around the restaurant. "Looks like you landed very nicely."

"Better than I ever dreamed."

Meme arrived with a plate piled high with food.

"*Buen apetito*," he said before he walked away.

"I'll need a doggie bag unless you can help me eat all this," Mario said.

"Thanks, but I've already eaten."

"Could I at least buy you a cup of coffee?"

"Breakfast and coffee are on me today."

I poured a cup for him and half of one for myself. He ate slowly and, as I watched him, I realized that even with

Jorge, my job and my friends at the restaurant, there had still been a void I hadn't been able to fill until then.

"The food's great," Mario said. "Wish I lived nearby." He stopped eating and looked at me. "We've got a lot of catching up to do. Think you can take some time off?"

"You kidding? I'm on vacation as of right now."

"Good." He leaned back, patted his flat stomach and groaned. "I can't believe I ate all that food. It really is great to see that you've made a new life for yourself, Lu."

"Sounds like you've done pretty well yourself. Will you be staying for a whole week?"

"I was hoping to spend a couple of days with you, if that's okay. Then I have to get back to San Diego to take care of a few things before I report to work."

"I wish it were longer, but I'll take a couple of days." I reached across the table to take his hand. "Come on, there's someone upstairs I want you to meet."

"Hmmm!" Mario raised his eyebrows and bobbed his head a few times.

"We're going to see you-know-who," I said to Meme on the way out. "You all are on your own for the next couple of days."

"We'll try to manage without you." Meme said. He turned to Mario. "Welcome to Maguey."

❧ ❧ ❧

"I live upstairs," I said as I led Mario to the patio. "We can go up there later, but first I'll bring my baby down to meet you."

I raced upstairs and let Lucky out. He tramped down the steps, jumped up on Mario and planted his paws on his chest. Mario petted him while I looked around for one of his toys.

"We need to wear him out a bit before we take him back up," I said. I threw a ball toward a corner of the yard, and Lucky ran off to retrieve it. After about twenty minutes of non-stop romping, he was panting, still waiting for more.

"Enough for now," I said before leading Mario up the stairs.

Lucky tore past us and stood at the door whipping his tail from side to side and looking down at us as if he couldn't believe how slow we were. He followed us from room to room when I gave Mario a quick tour of the apartment.

"Pretty basic," I said.

"You haven't seen basic until you've seen my quarters," Mario said.

Excited as he was to have company, Lucky finally settled down on the couch next to Mario and was soon snoring.

I sat in my favorite chair across from them. "I'm so glad you found me. I've been dreaming of this day since the last time I saw you. It was one of the things that helped me cope."

"I worried about you after I left and kept trying to figure out a way to help you get away from them. When I heard you were in El Paso, I wasn't sure whether to be glad or worry even more."

"After you left, I became Pedro's punching bag."

"Oh, Lulu!" Mario said. He leaped up, came to kneel in front of me and took my hand. "I'm sorry I wasn't there for you, Baby Lu."

I squeezed his hand. "Delia and I had a chance to get to know each other a little better during the short time I spent with her. She's a little strange, but she has a good heart."

"Which is more than anybody can say about Pedro."

"I used to think they were both adopted."

"You obviously couldn't see it, but they both look just like Nana."

I thought about it for a moment, unable to see any resemblance.

"I called Sara when Fernando told me about Pedro's stroke," Mario said. "As soon as she realized it was me, she went nuts. 'You ungrateful little brat! Where were you when your father needed you?' She had nothing good to say about either of us. Then she asked about you, when I told her you were doing great, she started sobbing and hung up."

"Pretty pathetic, huh? Last I heard, Pedro was getting physical therapy. I used to wonder why Sara didn't leave him. I finally realized he'd beaten every ounce of confidence out of her, if she ever had any to begin with."

※ ※ ※

Mario took my hands in his. I didn't even realize I was crying until he wiped my tears away.

"Lu, sorry I brought any of it up. It's all behind us now. The important thing is that we're both safe and that we've found each other. Now that I know where you are, you won't be able to get rid of me."

I put my arms around his neck. "For a while I felt like I'd always attract violence, no matter where I went. When something bad happened, I felt like Sara had put a hex on me."

Mario laughed. "No way. She's never been a real witch. It was just a mind game she played. It's her way of coping with Pedro and his crap."

His words reminded me of the wedding picture Nana had kept on a table in her living room. Pedro was already pretty "husky," as Nana liked to say, but Sara's collarbone, elbows and ankles stuck out at sharp angles. Her hair was piled on top of her head in a loose knot. I'd never seen it any other way. Her dress hung on her like a shapeless sack. In the picture, she clutched a bouquet of pink carnations. Neither she nor Pedro was smiling. It made me wonder when she had stopped smiling or if she'd ever had a reason to smile.

"Enough about them," I said, my voice still a little shaky. "Tell me about you."

Mario settled on the floor next to my chair and leaned against the wall. "I do okay. The Navy saved my life. I'm not saying my life's been one long picnic, but the military's provided a steady paycheck. I've learned a few skills, traveled a bit, even earned some college credits. Best of all, I don't have anybody beating the crap out of me for no reason."

Lucky, probably feeling a little left out, jumped off the couch and walked over to lick my foot. I kissed the top of his head to reassure him he was still king of our little castle. He butted his head against Mario's shoulder before he wandered off. A few minutes later, we heard him crunching kibble and slurping water in the kitchen.

"Maguey is the last place I would've thought of looking for you," Mario said. "I'd never even heard of it until Fernando told me you were here. How do you like it?"

"The Navy was your lifesaver and Maguey was mine. Life here was a little bumpy at first, until I started meeting people and making friends, one very special friend in particular. I'm happy. Oh, that reminds me, I've got something to show you."

I went to the nightstand where I kept the framed *Desert News* article.

I watched Mario's smile grow bigger as he read the article. When he was done reading, he let out a low whistle.

"You've come a long way, Baby Lu! I'm so proud of you. But I'm not surprised."

"It's good to know that people like our food because I get to do what I love."

I told him about my dishwashing days and about the party that led to my promotion.

"So, tell me more about your special friend. He better be good to you."

"Jorge. He's the best. Unfortunately, hanging around with me almost got him killed." I told him about Rigo and all the problems he'd caused.

"Son of a bitch! I hope you reported everything to the cops."

"They watched me like hawks. Still, it wasn't until the woman who'd been covering his back got tired of his crap and turned against him that he got what he deserved."

"Is Jorge going to be all right?"

"He still gets physical therapy several times a week and will be wearing a brace for a while longer. At least he can talk and eat now. He's even thinking of going back to school soon."

"When do I get to meet him?"

"How about tomorrow?"

We didn't realize how long we'd been talking until we heard a knock at the door and noticed we were sitting in near darkness. I turned on a lamp and went to the door.

Meme was standing there holding a tray with two plates of food and a couple of beers.

"Thought you might be getting hungry," he said.

I had to grab Lucky's collar to keep him from jumping up and knocking the tray out of Meme's hands.

"Wow! This is what I call service," Mario said as Meme carried the food inside. "Good thing I'm only here for a couple of days. I have a feeling I'll be putting on at least five pounds in that time."

Lucky followed us out to the balcony and sat under the table, waiting for us to drop a scrap or two on the floor.

We were still sitting outside when the phone rang at ten. I jumped up and ran to answer it.

"Jorge," I said. "How was PT?"

"Barrels of fun as usual."

"I'll take Lucky out for a break," Mario said.

I turned away from the phone and whispered, "Thanks."

"Who's there?" Jorge asked.

"My brother. He surprised me this morning. He's only here for two days, so we've been talking nonstop since he got in. I'll bring him by tomorrow, okay?"

"Sure. I look forward to meeting him, and I'll be dreaming of you until then."

Ever since he'd come out of his coma, I never missed a chance to tell him I loved him. The first time, he'd try to mouth the words back to me, until the effort made him wince in pain.

❈　❈　❈

"You look and sound happy," Mario said when he brought Lucky back in. "I assume with your job, your boyfriend and your dog, you've got every reason to be happy now."

"Jorge's great. You'll see for yourself when you meet him tomorrow. When I almost lost him, I realized that all my other goals and dreams were nothing without him in my life. What about you? Do you have a girlfriend?"

"Her name's Brigitta. I call her Brig. She's German, but we have a lot more in common than you'd think. Hopefully, you'll meet her someday."

The next morning, it was obvious that everyone had already heard about Mario from Meme. Even though they were as busy as ever during the lunch hour, they all stopped what they were doing to talk for a few minutes . . . even Berta. After I'd introduced him to the rest of the crew, I took his arm and we walked toward her.

"You must be very proud of your sister," she said. "She's really turned this place around."

Is this the same Berta who . . . ? I could feel everyone's eyes on us when she turned, took my hand and squeezed it.

❧   ❧   ❧

Mrs. Flores was beyond excited, gushing on and on about how Maguey hadn't been the same since my cooking talents were discovered. Mr. Flores had all kinds of questions about life at sea and about Mario's job. We were only able to get away when I said Jorge was waiting for us.

Jorge was sitting on the back patio when we got to his house. I walked up behind him, put my arms around him and kissed his head. He took my arms and leaned against me.

"So, you're the lucky guy," Mario said when I introduced them.

"Even my family calls me that," Jorge said.

"I brought lunch for you." I set a thermos of juice and a sealed bowl of fruit salad in front of him. "Lucky's waiting for us in the car."

"Tell him I'll see him as soon as I'm able to stand on my own." He turned to Mario and added, "Otherwise, he'll knock me down and I won't be able to get back up."

Mario laughed. "Yeah, I'm surprised Lucy's still standing."

⁂

Mario would be leaving early the next morning, so I felt like this was our chance to bring our ghosts out into the open and be rid of them for good.

"My trip to LA made me realize that so many people go there in search of fame and end up getting lost in the crowd, just one more anonymous face," I said. "It made me wonder how many of them go to the big city to escape their past. I guess we all do what we have to do to cope."

Mario looked at his hands and nodded. "In our case, we were a family of Houdinis, each of us wanting to escape reality in our own way. Just as Nana never seemed to see what a monster Pedro was, she always pretended Sara's craziness was just 'nerves.'" Do you remember Sara's favorite holiday?"

"Día de los Muertos," I said. "Remember all the amulets she used to wear? I always admired her jewelry, until I was old enough to realize what it really was."

"What a sick joke," Mario said, "wearing all that crap while she was living with the devil himself. If she had relatives, I'm glad we never met them."

"I asked Nana about that once. She only knew of the aunt who raised her. It wasn't until I heard Berta's story that I began to wonder what Sara's childhood was like."

Mario gripped my hand.

"I used to think that, except for Nana, we came from bad seeds, from a herd of lunatics hatched in some insane asylum. That made me more determined to escape the madness. And now, with Jorge, my friends and you in my life, I finally feel like I have."

"You're very strong, Lulu, stronger than me. I decided no one would ever beat me up again, so I bulked up physically but I never developed the mental toughness to match the muscle. I told myself I wanted to find you so I could protect you. The truth is I needed you. I needed to find something good and positive and beautiful among all the rubbish that surrounded us as kids."

"We've both come a long way. After Berta shared her story and why she put up with Rigo, I kind of understood why Sara felt trapped."

"Maybe it's not too late to help her," Mario said. "I want to at least try, but I'll totally understand if you don't feel the same way."

"She first has to understand how messed up her life is. She has to want our help. I was just a broken, scared, skinny girl when I escaped. But even then, my survival instincts were very strong. I think my bosses saw that in me. As I got to know them, my other friends and Jorge's family, I realized there were actually normal people in the world. I slowly began to trust them and they drew me out of my cocoon."

"Now, you're the beautiful butterfly you were always meant to be," Mario said.

Lucky walked into the room just then, tail wagging. I scratched behind his ears. He licked my arm.

"Sometimes, I envy him. When I first found him, he seemed haunted by whatever trauma he'd been through. He'd whimper and twitch in his sleep."

Mario put his arm around me. "Maybe he was just dreaming about hunting or whatever dogs dream about," he said. "He's lucky to have found you."

I lay my head on his shoulder, knowing that I was the lucky one.

If you are a victim of domestic violence or workplace harassment, speak with a trusted adult, teacher or medical professional who can help you find the appropriate resources in your area. Be safe. Stay strong. Keep your eyes on your goals.

Please Note: The author's proceeds from this (and all of my writing) go toward three of my favorite causes—education, the environment and animal welfare. If you enjoyed reading Lucy's story, please tell your family, friends, teachers, librarians and favorite bookstore about it.

www.estelabernal.com